The Keepers of Stal[ingrad]

Author's Note

I have always been fascinated with the *Battle of Stalingrad,* which took place between 23rd August 1942 and the 2nd February 1943. It was a major battle on the Eastern Front of World War 2 where Nazi Germany and it's allies unsuccessfully fought the Soviet Union for control of the city of Stalingrad (later named Volgograd) in Southern Russia. The battle was marked by fierce close quarter combat and deadly air raids on the civilian population.

The Battle of Stalingrad was the deadliest battle to take place during World War 2 and is one of the bloodiest battles in the history of warfare, with over two million casualties. It was a turning point in WW2 as it forced the *Oberkommando Der Wehrmacht* or German High Command, to withdraw military forces from other theatres to replace it's losses there.

The battle degenerated into house to house fighting as both sides poured reinforcements into the city which had largely been reduced to rubble by prolonged Luftwaffe air raids. During November 1942, Russian forces launched a counter-offensive against the weaker Romanian and other axis armies and as a result, the German 6th Army was cut-off and surrounded. Hitler however, was determined to hold the city at all costs and forbade the 6th Army from breaking out or surrendering. The Soviets were successful in denying the German forces the ability to resupply through the air which stretched them to breaking point and in February 1943, having run out of food and ammunition, the German forces finally surrendered to the Russians, the first of Germany's field armies to surrender during World War 2.

The following is a story of a very small number of German soldiers who had the strength and will to make it out of Stalingrad during the terrible winter of 1942/43. Such people epitomise the triumph of the human spirit over adversity.

The Keepers of Stalingrad

Prologue

Near Warsaw Poland

Late September 1939

The Pripyat Marshes Russia

July 1941

It is very hard to kill a man when he doesn't want to die. Unteroffizier Karl Heinz Morgenstern knew this very well, and thought he had seen most things. Now an infantry section leader he was not the same man who joined the army in 1938. His experiences changed him of course. They would change anyone.

In 1938, at the age of 27, he joined the army to get away from life in an engineering factory, in Templehof, Berlin. It was a razor blade manufacturing facility that had just been bought by an American company, Gillette. Morgenstern hated his sixty hour week there and though his wages had gone up slightly, he dreamed of better things.

Swept along by national fervour and urged persistently by his friends, most of whom had already joined up, he signed on for the Wehrmacht in the summer of 1938 and wished he's done so years before. Suddenly, he commanded a new respect around friends and neighbours, but his decision was really made by the death of his mother. This sparked something inside him; He saw how short life could be and here was his chance to live it to the full, or so he thought at the time. Anyway, he told himself again and again, you would have joined the army eventually, whether you wanted to or not.

He was also engaged to Elke, his childhood sweetheart. Now they could get married. Elke laughed at how jealous her friends were. Karl looked so handsome in his uniform they said. But really they were jealous of Elke because she was escaping the rut they were in.

So here he was in Poland, changed forever. All the dreams and hopes he'd had were diluted by the harsh brutal realities of war. He was fascinated by how you could settle for less and less as time went by and events overtook you. What he'd wanted out of life and where it might have taken him was a distant embarrassing memory now, when all you could think of was survival and waking up to a new day.

Already a Lance Corporal or *Gefreiter*, before he'd left Germany and mainly due to his age, here he was standing in a town square, with his section, surveying the appalling scene around him, where a brief skirmish had taken place. Already, he'd decided he seen most things. Things that might give others nightmares. He'd seen a man crushed by a tank in a stupid accident, and the same man crawling away on his elbows, legless, looking for help. Another time he saw a man shot by a sniper and with half his head missing, walk around looking for a medic. Oh yes, he'd seen things, but not everything. Of course not.

His men were helping to clear the dead from the square. Horse drawn wagons were everywhere. German soldiers were to be separated from Polish soldiers, and civilians, of whom there were many. They'd been at it since early that morning. The temperature was hot and everyone was stripped down to their vests or bare chested altogether. They'd been taking a break, sitting around an empty dry fountain, smoking and drinking Tyskie lager from a local bar they had commandeered. One of their group suddenly stood up, pointing. A cigarette fell from his mouth.

"What the fuck?!" he muttered, still pointing. Everyone followed his gaze to see a dead German soldier fall off the back of a wagon, followed by another who was crawling his way out from under the pile of corpses. Now he thrust out two outstretched arms and was screaming for help. When they got him out, they could see he'd been hit several times. Bullet holes covered his body. Fourteen separate wounds they found out later.

*

Morgenstern had nightmares after that. A wagon with the same pile of corpses, but his mother crawling her way out in tears and anguish; the same tears and anguish he'd remembered seeing as she lay in her hospital bed, looking as small as a bird. He would have many more nightmares, each of which would chip away at his soul. Sleep became another ordeal and he was grateful for the amphetamines the army medics doled out, 'to keep you alert', but were in fact designed to keep soldiers awake so they could out perform their enemy. Morgenstern and his fellow comrades would sleep two or three hours every three or four days. It would catch up with them all eventually, but it went a long way in explaining their recent sudden successes.

Now in Russia, more than eighteen months later, he tossed and turned on his groundsheet in a tent where his section had camped for the night. Another nightmare. He woke and lit a cigarette from a drum of Juno's beside him. He smoked and watched the smoke rise above him. I'll never sleep again, he decided.

His section had been making their way back to their lines, having been involved in a skirmish that had lasted what? Maybe ten minutes. As he made his way at the rear of a column, he stopped to look into a shell hole that was half full of dirty brown water. What caught his attention was the corpse floating in that water. Head down and with it's back torn wide open, Morgenstern stared at it, trying to determine if the dead man was German or Russian. He couldn't tell looking at all the mess.

Then suddenly he was propelled by a force that swept him off his feet and into the crater's pool of fetid water. His weapon had been knocked from his right hand and he nearly swallowed his cigarette as he hit the water. Panic engulfed him and then he was breaching the surface trying to regain his senses. Now a shape was forcing him back down under the water and he struggled violently, kicking out and using his hands to find the shape's neck which he squeezed with all of his strength. The pressure on his shoulders lessened though he felt a collarbone snap and he fumbled blindly for his combat knife as he fought to stand and face his adversary, who'd let go of him.

Morgenstern faced a Russian officer who stood opposite him with two bare hands; Fists clenched. The Russian spat a mouthful of blood at him. "Nemetskiy ublyudok!" he hissed. Both men ignored the corpse bobbing in the water between them.

Morgenstern gritted his teeth and slashed at the man who flinched backwards. A bolt of pain shot down his arm and abdomen from his broken collarbone and he switched his knife to his left hand. He lunged again. The Russian reached for a piece of timber, perhaps a small fencing post and swung at him, catching his left arm. His knife disappeared under the water and he had to quickly raise his arm again to fend off another blow from the Russian who had momentum behind him. A third blow threw him down into the water and as the Russian moved towards him, he looked up at him, apparently helpless.

Miraculously, he moved a hand and then he felt something under the water. Grabbing it, he produced a broken trench spade, most of it's handle missing. He grasped the spade where it met the handle and swung it towards the Russian's ankles, hitting home with a thud that almost took the man's foot off. He cried out in agony and fell back into the water. Morgenstern was upright now and it was his turn to stand over his opponent who scrambled backwards in the water until he ran out of space, having reached the edge of the crater. Then he flung himself forward, catching Morgenstern around the waist who stabbed downwards with his spade as both men crashed into the water thrashing around in a blurring chaos.

He cried out as he felt a thumb over both eyes that wanted to either gouge them out or push them to the back of his skull and he had to let go of the spade to grab the Russian's wrists and force him away. Then there were hands around his throat and he was forced back down under the water. Somehow he forced himself up and sideways and the two men were side by side, kicking, punching, biting.

Morgenstern felt his strength draining away and he clawed at a rock to his right, embedded in the crater's muddy walls. He desperately tried to free it from the earth, breaking some nails and now he

v

swung it towards the Russian's head catching him with a sickening dull crack. He kept pounding until he could see the glistening white of his skull as it shattered like eggshell beneath him. Blood was everywhere, forming tiny rivulets in the brown water around him.

The Russian slumped back against the crater's edge; his arms limp beside him. Morgenstern then turned but he couldn't seem to control his breathing and something inside him was stuck under his ribcage. He fought to breathe and was close to passing out from hyperventilation. But he still looked down at the Russian, blood now seeping from the cracks in his skull.

After a few minutes, his breathing became easier and he felt he had to get out of there or he would surely die. He flinched in great pain as he reached upwards to start climbing out of the crater, but inexplicably, he felt a vice like grip around his lower legs and he was being pulled back down. He cried out in pain and alarm and then he was straddling the Russian and with his hands around the man's throat, forced his head under the water. He thrashed and fought; his legs kicking and his hands clawing at Morgenstern's chest and face, but eventually he was still. Then he moved again and he resumed his grip around the man's throat. It was impossible surely?

But the Russian died after maybe another minute and near exhaustion and with tears streaming down his face, Morgenstern was finally out of the shell hole and lying on his back, breathing hard while he stared at the sky. Suddenly a bird flew past a cloud. A swallow perhaps, he wondered as familiar voices gathered around him.

*

Already A Veteran

Stalingrad

January 1943

The cold! The vicious unrelenting freezing cold! Where a sentry on duty at night could freeze to death where he stood. Where columns of Russian tanks could cross mighty frozen rivers like the Don at will. It tormented the very depth of one's being. It was merciless, unforgiving and as Morgenstern huddled in an open doorway while he surveyed the square before him, he thought only the Devil himself could be responsible for it. Temperatures would often drop to below -20C with winds that cut and stabbed you over and over without mercy. But that was Stalingrad, wasn't it? In January 1943? Totally and utterly merciless. In the mind of the common man and a stranger to this part of the world, Stalingrad became the epitome of all human suffering. A place so unique that nothing in this world or the next could be imagined that could possibly be worse.

Unteroffizier Morgenstern wept with the pain it took just to stay alive and his tears froze instantly. He had to blink continuously and wipe his eyes lest they freeze in their sockets. Not having eaten in days and in poor general health, his core temperature was fighting a losing battle with the weather and if he ever felt like doing so, it was a battle he could admit defeat to in under thirty seconds if he just simply sat or lay down and stayed still.

He adjusted the various rags wrapped around his head and grasped the collar of his greatcoat that he stuffed with other rags and old newspapers to keep out the worst of the cold. People here now wore everything and anything they could find to keep from dying of the cold. There was no such thing as keeping warm; It was just about not freezing to death, and led to a bizarre and sometimes unsettling parade of men dressed in rags and clothing from a dark nightmare.

Morgenstern tried to imagine, as he often did, what it had been like back in France in 1940 as if those thoughts could somehow warm him. Christ! But those were great days! The sun! The wine!

The women! Was Stalingrad the price he and others were paying for those days? And what about where it all began in Poland in 1939? If God himself appeared to Morgenstern and said, 'Yes! For your sins! This is Stalingrad!', he would bow his head and accept it as the absolute truth. It wasn't of course, but for now he saw it as God's revenge and who could blame him?

He looked across the square. There was a bunker under what once had been a milliner's shop. He remembered it and even the woman who had worked there before the place was shelled to rubble and dust. Then he remembered the woman later. The top half of her body had ended up somewhere on the square upright, as if she'd sunk into the ground. A hat, still in her hand, had remained strangely untouched.

Now someone appeared from the bunker, as if crawling out of the very depths of the earth. A tall, slim figure, wrapped in furs and almost doubled over. Morgenstern recognised him as a Flak Officer he'd met some time before. Had he got any bread from the bunker? Rumour had it that a foraging party from the bunker had come across a rare airdrop of food, purely by chance! It was said it contained 200 loaves of bread! More valuable than it's weight in gold or diamonds here where the last daily ration had been 100 grams of bread per day per man.

Food drops, if recovered, were supposed to have been handed in to Headquarters. Failure to do so meant a firing squad if you were caught. But that meant shit these days! Doing the right thing; Morality; Comradeship? Words that meant nothing any more. You did what you had to do in order to survive another day. But keeping 200 loaves of bread had a more relevant danger. If the wild, feral mobs of wretches that roamed the city these days found out about it, they would tear to pieces anyone who stopped them getting their hands on such a bounty.

Morgenstern thought it impossible to try and enter the bunker in the end. The occupants wouldn't know him and he'd be beaten to death the moment he stepped inside. Instead, he decided to follow the Flak Officer. He knew where he was going, but he'd have to hurry. There were others around, watching and waiting.

The Padre

Padre Eduard Huber shuffled through the freezing corridors of a shattered warehouse. In one dark corner of this particular hellhole was what passed these days for a Field Hospital. Huber struggled to remain upright, slipping on the ice covered tiles while he tried desperately not to walk on some poor unfortunate who lay writhing on the floor beneath him. It was impossible though as every available space was taken by the suffering wounded or seriously ill, who had gathered or were brought here in the lost hope they might get something, anything, to relieve their pitiable existence.

The stench was appalling. Men screamed out, covered in their own filth where they lay, while other shapeless heaps heaved with lice and fleas. Huber felt increasingly useless as some would openly sneer and mock him as he stooped over them, trying to offer some comfort.

"What do you want here!? You fucking crow!" said one, the blood soaked stumps of what remained of his legs now black with frostbite. The rest of his legs were gangrenous and foul smelling.

"I...I want to help you. Pray...with you...Pray for you," said Huber, visibly wincing under the vehement hostility shown him. 'Crow' was the common soldier's term for the traditional black robes of a priest. Huber however as a Field Chaplain, wore an ordinary field grey uniform with a cross on his cap and a red cross armband. The cross and chain he would have worn around his neck in ordinary times was now long gone.

"You want to fucking help me? Then kill me!" the wounded man screamed, tears in his eyes as he tried to sit up. Huber bent to help him. "Get your hands off me!" said the man. Eventually he gave up and lay back down.

Huber's face betrayed his own agony. That of the complete futility around him. There certainly was no room for God in Stalingrad. He had long abandoned the place.

"You still believe in your God?" the wounded man asked.

"He's your God too," said Huber, without conviction. He began a silent prayer.

"Of all the fucking lies and betrayals here, Padre, yours is the worst!" The wounded man was laughing now in a manner that betrayed his state of mind. "Look around you Padre! Show me one sign of your God! Or step outside and look for one!"

"Let me help-."

"Get away from me Padre! If you won't kill me, then get away. Leave me be."

Huber finished his prayer for the man despite his malevolent look of hatred and stood up, surveying the scene around him which assaulted his senses. He moved on, clawed hands grabbing at his legs as he made his way to a group of Medics and a Doctor, who despite everything, continued to go through the motions of treating those here. Huber stood to one side and observed the scene.

"Clear this fucking mess around me, you Russian scum!" the Doctor yelled at a prisoner who had been forced to work here. The man dutifully tried to sweep the blood and filth from around the Doctor's feet with a besom that was almost worn down to the stubs.

"Shit! This one's dead! Get rid of it!" the Doctor went on. "Bring another!"

Two more prisoners heaved the dead man off the field table and on to a cart, which they wheeled outside, stacking the dead man beside hundreds of others like so many logs. Later, maybe, other prisoners would come and throw a few more of the dead into a pit that was filling up fast with each passing day.

Back inside, the way the Doctor referred to the dead man as 'it' instead of 'he', was not lost on Huber. There seemed to be no more room here any more for the most basic form of humanity. Watching the man, in his late twenties, Huber knew he was lost in his own agonies. Heavily addicted to morphine, the meagre supply he kept from his patients who constantly pleaded with him for it, was fast running out. When it did, what would the Doctor do then?

"Is there anything I can do?" Huber asked repeatedly. The Medics stared at him in silence, frowning. Eventually, the Doctor took notice of him.

"Yes Padre," said the Doctor. Huber's face brightened. "You can write to the families of every dead hero here and explain why their loved one had to die. But you must be open and truthful mind! No bullshit. No flowery religious shit! The families deserve it, don't you think? That should keep you busy and out of my fucking sight!" Huber turned and fled, bursting into tears as he did so. The sound of mocking laughter followed him out into the freezing air.

*

The Leutnant

Elsewhere, 19 year old Artillery Leutnant Heinrich Reuters was squatting with his back to the wall of an abandoned bunker that had become just another hole in the ground. He was still in permanent shock at how his first posting in September 1942 to Stalingrad had ended in the situation he now found himself in. He could look back say, a year ago, to his Officer training and remember a young, confident man at the start of his adult life that had matured in the Army and was on the brink of taking part in something unprecedented. Led by the Fuhrer, a man with vision and a sense of history, victory was not only assured, it was guaranteed. Reuters didn't recognise that young man any more and grimaced at the distant memory of himself. That young fool had become an uncomfortable personal embarrassment.

Hearing noises, he stood now with his arms clenched around him, shaking uncontrollably with the freezing cold. He couldn't feel his feet any more. They were probably frostbitten but he felt no pain and was terrified of removing his boots. He'd seen a Corporal do that once. The flesh of the man's foot came off with his boot, leaving just the gleaming white bones showing.

Reuters peered over the rim of the bunker. It was a truck, now gone, disappearing into the distance. Could have been anyone, he decided, maybe even the Russians. So what? He was very close to his limit of endurance. Aware that his mind was slowly going, he was often confused and fought to think through even the most basic things, but at times, he would also seem to recover a sense of purpose which enabled him to get through his day. But more often than not, he just wanted everything to end. His youth and courage forbade him from taking his own life but maybe his sanity would solve that problem one day.

Now he saw a figure trudging through the snow and coming towards him. Eventually he could make out the man's rank and regimental flash. He was a Major in a Flak regiment. Reuters thought he should call out. The man was going to fall straight into the bunker if he kept going. But he kept silent, not wanting to draw attention from others who might be around.

Then another dark shape came out of nowhere and pounced on the Flak Major, bringing him to the ground. It was Morgenstern. The two men fought and thrashed about, crashing down into the bunker at Reuters' feet, who gave a yelp of terror as he scrambled away into a corner.

Morgenstern proved the stronger of the two struggling men and it was over quickly. Looking at the Major, he could see he was dead and withdrew his combat knife from the man's throat. He wiped his blade on the Major's sleeve and became aware of Reuters, skulking in a corner. He was over there in a second, ready to kill him too if need be.

"Please! Jesus, no!" said Reuters, his arms crossed over his head in a pitiful defence.

Morgenstern stopped and his eyes darted around to check they were alone. Satisfied, he backed away from Reuters and began to search the dead Major for the bread he so desperately needed. His eyes suddenly widened. Two whole loaves! My God! What luck! He quickly bit off a corner of one and stuffed the loaves into his greatcoat pockets. Then he sat and contemplated the quivering Leutnant before him.

"Who are you boy?" Morgenstern asked finally. "Sit still!" he snapped in his best Sergeant's voice.

"R..Reuters. Leutnant Heinrich Reuters. 112th Artillery. Please don't hurt me."

"Why would I hurt you boy?" Morgenstern relaxed, sitting back against the bunker wall. "You've seen what I've done? This man stole the bread. What else am I to do?"

"Now you have stolen it from him. And killed him besides," said Reuters, recovering slightly.

"And what are you going to do about it? Report me? Kill me?" Morgenstern asked, laughing. "What does it matter any more? Is there anyone left who would care?"

"Exactly!" said Morgenstern. "Save your strength boy."

The two men sat in silence for some time. Reuters asked for a piece of the bread and Morgenstern reluctantly broke off a small piece before throwing it across to him. The young Leutnant wolfed it down like a starving dog and Morgenstern laughed again.

"Th..Thank you," said Reuters. "Who are you? Where..?-."

"Never mind who I fucking am!" Morgenstern snapped. "How will it help you knowing who I am?"

"I..just wondered. I'm interested to know."

Eventually Morgenstern sighed heavily and spoke. "I'm Morgenstern. I was a section leader with the 21st Infantry. All the men I've ever served with or known are dead. I don't know how I am still alive. It's a mystery I've given up trying to solve. I don't know anything any more except the fact that we will all surely die, if we are not dead already. Perhaps we are and this *is* Hell! Wouldn't surprise me in the least."

"Yes, perhaps," said Reuters. Nothing about that statement struck him as odd. "Do you have a family? Back home I mean. A wife? Children?"

Morgenstern frowned as he looked at the young Leutnant. Then he stood up, making to go.

"Wait!" said Reuters, standing also.

"What for?" said Morgenstern, heaving himself out of the bunker.

"Take me..I mean..Can I come with you?"

Morgenstern smirked with contempt. "Are you joking?" he asked.

"Please. I've been alone for several days. I just.."

Then Morgenstern was gone over the top and out of sight. Reuters slumped back down into the bunker, weeping as his tears froze on his cheeks. The man had represented a glimmer of hope. Help in the darkness. Now he was alone again and bereft. After some minutes, Morgenstern reappeared.

"Well come if you're coming boy!" he said, before disappearing again. Reuters leapt to his feet and scrambled out after him into the freezing white distance.

*

The Cook and the Signaller

Wilhelm Stark, previously a Field Cook, carefully opened the rear door of the Opel Blitz truck and peered out into the frozen white and grey wasteland. His companion, Hugo Wagner, a Signaller from Staff Headquarters, opened his eyes and followed Stark's gaze from where he lay on the truck's floor.

They were on the Bone Road, so called for the frozen solid corpses that had been hammered into the ditches on either side to act as signposts or telegraph poles. Nobody could remember who started this particularly macabre use of available resources, or when, but rumour had it that it was probably the Romanians. It was their way of showing how much they detested their German allies and overseers. The ordinary Romanian soldier had been forced kicking and screaming into this nightmare and suffered as much if not more so, than others here.

Stark jumped down from the truck and looked around him. He began to relieve himself into the ditch, wincing at the freezing temperature. Buttoning his flies, he turned and immediately gave a start at a figure standing across the road. But then he realised it was just one of the 'signposts' whose arm was raised, pointing to a workshop according to the sign that was nailed to it.

Stark opened the other door of the truck. Wagner met his eyes. The man was dying; Sick with, well, God knew what? Typhus? Dysentery? Starvation? Whatever. It was a miracle how anyone could survive here, day after day. The limits of human endurance were a mystery to Stark that he spent little time trying to fathom.

"We should get going," he said now. "Try and find some shelter in the city. We'll die here if we don't."

"We'll die anyway," said Wagner. "Why bother?"

Stark didn't reply. He was used to Wagner by now. They'd been together for some weeks now and the man hardly spoke these days. When he did, it was usually just his stock phrase; 'We'll die anyway. Why bother?' that he so often used.

Stark had met Wagner after the Russians had overrun a forward defensive position near Dubovka. Stark had fled south with the remnants of an army brigade to a Staff HQ and shared a bunker with Wagner and others during a period of intense shelling that had lasted for three days. It was the sort of situation that created a bond between men who'd shared an experience unique to them alone.

But Wagner wasn't cut out for life outside the relative comforts of a Staff HQ and had deteriorated rapidly both physically and mentally. In a place where lives meant so little, and the scale of human suffering had become so severe, Stark, like others, had felt obliged to preserve the lives of those around him where possible and as best he could. But it had become an added burden he could well do without and he struggled with the thought of just walking away and leaving Wagner to his inevitable fate.

Back inside the truck, with the doors now closed, Stark picked up some rags and checked the meagre scraps of food they held. Some frozen potato peelings and half a can of some yellow paste that was beginning to turn black and foul. He threw the can away over his shoulder. What we are reduced to, he thought. He offered Wagner a potato peel to suck on. The man shut his eyes and turned his head away. Stark placed the peel in his mouth and let it melt against his gums. He winced. His teeth were getting sore lately. Most were so loose that if he chewed anything, at least one would simply fall out and he'd spit it out without thinking.

He thought about their next move. They'd stumbled upon this road two nights ago, aimlessly wandering and looking for some shelter from the weather. Wagner had screamed at the figures standing upright in the ditches, thinking them grim sentries on a road that led to Hell. Stark had come across the broken down truck and decided they could rest inside for a while, but only after he dragged the bloated corpse of someone who'd had the same idea out of it first.

"Hugo? Are you ready to go? We can't stay here," said Stark.

"You go. Leave me. I can't go on. I'm finished," said Wagner, his voice a whisper.

"Stop being a selfish bastard for five minutes, can't you?" said Stark.

Wagner managed a brief smile despite himself, and stared at the roof of the truck while he summoned the strength to move. Then later, they were outside, Stark supporting Wagner as best he could as they shuffled onwards past the signposts of the dead who seemed to mock and jeer them with complete contempt. After all, they still lived.

*

The Medical Orderly

Sanitatsobersoldat Theodore Benz had had enough. He was standing knee deep in snow watching two Russian prisoners empty a barrel of body parts into a pit that had been hacked out of the frozen ground perhaps a week ago. Now it was almost full and one of the prisoners dutifully threw a shovel full of lime over this new layer. Soon they would have to think about digging a new pit.

The Field Hospital where Benz now was had become nothing more than a morgue. The sick and wounded would arrive day after day. And everyday, most would die because there was simply nothing to be done for them. Benz would also supervise their disposal outside before returning to meet the new influx of wretched souls that gathered here. There were no medicines; No drugs; No supplies of any kind. Air drops were prioritised for food. Better, it had been decided, to feed the healthy and hungry, than try and treat the sick and dying.

Bandages were cut from sheets; though these had run out and the last few that remained were made from a parachute that had been attached to one of the canisters used in the air drops. Morphine supplies were pilfered long ago, and those that hadn't surfaced on the black market were hoarded by the Doctors themselves or Medics, for their own personal use.

It was an impossible situation to live and work in. Yesterday, Benz had started to try and wash a wounded Panzer driver who had lain here for days before they got to him. Benz had begun to cut his tunic off as he lay on a table. His arm and shoulder had immediately been covered with lice where his hand had touched the wounded man's sleeve.

For a man who only wanted to help the sick, wounded and suffering, Benz had been driven to despair by the conditions here. Stalingrad to him, was a Nether World, that had taken on a supernatural entity all it's own. He'd watched Russian prisoners gnawing at the amputated limbs before now, to quell their agonies of starvation. The dead or dying that lay around waiting for treatment, were often stripped naked by others for their coats or boots. Once, the Military Field Police, commonly known as the Chain Dogs because of the gorgets they wore around their necks, had found two wounded men with pliers and bags of gold teeth they had extracted from the dead around them. They were dragged outside into the snow and summarily executed.

But the final straw of Benz' torment was one of the Doctors who was fast losing his mind. Lately, he had started having random wounded men brought to the operating table and regardless of their injuries, he would always amputate a limb. An arm here; A leg there. And without ether, which had long run out. It was a harrowing experience, not least for the poor souls lying underneath the Doctor, unknowing and ignorant, as they bit down on a thick dowel of wood placed in their mouth, their sunken eyes wide with terror.

Benz had tried to stop it, but the Doctor would produce a pistol and threaten to shoot him, or attack him with a surgical cleaver like he did the day before. So now, he waved the prisoners back inside and simply walked off into the snow, having little idea where he was going, but fully aware that he must get away from here if he was to survive intact and sane.

*

The Panzer Commander

Morgenstern and Reuters stood behind the burnt out shell of a Panzer Mark IV that was parked in a mechanics workshop where it come to be repaired before shelling had reduced it and those inside it to ashes. The faint smell of the incendiary rounds still clung obstinately in the fetid air. They were looking across a large open yard at a shattered building, a corner of which still remained virtually intact. They had taken shelter here the night before but had become aware of various comings and goings across the yard, with several open gateways serving as points of entry.

"It seems safe enough," said Reuters, his teeth chattering loudly.

"No worse than anywhere else, I suppose," said Morgenstern. "Least they're our lot. Let's go then."

Together the two men crossed the yard and came to a barn-like door at one corner of the building where they had watched several others enter or leave, either alone or in groups. They went inside. It was dark but holes in the roof lit some areas of the place showing groups of men huddled together or others alone, lying down or sitting with their backs to the stone walls. Morgenstern felt for the knife in the pocket of his greatcoat as he and Reuters made for a space to their right. Here they sat down and waited to see what was happening while they tried to gauge what sort of men were gathering here.

"You're new, aren't you!" said a shape in the dark, suddenly dropping down in front of them. Reuters flinched.

"Yes," said Morgenstern, gripping his knife. "We've been stumbling around outside for days. Came across this place by chance. Thought we'd come in and see what was happening here."

"Did you?" said the stranger. "Did you really? Well, well. I'm Hauptmann Voss, Conrad Voss. Used to be in command of a company of tanks. But well, I'm not any more. I think I must be the only member of my regiment that's still alive. At least, I think so. I've been looking for them for weeks. Can't find a single one. You'd think if there was someone still alive, I'd have found them by now. Ended up here days ago."

"I'm Morgenstern; Infantry. This is Reuters; Artillery."

"Well, well," said Voss then, beaming at Reuters. "All we need now is a Sailor and a Pilot and we'd have our own little army!" he laughed, though no one joined him. Morgenstern quickly decided he was half mad, but pressed him nonetheless.

"So what is this place? What's happening here?" he asked, looking around. Reuters couldn't help staring at the Tank Commander.

"Oh it's not so bad," said Voss. "A refuge if you like. Everyone keeps to themselves.....You know," he added, his eyes flicking around him as if he was wary of being overheard or constantly expecting some new threat.

Morgenstern nodded. "Any food or water?" he asked.

"What do you think?" said Voss, laughing. "At least there's the snow! What would we fucking do if it was summer?" Voss laughed again. Morgenstern frowned. Reuters kept staring.

Just then a shape appeared out of some recess in the darkness. The three men could eventually see it was a man without legs, dragging himself along the ground with the stumps of his hands. "Mutti!" he said as he went by. He left a trial behind him. A faintly yellow, watery substance, that came from badly infected pressure sores on his buttocks and what remained of his legs.

"They call him the Snail," said Voss. Morgenstern couldn't believe it; his stomach contracting. Reuters gave a whimper as he shut his eyes; tears streaming down his face.

"They say he chewed his own fingers off," Voss went on. "When they became frostbitten. Wanted to save his hands and arms I suppose. Well, you would, wouldn't you? Especially when you'd lost your legs."

"But..the fluid..The trail," said Morgenstern.

"According to a Medical chap I spoke to, it's the inevitable result of the conditions here. Bad infection of blisters or something, because he's always on the ground, do you see? Suppurations? No idea why he isn't dead. If that was me, well...Anyway, I've seen far worse than that."

Morgenstern looked at Voss. He tried to think of what could possibly be worse. Eventually he came to the same conclusion. Yes, there was probably a lot worse than that.

"I knew of a chap once. Oh ages ago it was now. What was his name again? Anyway, his tank had been hit several times. Including a phosphorous shell. Managed to crawl out through the escape hatch underneath, didn't he? Miracle he survived. Trouble was, one of his legs got caught. So he starts pulling and tugging and finally he's free! But he left the lower part of one leg behind in the hatch. Sounds like he would have lost it anyway, I'd say.

"So now he's free and all his mates are gone. What does he do? Well, he only crawls four kilometres back to camp, would you believe! Crawls with one arm mind, because one is just a withered stump thanks to the phosphorous. Apparently he left a trial too, though I don't know of what. Still, he got patched up and sent home. Any amount of Wound badges weighing him down, I'll bet," said Voss.

Morgenstern and Reuters looked at him with their mouths wide open. What sort of place was this? they wondered. What have we gotten ourselves into now?

*

The Padre Warns of Captivity

Time passed slowly in what Morgenstern and Reuters had been told was a cowshed. Others knew it as a stables and some would insist it had once been used to store grain in the days long passed. Whatever it had been, it was none of these things now. It was a gathering point of abject suffering where the strongest were the one who suffered most. They found themselves in a situation so alien and surreal that it tested their sense of reality to the limit. But still, they persisted and endured.

Most had felt part of something noble, even glorious. Their leaders, who they had looked up to, had abandoned them in a most heinous way. They were forgotten and isolated in a betrayal like no other. They had been written off like a bad debt in some bookkeeper's ledger.

The obscenity of the decision to forfeit half a million men, 320,000 of whom were already dead, was matched only by the appalling conditions they had been left to. Names, individuals, who sacrificed their lives for a cause that ultimately spat at them while they did so. None of it was lost to people like Morgenstern, Reuters or Voss. It was common knowledge everywhere in Stalingrad, from Field Marshal Paulus' bunker to the foxholes and shell craters where men huddled, freezing to death while they starved. Many strove to survive so that one day perhaps, they might return home and exact their revenge.

"Will we ever get out? Get away?" Reuters asked now, his head bowed as if in prayer.

"Give up any hope of that," said Morgenstern, looking at Voss, who seemed to have attached himself to the two men.

"Well, one never knows," said Voss then, feeling he should try and say something to allay the young Leutnant's fears. Morgenstern looked at the Tank Commander contemptuously, shaking his head as he looked away. What did he care? he thought. If the boy thinks he is going to escape this place, let him.

"It's said we're part of a great sacrifice," Reuters went on. "So that others may survive and create a front elsewhere. It's said then we'll show the Reds what we can do and make them wish they'd never been born."

"Where do you get this shit from?!" asked Morgenstern angrily. "And is that alright with you? For Christ's sake, the bit about sacrifice may be true; The bastards at home have certainly done that to us, but for a new front? A final victory? Or whatever! Bullshit! We're beaten! This war is lost! And the Reds will make sure they wipe us off the face of the earth. It's over! We're already dead and this is hell!" With that, Morgenstern got up with some effort and decided once he'd done so, to explore this place and see if there was something, anything to be gained in doing so.

"He's...just tired," said Voss, feeling embarrassed at Morgenstern's outburst. "Those of us with most to lose feel it worse."

"He's right," said Reuters, feeling foolish for talking such nonsense. "And you know it, Conrad. But my God, I cannot come to terms with what has happened to us."

"None of us can," said Voss. "But it affects us all in different ways. The worst of it is really, is that we can't right the wrong. We are in no position to be able to do anything about our situation. The frustration of that alone is monumental."

"Is there really no hope?" Reuters asked. In his heart and soul, he felt there had to be.

"Well, my boy," said Voss, smiling. "We could all march, as one, out into the snow towards the Russian lines and get it over with. That alone would be a page of history. But I do believe that while we breathe and live, there is hope...of something at least. Our flickers of hope burn on as our appalling situation deteriorates. It's why we continue to endure."

Reuters looked at Voss in a new light. What he said warmed something inside him. Then the door to the barn was suddenly flung open and those near it recoiled at the blast of cold air that entered the space, flurries of snow dancing in the pale light before it was hurriedly shut again.

A figure stood then momentarily before sinking to his knees, as if having endured a journey here of a thousand miles. Voss was immediately alert to the man; A promise of something new and curious. "Here friend," he said. "Join us here."

It was Padre Huber. He had walked non-stop since his humiliation at the Field Hospital. He had wandered aimlessly and eventually followed others to this place. He looked up. Who had spoken? A voice in the darkness. Was he dreaming again?

Voss held out a hand, beckoning the young Chaplain. He hadn't the strength to get up and go to him. Huber shuffled towards them on his hands and knees. "What is this place?" he asked finally.

"Oh, it's just one of many places, I imagine," said Voss. "Perhaps a candle in the darkness."

Just then, the Snail passed between them in a blur as if from nowhere, and Huber's eyes widened with a new horror. He crumpled over and lay down, staring upwards at a hole in the broken thatched roof. Voss studied him as if looking at something interesting in a magazine. Reuters stopped thinking about hope and blinked several times while he contemplated this newcomer.

"Where have you come from," they asked him. "Any sign of the Reds?"

There was no reply. Voss and Reuters left him to gather himself. Then Morgenstern reappeared, reclaiming the space against the wall where he had sat previously. He finally noticed Huber and looked at Voss, who merely shrugged. Reuters seemed to be asleep.

"There must be a couple of hundred men here," said Morgenstern later. "There's even some civilians among them. Every regiment you can think of is represented. But not a hint of any food."

"Not going to be, is there?" said Reuters, his eyes still closed.

"It's a substantial place really, or it was at least. A Depot of some kind. The outskirts of the factory district are over that way," said Morgenstern, waving a hand. "Open countryside that way after a kilometre or so. As good a place as any to hole up, I suppose."

"We can't wander around for ever," said Reuters.

"Indeed not," said Voss, still looking at Huber who hadn't moved, his eyes now closed.

Morgenstern contemplated the new arrival.

"He's just joined us," said Voss. "While you were away."

"What's your name Padre?" the Veteran asked him, noticing the cross sewn onto his cap.

"Huber," he said after some minutes. "Eduard."

"I'm Morgenstern."

"And I'm Voss, Conrad Voss."

"Reuters," said the young Leutnant, completing the introductions.

"Is there any news?" asked Huber. "Any hint of when this might end? I heard outside that Paulus is dead."

"Some days ago, I was sure the Reds would swamp us within hours. But now? They're hitting us from everywhere and still we hold them off. How?" said Morgenstern, picking at something wedged between two cobblestones at his feet. "I can only guess they're in as bad a shape as we are. But once their reserves arrive, well, then you can measure your lives in minutes, not days."

There was a silence while everyone digested that. It wasn't exactly a revelation. In fact, it was a fairly well known certainty. But hearing it again in this place and coming from someone like Morgenstern, made it sound more ominous. As if it had already taken place.

"Could capture by the Reds be any more worse than this?" asked Reuters. "If we survive I mean. I can't see how it could be."

"You fucking bet it could!" said Morgenstern. "Crammed into a cattle car for weeks on end while they transport you east to a Siberian Gulag? Most of us would die before we got there. Then-."

"Whatever you've heard boy," said Voss, cutting across Morgenstern, "is lies! They'd work us to death in a matter of weeks in the mines."

"But they keep telling us we'd be treated well. Fed properly and-."

"Here there are glimmers of hope," said Huber, suddenly sitting up. He had everyone's attention. "If we live that long, we'll probably die of starvation or the cold or at the hands of the Russians. And who would blame them? For what we have done? What we have become? You should pray for death before you think about surviving captivity. There, all hope is gone."

Reuters couldn't believe that. His youth wouldn't let him. "You exaggerate Padre", he said. "I've heard of men who escaped and returned to us. They spoke well of their time as prisoners."

"I heard of an officer," said Morgenstern. "He wasn't even in the SS. He was a Major, waiting for a promotion, because his C.O. had been killed. A Grenadier regiment they were. This was over near the Tractor Factory.

"So one night, he was captured in a trench raid. The Reds held him for two days. Suddenly, one morning, there he is standing in the middle of no man's land in a minefield! The bastards had gouged his eyes out and cut off his fingers. There was also a horse-shoe nail through his tongue. And all because he refused to talk," Morgenstern finished with, shaking his head.

"It's unbelievable," said Voss, who had heard similar tales. "What about the crucifixions?"

"Well, SS scum started that!" said Morgenstern. "They'd roll into a village behind the advance back in the early days. I heard of one place where they'd nailed whole families to barn doors. Including kids! Now it seems like a game to see who can be more cruel and sadistic. Us or them. I tell you this, we are lost!"

After a few minutes of silence, Huber spoke again. "I was privy to an interrogation once. Long time ago now; perhaps a year?" Everyone looked at him. He seemed detached from his surroundings. Lost in his memories. He sat with his legs under him, trying to ease some discomfort. He rocked slightly, to and fro.

"I was friends with an Intelligence Officer. A young Hauptmann. We were both from Cologne, so...Anyway, one day a raiding commando came back from the Russian lines with two prisoners.

Nothing unusual about that, as you know. Happened all the time. Some Colonel however asked the young Hauptmann-."

"What was his name?" asked Voss, details like that important to him.

"Do you know, I can't honestly remember," said Huber, silent then for a time. "I think his first name was Erich..Yes, Erich."

"Oh very good," said Voss, satisfied. "Go on, please."

"The Colonel had heard Erich could speak pretty good Russian, and being with Intelligence, well naturally, he wanted Erich to interrogate the new prisoners because his own Intelligence Officer was dead. Erich's C.O. agreed and so eventually, he sits down with the two Russians; an Infantry Corporal and an NKVD type. At least everyone suspected he was NKVD. He was the real prize, so Erich starts with him. He stayed silent throughout. Not a single word.

"Then Erich starts on the Corporal and what do you know, he is singing like a songbird! All he knows. The NKVD man suddenly jumps on him and the two of them end up on the floor, rolling around and thrashing each other senseless. Well Erich gets the guards in there to drag the NKVD man out. I heard later they shot him that afternoon."

"NKVD are trash," said Morgenstern. "Fucking animals! Any we ever came across were shot out of hand. They're fanatics. Crazy bastards!"

"Quite," said Huber. Everyone was nodding. "So the Corporal back with Erich tells all he can about troop strengths, tank numbers and so on. Small stuff really, that any reconnaissance patrol could find out, but Erich is happy to hear it, and he decides he'll get the Corporal some proper coffee and cigarettes. The Russian thinks it's his birthday and Christmas on the same day. Over coffee, Erich asks him about the treatment of German prisoners sent to the Gulags. Would you believe this Corporal used to be with the Police Militia, attached to a detail that transported prisoners from Moscow Central out east?"

"What luck!" said Voss, enjoying the story.

"How did he end up at the front?" asked Reuters.

"I don't know," said Huber, looking at the young Leutnant. "Who can say?" he added.

"What difference does it make?" said Morgenstern, irritably. "Go on Padre."

"So Erich pressed him for details. More out of curiosity than anything else. Nothing he was saying was going to help the situation where they were. Erich was just curious to know.

"The Corporal spoke of hundreds of German prisoners arriving at a processing station near Moscow Central. Most arrived on trains but some would come by truck. A lot of them were in bad shape, wounded or sick, but they were given no treatment. They were herded into large groups and left standing in pens for hours on end, sometimes even days, before being put on other trains heading east. Anyone who tried to escape were shot or clubbed to death to save ammunition. Perhaps they were the lucky ones, Erich told me later.

"The train journey could last for several days, even weeks. It was almost 5,000 kilometres after all. Often a train would just stop in a siding for days on end for no apparent reason."

"My God!" said Reuters, closing his eyes.

"Once arrived at their destination, the prisoners were ordered off their cattle-cars after collecting their dead comrades who hadn't survived the trip, and that was most of them. Guards from the prison camp would chain the prisoners at the ankles; sometimes together, sometimes not. Then they were forced march for hours to the camp; the Guards following behind in trucks or cars, taking it in turns as escorts on foot.

"The prisoners were whipped repeatedly for falling behind or simply falling down. Some would be shot or clubbed to death. A common injury was a broken ankle from the chains if you fell or tripped. If that happened, the poor unfortunate was unchained and tossed in a ditch where he was left to die. There was nowhere to go; not with a broken ankle and the weather would do for you anyway in no time. Sometimes, the Corporal said, the Guards would cut the prisoner's Achilles Tendon to make sure they couldn't go anywhere."

"Jesus Christ!" said Voss, biting his fist.

"At the camp, the men were simply worked to death," Huber continued. "Breaking rocks or clearing forest. Beatings and torture happened every day. Food was black bread, frozen solid like a brick, with a watery soup that might have some fish heads in it, but not everyday. Life expectancy was around forty days for the strongest. If the work and conditions didn't kill you, other prisoners would for any reason you can think of," said Huber, ending his tale. He lay back down, exhausted with the effort of sitting up for so long.

"That's a grim tale, Padre," said Voss.

"Is it any worse than what the Einzatsgruppen got up to?" Morgenstern asked. "I remember the early days. A matter of weeks after we entered Russia. There was a prison camp run by those bastards close to the border with Poland. They kept 75,000 Reds inside a fence that was what, 500 square metres? They were simply left to starve or die of thirst. In the end, the Reds turned on each other. The strong preyed on the weak and ate them. They had become cannibals. The SS guards, mainly Ukrainian or Latvians, would amuse themselves by cheering them on."

Reuters suddenly leapt forward and grabbed Morgenstern's lapels. "It's not true!" he yelled. "Lies! Damn lies! How can you say such things about our side!" Tears streamed down his face as he shook the Veteran back and forth with the strength of a child. Then he collapsed back into his space, whimpering with despair.

Huber was staring at the roof again. Voss closed his eyes. Morgenstern returned to picking at the gap between the cobblestones.

*

Benz' Army of the Dead

Time dragged ever on. The following night, there was a tremendous commotion. It seemed as if a dozen people were pounding on the doors to the depot across from Morgenstern and the small group around him.

"What the hell?" he said, sitting up.

Reuters yelped and recoiled against the wall. "It's the Reds!" he screamed in panic. This caused everyone to shout and yell in the depot while they scrambled to somewhere away from the apparent danger.

But the door suddenly fell open and a figure in the darkness dropped to his knees, breathing hard. He lay on his back, clutching at the cobblestones as if trying to gain some purchase. Morgenstern and Voss went over to shut the large wooden door which creaked loudly in protest. Then it was closed and while Morgenstern peered out through a gap to see what was outside, Voss leant over the new arrival and could see he was a Medical Orderly.

"There's nothing out there," said Morgenstern, joining him.

"It's alright," Voss told the Medic. "You're among friends."

"Take it easy," said Morgenstern, who could see the man was terrified.

"What's your name?" Voss asked him.

"B..B..Benz," he said, his teeth chattering madly. His eyes were wide and this emphasised the dark rings around his sunken sockets. He kept looking at the door, as if expecting someone or something. "They're coming!" he said, rolling himself into a ball.

"There's no one out there," said Morgenstern, looking at Voss, frowning.

"You're safe now," said Voss.

Then Huber came over to them. Reuters had calmed down, but not enough to move. "Tell us what happened," said Huber. "Where have you come from?" It took a while, but eventually Benz spoke.

"I came from the Ring, near the Tractor factory. I walked and walked, not really knowing where I was going. Last night, I slept in a foxhole which I covered with branches. The snow did the rest. When I started walking again at dawn, I thought I could hear the Reds behind me, so I ran and ran! After some time, I collapsed. My legs simply gave out and everything was quiet. I looked up behind me and couldn't believe what I was seeing! It was a Battalion, at least, of our boys marching towards me!"

"Impossible!" said Morgenstern. "You're dreaming."

"Why not," said Reuters. "It could be true!" Morgenstern rolled his eyes.

"Let him speak!" said Huber. "He has more to tell." Voss stared at the Medic in disbelief. Could it possibly be the head of a rescue force? The rescue force they'd heard so much about?

"So I got up as this hoard drew nearer, perhaps a hundred metres by now. I called out and waved, but no one answered. They drew nearer. The snow made it hard to see, but you could tell from where I stood they were our boys."

Benz got to his knees and allowed the others to bring him over to their space, where he sat against the wall. "Then,...oh Jesus!" he said, tears coming as he shook with fear. "They got nearer and nearer. I still waved. Now I see they're wearing snow masks. Except..except they weren't snow masks! They were the whites of their skulls! They were skeletons in uniforms! A thousand fucking skeletons marching through the snow! And they're coming this way!" Benz buried his face in his hands and wept like a child.

"For Christ's sake," said Morgenstern. "He's cracked! What shit."

"What did he see then?" asked Reuters. "The Reds?"

"Well it wasn't our boys," said Voss, frowning deeply as he looked at Benz.

"And it wasn't the Reds," said Morgenstern. "At least, not yet."

"Well he saw something," said Huber, scratching the stubble on his chin. "I mean, look at him."

"Oh really?" said Morgenstern. "A battalion of fucking ghosts?! Come now Padre; You of all people!" Morgenstern felt like laughing, but one look at the Medic stopped him.

"I tell you, it's the truth!" Benz insisted.

*

Stark Buries Wagner

The strong wind and driving snow made it impossible to go on for now. In their weakened state, Stark and Wagner slumped to the ground, exhausted. The biting cold was a torture no one could stand for long.

Stark remembered last September, in the Field Depot he'd worked in. The talk then was all about a winter campaign that nobody wanted. Many of the Officers from the different regiments that had passed through the Depot, were critical of the planners back in Berlin. Their objectives were whimsical and what they asked the Senior Officers for on the ground, was seen as pie in the sky fantasies. Some objectives were achieved, but this was due to the quality of the forces involved or the lack of quality on the Russian side.

Many requests were made; for equipment or replacements; for more men; for better air support that Goering kept promising but never delivered, but also, and this was seen as crucial, winter clothing. Even Paulus it was said, had personally asked for that. But none ever came. One rumour was put forward that everything was supposed to be finished by October at the latest, so there was no need for 'winter clothing'. Another rumour was that it was a supply issue; there simply wasn't any winter supplies to send.

Whatever the reason, by November and December, men were freezing to death in summer uniforms or greatcoats that kept you warm on a chilly autumnal day. Men gathered around drums of petrol which they lit as fires. Tank and truck engines had to be kept running all the time or they froze solid. Even the rifle oil in men's weapons froze, making them useless. The Russians were more used to the weather conditions and had proper winter gear for their men. The Germans sent many raiding parties out into the night, not for intelligence or prisoners, but to simply get their hands on the coveted quilted field jackets the average Russian soldier wore.

"We've got to get out of this," said Stark, more to himself than Wagner, who now seemed asleep or unconscious. Stark rolled him onto his back and getting to his feet with some effort, dragged the man off the path they were on and into a hedgerow on one side, where a hollow in the frozen ground offered some respite from the dreadful weather.

"Alright Hugo," said Stark, breathing hard. "We'll rest here."

Wagner was still out of it, but at least he was still breathing. It was eerily quiet, Stark noticed. There was no shelling any more but wherever you looked, smoke could be seen billowing from various points n the distance. Even the Reds were servants of the weather, he thought. What a fucking hellhole this country is! So desolate and so unforgiving. How could anyone in their right mind come to settle here?

Stark thought about the first time he had come to Russia. Was it really twenty months ago? A convoy of trucks from Poland that kept leapfrogging the trains that ran parallel to the roads they used, and all the while feeling like territory Germany had held for decades. What a trip that had been! It was weeks before they caught up with the forward lines. It was another stroll in the park; like France had been. Everyone was so confident and bullish. Soon Germany would rule the world if she wanted to!

On a platform in Berlin, while waiting for a troop train to Warsaw, Stark felt uncomfortably hot in his uniform. That warm April day was cloudless and he could remember looking across at his wife of six months, Greta, as she stood in the doorway of the waiting lounge, the bright sunlight showing her lovely figure through the yellow summer dress she wore. Her blonde hair shone under a wide-brimmed hat that she kept touching as if to make sure it was still there. She turned and came back to him.

"Mama said she would come!" said Greta, sitting down beside him once more.

"There's time," said Stark. "Perhaps she got held up. You know how the trams can be."

"Yes, perhaps," said Greta, resting her head on Stark's shoulder. "Oh Wilhelm, you must promise me to take care. Look after yourself and-."

"Come now! I'm a Cook! What can happen to me? I'm never near any fighting. You know that."

"Yes, but I hear all sorts of tales about Russia. Last week, Ingrid spoke of-."

"Well Ingrid should stop speaking. What a gossip she is! I'll be fine and nothing will happen to me."

But Greta started crying nonetheless. Stark hugged her and held her close. "Hush now," he said.

"But when will I see you again? Christmas? Oh, I can't stand it Wilhelm!"

Stark held her closer and now, lying in this filthy freezing ditch on the outskirts of Stalingrad, he hugged Greta again, wrapping his arms around him tightly, his eyes shut as he imagined his beautiful girl once more in his arms. He hadn't seen her since. He'd been due leave last October, but this had been cancelled due to the frantic events that had led to the 6th Army taking this Godforsaken place. Leave was promised again before Christmas last year, but now, well, Stark was sure he would never get home again.

He'd even stopped writing to his wife, wanting her to forget him and move on. He didn't think she would. She would cling to his memory, hoping he'd return to her, unless she received notice of his death. Stark couldn't bring himself to write of the horrors he had witnessed and endured here. He wouldn't want Greta to read such things anyway. How do you put such things down on paper? he wondered. The last letter he'd written in November spoke of his hopes to see Greta for Christmas, before everything fell apart around him.

He wept. He wept for his wife. He wept for his life and hers. All their hopes and dreams; Cut short and abruptly pulled from under them in a vast betrayal.

Some time later, he started awake. Had he really been asleep? That was a dangerous mistake, unless you were prepared. What had woken him then? If he closed his eyes, he could still see Greta, but he forced himself to rub snow in his eyes and feeling alert once more, he turned to look at Wagner, lying beside him and covered in a thick frost. Stark knew immediately he was dead. He placed a hand on his chest. Nothing. Oh my poor friend, he thought. How you suffered. But you can rest now.

The earth was frozen like concrete, so it was impossible to dig a grave. Instead, Stark covered Wagner with branches and leaves. It took him a long time but finally he was done. He struggled to his feet and thought of saying some words before leaving Wagner and moving on. But what was there to say? Even if there was a God, he wasn't listening to anyone here.

*

The Snail's Tale

Reuters awoke in the early hours to the piercing shrieks of someone who sounded like they were being repeatedly stabbed. As he started awake, he disturbed everyone else around him and once they had fully woken and became aware of their surroundings, they all stared open-mouthed at the spectacle in their midst. The Snail was over by the entrance, going round and round in circles, yelping continuously as he pounded the cobblestones with the stumps of his hands to propel himself in his frenzy. "Mutti! Mutti!" he cried every so often.

"Jesus Christ Almighty!" said Morgenstern, though it was barely a whisper.

Several men who had woken to the noise spaced around the rough walls of the depot started hurling abuse at him. Some threw stones or whatever came to hand.

Benz got up and went over to the man in an effort to try and calm him down.

"What's wrong with him?" asked Reuters, looking around in the darkness.

"What's got him so worked up?" said Voss, expecting some new threat.

Benz knelt down near the Snail and said, "Alright friend. Let me help you." But he just kept going, dodging Benz and continuing on like some ghastly bumper-car. He spun around the cripple, trying to keep him in view.

"Leave him," said a voice, coming out of the darkness, getting nearer. "Let him be." A crumpled figure who looked more dead than alive stood beside Benz. The Snail then stopped his circuitous motion and darted off to everyone's left, yelping dementedly into the recesses beyond.

"He'll stop soon," said the crumpled figure. "Every so often, he carries on like that. There's nothing to be done. In time he'll just wear himself out."

"But what's this?" asked Benz, looking down to the ground at the trail. Then he realised what it was. "My God!" he muttered, shocked, even though as a Medic he thought there were no more surprises left in the world.

"Why don't you join us?" said Voss to the crumpled figure.

The frail man came over and sat with the group. Benz followed him, shaking his head in despair.

"I'm Huber," said the Padre, starting the introductions. When everyone followed suit, the stranger spoke.

"Names' Jürgen," he began. "I was a Senior Sergeant with the 289th. I've been a soldier since I was 17. That's damn near thirty years now. I went all the way through the Great War without a scratch and I did two years in Spain with the Condor Legion. But I've never in all my time seen anything like this fucking place. How we ended up like this I'll never know!"

"We're all with you in that friend," said Morgenstern.

"How do you know this poor soul?" asked Huber, referring to the Snail.

"Oh hell, let me see," said Jürgen, trawling through his memories. "Last November it was, yeah. One late afternoon, I was summoned to the Colonel's bunker. There's a young Leutnant already there. I was to take this Leutnant and six men behind Russian lines to scout out their Katushya positions. Those fucking rockets were playing havoc with us and it was felt we were wasting time and effort shelling them blindly."

"Bloody stupid idea!" said Morgenstern. "They're usually mobile. You can move 'em about like chess-pieces."

"Very true," said Jürgen.

"Some are fixed," said Reuters. "Depends on your intelligence reports. If-."

"You don't say," said Morgenstern, rolling his eyes.

"Go on," said Voss, as Huber closed his eyes. Benz was staring into space.

"Anyway, it was a total fuck-up," Jürgen continued. "Eight of us left in the middle of the night. Three of us got back. There was no sign of the rocket batteries and we had to fight our way back the following night. Nothing unusual about that you might say. Intelligence reports always lag behind a job like that. It becomes a fool's errand that's accepted as part of life on the front line.

"At dawn, we found ourselves about a kilometre from our trenches. We could see them clearly in the distance. There was me, a young Private, and the Leutnant, name of Haase. Five of our comrades lay in the snow behind us; three dead and two wounded. We couldn't do anything for them. The Leutnant wanted to bring them with us and we almost came to blows I can tell you as I said there was no point. They wouldn't have survived being moved, but this kid was still fresh and green. Typical young officer; wanting something out of nothing."

Morgenstern nodded while Reuters blanched.

"So we started to make our way home. The Leutnant was on point. I was next while the Private took up the rear. As we got nearer, someone in our trenches called out and started waving his arms frantically. It was obviously a warning. The kid behind me suddenly took off, running towards our lines! He was waving back, thinking our boys were welcoming us home! I tried to grab the stupid bastard as he tore past me, but he was like a hare being chased by a wolf! The Leutnant yelled but it was no good." Jürgen paused, closing his eyes. He ran a hand through his thinning hair. He was haunted by guilt.

"What happened?" asked Voss, eager to hear the outcome.

"Seconds later, there was an almighty explosion! The young Private disappeared in a red mist. I was blown off my feet and the Leutnant to one side, a bit further on. In our dazed state, we both got to our feet instinctively. Then I looked at the Leutnant. One side of him was wet with blood, but he seemed oblivious to whatever injury caused it.

"I looked around quickly, thinking the Reds were on us! They were firing mortars and caught the Private by chance. But there was no one else around and anyway, there was only one explosion. Next thing, the Leutnant is doubled over, looking at his boots, like he's stepped in a pile of cow-shit and I knew then what had happened. We were in a fucking minefield! The Private had trodden on one in his dash home and now the Leutnant was standing on one! I checked my own position but I was lucky; fate had spared me that day.

"'Don't move', I called to him. 'For Christ's sake! Don't fucking move!' He looked at me with the most pitiable face. 'What can I do?' he said. 'Oh Jesus help me!'

"I took off my gear and as many layers of clothing as I dared in the cold and threw them to him. 'Wrap them around your legs! Tight as you can!' I said. When he'd done that, I said, 'you're going to have to jump. Wait till I've backed up! It's the only way. The only thing you can do!'

"Well, it took forever. I was close to hypothermia and knew I'd have to leave him soon if I didn't want to freeze to death. I was lying on my stomach, watching him. Urging him on. He wasn't going to move. I closed my eyes, giving up and thinking how was I going to get out of this mess. Then there was another explosion. Perhaps the Leutnant's weight took it's effect on the mine. Perhaps he'd flexed a muscle, or jumped. Whatever.

"When I looked again, he'd been blown about twenty metres further on, towards our trenches. I inched myself towards him, crawling all the way. I was waiting to be blown sky-high myself; terrified I wouldn't die outright. Then I was there beside him, and well, you can guess the state he was in. Both legs gone; A hole in his back the size of your fist! Blood everywhere. The wound he'd got from the first explosion had widened. I could see a lung through all the mess. I lay beside him and dragged him bit by bit towards our trenches. When I got half-way, I felt I couldn't go on and must have passed out or something.

"When I woke up, I was in a Field Hospital! So I'd been rescued. I'd been there for a couple of days. I asked about the Leutnant, expecting to hear he' died. No, no! I was told. Young Leutnant Haase was in the next ward, recovering!"

"But how?!" said Morgenstern, incredulous. "How could he possibly have survived?"

"Incredible," said Voss and Benz, almost as one.

"A miracle," said Huber. Reuters nodded in agreement.

"Well fuck knows," said Jürgen. "Wherever that hospital was vanished one night under heavy shelling. I was long out of it by then but somehow, Haase had lived through it and I came across him in a shelter near the sulphur works. Long story short, we ended up here.

"He suffered with frostbite early on, because his hands were always on the ground, in the snow. He cut his fingers off with the lid of a tin can. When he couldn't hold the lid any more, because he was running out of fingers, he chewed his own thumbs off! It's true I'm telling you! I watched him do it!" said Jürgen, looking at everyone who stared back at him in disbelief. "And that poor wretch, just now, is young Leutnant Haase. Crazy as can be, but he lives! Covered in festering sores and always bleeding from somewhere, but he lives!"

"I bless the fact that I'm uninjured," said Morgenstern, after a while. Everyone was still coming to terms with Haase's story. Reuters and Voss nodded their agreement. "Imagine the hell of a bad wound on top of the hunger, the cold, the lice, and-."

"And as we all know," said Huber, "The Russians aren't going to treat anyone. Why waste resources on those who came to kill you and take your country. Rules don't apply here. Those they don't kill immediately, they'll let die in some hole out east."

"Do you really think they'll bother transporting us out east?" said Voss.

"Most likely we'll just be herded somewhere while they wait for us to die. But if they have a use for us? Why not transport us?"

"Work us to death," said Morgenstern.

"But not until they get some use out of us," said Jurgen, getting up now. "I must find young Haase," he said then, disappearing into the darkness.

"I admire his loyalty to that poor wretch," said Huber, watching him go.

"There must be more to that story," said Voss.

"Maybe," said Huber. "He's right though, about the Russians. They're not stupid. I'll bet they'll have us clear up the mess we made and then start us rebuilding all that we've destroyed."

"It'll take years," said Morgenstern. "We won't live through it, that's for sure."

"It'll be the cheapest labouring job in history," said Voss.

"They'll have to treat us well," said Reuters naively. "They have to."

"And who is going to care if they don't boy?" said Morgenstern, shaking his head.

"Have you ever thought about getting out?" Benz asked. "Getting away?"

"What do you think?" said Morgenstern dismissively. "For Christ's sake, where do you think we should go?"

"There is nowhere to go," said Voss. "We're trapped here."

"But we could try!" said Reuters, sounding excited, as if the idea had never occurred to him. "As a group, we'd have a chance!"

Morgenstern rounded on him angrily. "How far could you walk in this weather? Without food! Without your health! Unarmed! Think about it! And that's if the Reds let you walk right by 'em!"

"It's better than sitting here! Waiting to die!" said Reuters, tears streaming down his face.

"Then go!" said Morgenstern. "There's the fucking door! Off with you!"

Reuters started shaking. He wept and withdrew into himself. Nobody said anything. What was there to say? It was like a Doctor suddenly telling you that you had days to live. There was nothing you could do about it.

*

Stark and the Angel of Death

Pain racked Stark's emaciated body while he struggled to remain upright in the freezing wind as he stumbled through the knee-deep snow. He had no idea where he was going and could make nothing out in the surrounding whiteness.

His thoughts returned to Wagner, whom he'd left maybe two or three hours earlier. Poor Hugo. Twenty years old. He had studied engineering at Freiburg University and had been engaged to a girl called Lara, of whom Stark knew next to nothing. Wagner hardly spoke of her, saying it upset him to even think about her.

Wagner didn't get caught up in the mad fervour of the mid-thirties. All he dreamt of was building bridges and great civic works that would endure for centuries. But unusually, his father pressed him to join the Army in 1939, thinking that a new era of greatness was coming to Germany and that his son should be part of it. Wagner resisted but his father's domineering personality won out in the end.

And now poor Hugo is dead, thought Stark. Another frozen corpse among hundreds of thousands in this dreadful, awful place. A pain shot through him then, and he collapsed into the snow, gasping for breath. His eyes widened and despite the cold, sweat broke out all over him. Stark remained on all fours and clutched his chest as he struggled to control his breathing. Then he was aware of somebody near him and looking up, he yelped at the figure standing over him.

"Take my hand Wilhelm," said the figure. "I'll help you up."

Stark saw little through his pain and through the snow which the wind sent howling all around him. The figure wore a dark habit with a hood. Stark flinched backwards and ended up lying on his back, looking up at this new image towering over him. The figure extended a hand.

"Come Wilhelm, enough of this now. We'll find your friends. Your loved ones."

Stark screamed then. He kicked himself backwards into the snow in terror. He had to get away. Was this the 'Todesengel' his grandmother used to speak of? The Reaper? Surely not! But here? Could it be?

"Get away!" Stark yelled, his voice sounding weak and feeble.

Now the figure knelt over him. "Why do you willingly suffer this hell, Wilhelm? There's no escape from it. No end. It will always be thus. Look around you. Don't you despair? Those still living are dead but they die over and over again. Free yourself from this agony. Come with me and one day Greta will find you, and you will both know peace. Stay and this will be your resting place. Your mother is with me, and your grandmother, Wilhelm. They weep for you. They despair seeing you like this. Come with me Wilhelm and join them in peace."

Stark screamed until he was capable of no more sound. Then all went black. Suddenly he started awake. Had he been dreaming? A terrible nightmare among so many others. He managed to get to his feet. What else could it have been? Dismissing it then, he stumbled on. The pain that had consumed him had eased and he was able to concentrate on making some progress, though every step was liking climbing a mountain. Every so often, he would fall into the snow, gasping for breath and with much effort he would regain his feet, stumbling on and on. Once or twice if he looked into the white distance, he could see the hooded figure looking after him, one hand gripping a scythe, the other held upright, beckoning him.

"No!" he cried to himself. "I will not! I will endure! I will live!"

Finally, when he thought he couldn't go on, he saw the depot ahead of him which to him was a grey shape in the gloom. As he got nearer, he could just make out the wooden door and then he was on all fours, crawling towards it. Eventually, he was there and he placed his hands against it, pushing with the strength of someone without any. Then the door was open and someone was helping him inside.

*

Morgenstern Remembers

While Stark was escaping the clutches of his grandmother's Todesengel, Morgenstern broke bread, literally, with the small group around him. They had become a tight-knit unit in a short time in the way that only heartfelt personal exchanges could forge. Breaking up the hard bread in his overcoat pocket, Morgenstern looked around him anxiously. If anyone knew what was going on, they would pounce on him and the group for the precious food.

"Gather round, facing me," he said. "Don't make it obvious for fuck sake! I'll pass out the bread, you palm it and no chewing! Pretend you've got two Reds watching you in prison!"

It went on for what seemed a long time but eventually they had all finished one loaf. Everyone beamed in satisfaction and expressed their gratitude to Morgenstern as if he'd saved their lives, and was bundling them up the steps of a plane out of here. A whole loaf! Between only six of them? It was a feast! They talked of the possibility of rescue again; They talked of escape, again; They talked of the Snail, poor young Leutnant Haase. Benz also spoke of his Battalion of Skeletons, marching towards them, amid responses of derision, doubt and fear. "It's true!" he kept saying. "They're coming this way and we will join them!"

Morgenstern left them to it and leant back against the stone wall, shutting his eyes. In a short while, he drifted away and was back home in his parlour in Berlin. He was with his father and brother. His late mother had died the previous year of cancer at the age of 47 and to his deep regret, had missed the arrival of his first child. His wife Elke was in hospital, having just given birth to a baby girl that afternoon. It was August 1939.

"I don't know what to say," his father, a stern Lutheran, was saying.

"It's a rough deal, Karl," said his brother, placing a hand on Morgenstern's shoulder.

It should have been a happy time and one of celebration but instead it felt like they had just come from a cemetery. Morgenstern wanted to shout and yell. How dare they refer to the birth of his daughter as a 'rough deal'! And say things like 'It may be God's will, but sometimes these things go terribly wrong..', as his father had said earlier. But if Morgenstern was to be true to himself, he'd felt the same way at first. Shattering disappointment.

He'd arrived at the Klinikum around midday dressed in his new uniform. "Obergefreiter Karl Morgenstern," he announced cheerfully to the severe looking woman at the desk. He wasn't sure if she was a nun or a nurse. "My wife Elke sent for me. She's having a baby, our baby," he said, feeling foolish.

He was ushered down a hall and shown into a room where he was told to wait. Before he could ask any questions, the door shut behind him and he was left alone in a bare room with two benches, a table between them, a steel jug of water and two steel tumblers. Being excited and not able to relax, he paced the small room, smoking all the while and stopping occasionally to look out the small window.

He was 28 years old. He'd escaped the factories and joined the Army a year ago, much to his father's dismay. Factory work was a sixty hour week of dull, repetitive hard labour. He and his friends would drink beer every Friday night and would talk of their futures which in reality, were already laid out in front of them, like their fathers before them.

His father disapproved of his son getting caught up in events associated with this Austrian bastard, Hitler and his cronies. He remembered the Munich Putsch in 1933. He looked on Hitler and his rabble of followers as nothing more than crooks. Ex-jailbirds who surrounded themselves with thugs who did their bidding for them with violence and intimidation. But what could he do? Karl was determined to escape his life of drudgery in the factory and that was that.

Morgenstern's brother had been more conciliatory. "You're leaving the known, with all it's certainties, for the unknown and all it's uncertainties," he'd told him. "Have you really thought about what you're getting involved in? War is coming Karl, and soon."

"Don't you ever wish for something better Johann?" Morgenstern asked his brother. "Something more? Don't you feel numbed by your life? Don't you wish for change? Something new?"

Johann, two years older than his brother, worked in the same factory, but in the offices as a clerk, where he spent his days tallying orders with supplies.

"I'm happy Karl. I like certainty," he'd told him. Morgenstern insisted these were great times and he wanted to be part of it all.

And now he was to be a father on top of everything! What days these were! he thought, looking out the window at the rain.

After what seemed an eternity, but was just a couple of hours, another nurse opened the door. Morgenstern sprang to his feet. He was taken down another hall and another, before being shown into a room with four beds, three of them empty. In the bed nearest to him was Elke, a small bundle in her arms. He smiled. "Close the door, Karl," said his wife. "Come and sit with me," she added. She wasn't smiling. Morgenstern sat.

Elke unfolded the bundle and he looked at the most beautiful, tiniest face he had ever seen. He smiled at his wife, kissing her, and looked down at the baby, tears coming to his eyes. "It's a girl!" he said, marvelling at the beauty of her. Elke nodded, smiling now. Was he disappointed? She couldn't tell. He'd wanted a son, like most expectant fathers in those days and very common for the times. "She's beautiful! Look what you've done Elke, you clever girl!" he said, kissing her again.

"Can I touch her?" Elke nodded again, her love for Morgenstern becoming overwhelming. He stroked his daughter's nose tenderly. "Be careful bringing her into the garden Elke," he said then, "or the birds will mistake her for a flower!"

Then Elke wept and reached out a hand to place on Morgenstern's cheek. "Oh Karl," she said. "What is it Elke?" he asked, taking her hand. "What is wrong?"

"She's our daughter, Karl. She's beautiful and complete, but she's deaf and dumb," said Elke. "The Doctor said that otherwise she is healthy and normal and fine."

"What?!" said Morgenstern, too quickly. "How can they say that? How can they know? How can she be deaf and dumb?!" He frowned and looked down at the baby, taking his finger away.

Elke forgave him his anger. She'd felt the same disappointment, but not the anger. All she endured the last nine months and the agony this morning delivering her daughter, was worth every minute when she was handed this beautiful little girl. Then the Doctor was muttering to a nurse, then both nurses, and the baby was taken off her while they gathered around her, their backs to Elke.

"They have ways of knowing, Karl. I don't know how," she said now. "But she's perfect in every other way. Can't you be happy with that?"

Morgenstern stayed an hour or so. Elke told him what she knew. What had been explained to her. Together they consoled each other. Told each other that everything would be alright. He felt guilty as he left them; his family. But he couldn't shake his crushing disappointment. How did Elke feel? The same? Have I been a selfish bastard? he asked himself. I'll make it up to her. He wanted to rush back and tell her he was sorry. He was happy. Of course he was! It was a shock, that's all. Unexpected. The baby, who they decided to call Marta, after Morgenstern's mother, was beautiful. Of course she was. But Elke was exhausted and needed to sleep. He'd say all of that tomorrow.

"If it's God's will, what is their to be done?" his father was saying again now, back in Morgenstern's parlour. He stood up abruptly, looking down at his father, who flinched.

"We should go father," his brother said. "Let Karl rest. He's had a long day. Wish Elke the best, eh? Send her our love," he added, ushering his father out.

Then Morgenstern was alone. He wept. He wept for the heinous betrayal his daughter had been dealt. He wept for his wife, beautiful Elke, who would bear the brunt of Marta's care after all. It was the last time. He would never weep again. He would love his daughter and cherish her. Give thanks for her. He would make everything alright.

Then there was another commotion which upset his thoughts; the last being watching Elke gently blow her breath over Marta's face, who smiled and moved her head, loving the sensation and the connection with her mother. Then he was fully awake and looking around him. Absently, he sought the tiny drum in his tunic pocket. It was a toy he'd found for Marta, so she could feel it's vibrations as she held it. Elke had given it to him at the train station to keep with him as he left for the last time, headed for the Russian front. That was over a year ago now and he was sure he would never see either of them again.

*

Stark Tells of Dark Things.

Benz knelt beside Stark who had collapsed now onto his face, his arms stretched out. He looked like a priest about to be ordained. Voss struggled with the door and quickly glancing left and right into the snow covered wasteland, finally managed to swing it shut. "There's nothing. No one," he said, answering Morgenstern's unspoken question.

Benz felt for a pulse; two fingers on Stark's neck. "Well, he's alive, just," he said, frowning heavily. "Help me someone!" Morgenstern nudged Reuters and got up. Together with Voss, the four men carried Stark over to their place by the wall and laid him down.

"He looks finished," said the Padre, Huber.

Suddenly Stark opened his eyes and began to struggle, a silent scream coming from his mouth. "Take it easy," said Benz. "You're with friends, comrades." Stark became still. He looked around the small group with wild eyes. "You're safe now," someone said. Then he looked around him again, and flinched at the huddled shapes in the shadows.

"There are more of us," said Huber. "We all gathered here."

"Where am I? What is this place?" asked Stark, calming down now.

Everyone relaxed a little. Morgenstern resumed his place; back against the wall. Reuters withdrew to his corner. The rest gathered around Stark, helping him to sit up.

"It's a depot," said Voss. "Or it was. Or a cowshed. Maybe-."

"It's a sanctuary," said Huber, believing it.

After some brief introductions, which still seemed important, Stark slept for a couple of hours. When he woke and became accustomed to his surroundings, he was welcomed again. Morgenstern gave him some bread. "Where did you come from?" he asked him.

"I'm a Cook," said Stark, letting the bread moisten and soften in his mouth. It was joyous. "I was at Group HQ. Sometimes I'd be sent out into the field, but that became rarer and rarer. No one left in the field to feed I think. We stayed on too long. Right up to the last minute. It was terrible," he said, closing his eyes. Everyone gave him the time to continue.

"I saw five officers, including a Generalleutnant, who Paulus himself had sent to us, trying to get away in a Kubelwagen," Stark said, looking into the distance. "The Reds surrounded the car and the officers must have thought they'd be taken away as prisoners. Instead, the Reds brought up a flamethrower and burned them all to death where they sat, there in the 'Wagen. The screams were hideous."

"My God," said Reuters. No one else spoke.

"There were five of us in the end. Somehow we managed to evade the Reds and get away. My strongest memory of it all were the fires. Bright red and yellow flames! They burnt everything. "We five of us ended up in a bunker, trapped for four days. The area was shelled continuously.

Eventually me and a friend, Wagner, a Signaller, took to our heels. No one else would come. Ended up yesterday on the Bone Road."

"Where is he?" asked Benz, sounding concerned. "You're friend, Wagner?"

"I buried him this morning," said Stark. "Least, I think it was this morning."

There was silence for a time. Then Huber placed a hand on Stark's shoulder. "Well you're safe now and with friends. How long for is anyone's guess, but for now..." his voice trailed off.

Looking at the door, Stark's eyes widened and he began to tremble. "I saw the Reaper today! Out there, in the snow. He knew my name."

Morgenstern sighed heavily, but said nothing. Everyone else stayed silent too. Then Voss said, "Yes friend, I saw him too." Benz was going to mention his Battalion of Skeletons, but one look at Morgenstern made him think better of it.

*

Voss and his Angel of Death

Voss' command vehicle, an eight-wheeled Puma, came to a slow halt, two wheels on it's right side hanging over a huge shell hole. He threw open his turret hatch and gulped in the cold air, as if he'd had to hold his breath for several minutes. The air inside the armoured car was foul. A mixture of cordite from the shells they'd fired or the MG34, engine fumes, stale body odours and heat from the engine.

"Oh Jesus! Oh Christ!" Voss gasped, ducking straight back down into the vehicle as he thought of his pursuers. He looked around the Puma's cabin. His gunner was dead, as was the radio-operator. They'd been killed by a grenade thrown through the hatch as they'd been stacking ammunition during a break.

Voss and his driver had been outside, smoking and chatting about what? He couldn't remember. The three Panthers under Voss' command (there had been eight), were parked nearby, their crews also stocking up on ammunition from a truck they had rendezvoused with. Then somehow, inexplicably, what seemed like a horde, but was probably ten or a dozen, Russian soldiers appeared from nowhere; out of the woods nearby? Maybe. Their surprise was total and the air was suddenly filled with small arms fire and exploding grenades.

Voss' splintered memory recalled his jumping into the Puma and closing the hatch. Then his driver who'd beaten him to it, started up the motor and by a miracle, they had escaped. The rest of his company he'd left to their fate. They were probably already dead. He had no qualms about it. He was afraid. He escaped. It was as simple as that. Was it cowardice in the face of the enemy? Maybe. Voss didn't think too much about it. He had got away and he was alive. That's all that mattered.

Then he noticed his dead gunner and radioman. "How…? he said aloud, frowning. "Willi! Don't stop for anything!"

His driver spat on the floor and looked over his shoulder. "I'm hit!" he yelled. "Stomach I think!"

"Drive! Head back to Group! The hospital!"

So Willi drove, at top speed. The damage caused by the Russian grenade that had killed the rest of Voss' crew was limited to some dials, the main 50mm gun and little else. By another miracle, the ammunition hadn't gone up and as he looked down at his two dead crew members, he could see they had absorbed most of the grenade's blast. Voss was shaken, terrified. But he was alive. What a few days it had been. Anywhere else under any other circumstances, he would have been taken out of the field. A nervous wreck. But this was Stalingrad. Normal rules didn't apply.

"How's the fuel Willi?" Voss asked now, the Puma tearing along as he clung to the side-panels while getting thrown around. "Willi! Fuel!"

"Enough..To make it," said his driver, the last words he ever spoke.

They carried on for maybe ten more minutes. Eventually Willi slumped forward on his seat and the Puma coasted to a halt, coming to a stop over the shell hole. Poor Willi was dead. Ashen-faced and shaken, Voss took some time to open his hatch. He climbed out looking around him like a frightened rabbit. The Puma swayed slightly as he did so, it's two wheels suspended over the shell hole still spinning.

Then Voss was out and down and he knelt against the Puma, looking around him while he groped for his pistol. It was gone! How? Where am I? he wondered, not recognising anything. He thought he could see a village up ahead, perhaps a kilometre away. When he was satisfied he was alone, he started to head in that direction. The snow had eased and it was starting to get near dusk. Strangely, the village ahead, if that's what it was, didn't appear to be getting nearer as he walked on, his arms wrapped around him against the cold.

All dead. They're all dead, he thought. All my lads, dead. Close to fifty men, gone. Questions would be asked he knew, as to how he, their Commander, was the sole survivor. But that was pure chance, wasn't it? He could just as well be lying back there in the snow, couldn't he? But you fled! Leaving them behind! Yes, but….

Voss stopped dead as looked up ahead where the track dipped. There was a figure standing maybe fifty metres in front of him. "Oh my sweet Jesus!" he muttered to himself. He couldn't move. Paralysed by fear. The figure moved though, slightly. Voss wanted to scream, but no sound came out. The figure was wearing a cowl; a habit? Was he a monk? Voss relaxed momentarily. Then the figure was pointing at him and he saw the large scythe in his left hand. His terror returned. Now the figure spoke.

"Conrad!"

"Who..How?" Voss managed.

"You think you are free? You think you have survived?" said the figure.

"I...don't.." his voice trailed off. Was he hallucinating? Yes, surely that was it.

"Why should you?! Why should there be hope for one such as you?!"

"I was scared...What was I to do?" Voss said. He was shaking now.

"Your duty! You left your men to die as you left your sister to die all those years ago! You think I had forgotten! You think I had forgotten how you left her to die in the fire while you got away, thinking of no one but yourself!"

"But...Oh Jesus!," said Voss. His head was spinning. Dark memories overwhelmed him.

"How you lied then! How you lie now!"

"I tried.."

"Liar!"

"I tried..my sister,..Oh Jesus! I tried.. to.." Voss was weeping like a child. He had been fourteen. His sister was ten. A house fire. Their house. He was standing in the hall. His sister stood at the top of the stairs. Everything was aflame. He looked up at her. She called his name; screaming! He turned and ran out of the house, leaving her to die, as he had left his men to die. He wept.

"You should be shot like a dog for your cowardice!"

"Yes..I'm sorry. I..will make amends."

"Go! There!" said the figure, in disgust, pointing. Voss looked. Amongst the gloom and shadows, he thought he could see a building. A stables? But he couldn't have missed it just now, on his walk to the village, could he? He glanced back towards where the figure had been. But there was no sign of him. Whoever and whatever he was.

Voss stumbled through the snow. Like the village, the stables seemed to get further way the more he walked. But then he was at the large barn-like door and he entered the darkness within, the door creaking shut behind him.

*

Reuter's Shattered Illusions

Time passed though no one knew how much or how little. Inside the depot, the light was dim at best; pitch black at worst. Watches long since bartered for food told the time to others in places where time still had some relevance. Talk was limited to the inane, the everyday or the deep and personal, which at times could produce conflict and disagreement. People slept a lot of the time or were lost in memories of their families, homes or past.

How much longer it would all continue and drag on to it's end, nobody wanted to guess. The best you would hear and agree with was just one word, 'Soon'. The sooner the better was an often expressed alternative. But mostly it was just, soon. How soon before the Reds shelled the place to dust and everyone with it?; Or how soon before the Reds kicked in the door and sprayed them all with machine-gun fire or flamethrowers?; How soon before they all turned on each other? And so on. No one spoke of rescue or salvation. It had been well known that Von Manstein had led a relief army that would have saved them all. That had been spoken of since last November. What had happened to it was a topic of great debate. It had been beaten back, some said. Others said it would reform and try again, but most doubted if any relief army had ever been sent in the first place.

If you wanted to survive or escape from Stalingrad, it was up to you to find a way yourself, but few had the will or strength of purpose to do so. Most were resigned to their fate. Everyday, men were dying but no one noticed. Men were still arriving, but in ones and twos and anyway, who knew or cared how many men were here? And everyone grew weaker, both physically and mentally, by the hour if not the day and the situation seemed to be testing how much men could endure and for how long.

One day, the Snail had suddenly stopped his frantic toing and froing and came to an abrupt halt between them and the door. He started to scream, his head tilted back, looking upwards as if beseeching the heavens. Voss stared at him in fascination. Huber sat still but clenched his eyes shut.

So did Reuters, but he also held his hands over his ears in a futile effort to block out the blood curdling sound. Stark lay on the floor, both arms folded across his face. He winced as if in pain. Benz made a move to offer the Snail some aid but Morgenstern grabbed his arm.

"Leave it," he snapped, gesturing towards a figure emerging from the darkness. It was Jurgen. Kneeling beside the Snail now who had stopped screaming and was slumped forward, he could hear the wreck of a man mutter 'Mutti', over and over, while tears streamed down his face. The Snail's voice was now barely a whisper. Jürgen placed an arm around his shoulder and a hand over his nose and mouth. Haase struggled but Jürgen held on, smothering the life out of him.

"Go to her, young Haase," said Jürgen, weeping now also. "Hush now lad."

Then Haase, the Snail, was still. "Murderer," said Benz, under his breath. Jürgen dragged Haase away with much effort. Nobody helped him but nobody said anything either. For Benz it was murder. For others it was a mercy killing. For most, it was nothing. Another death. So what?

Reuters saw it as a merciful act. Did this mean his world had finally come to a rest? The dust settling at last? An N.C.O. killing an Officer? Under any circumstances that was a Court Martial offence followed by immediate execution by firing squad. Reuters knew it had happened before. It was extremely rare but not unheard of. But here in this living hell, it just seemed routine and in this particular case, justified.

Reuters thought of his time, not so long ago, in the Officer Candidate School in Dresden. They were heady days. His father, a staunch party member, insisted his son joined the Army as an Officer. It was the last thing young Albert Reuters wanted to do. He dreamt of going to university to study the Sciences, but his father was adamant. He was also someone you didn't argue with and young Reuters didn't have the strength to stand up to him. He did however express a wish to join the Army as a common soldier, his lack of self confidence deciding it was the option he could best cope with. But his father would have none of it. He himself had been a Leutnant Colonel during the Great War. An Officer of the old school, like his father and grandfather before him.

"Your grandfather fought against Napoleon III at the Battle of Sedan! I myself as you know fought with honour at the Somme in 1916! Do you think I would let you join our glorious Army as a common trench rat?!"

"No father, but-."

"Albert! It is decided. You leave tomorrow for the Academy at Dresden. Eventually you will join the ranks of the 112th and serve with distinction and honour, or die trying to. And Albert, may God help you if you let me down or prove unworthy!"

Reuters' mother waved him off tearfully from the steps of their home. Her husband forbade her to accompany him to the station. He had left the house earlier without a word on his way to his position at the Reich Chancellery in Berlin. He tottered awkwardly on two wooden legs to his waiting car; His own legs lost and left behind in France.

Albert Reuters, eighteen at the time, and an only child, remembered that train journey to Dresden as one of fear and apprehension. He'd thought of running away but his father's domineering personality and the greater fear of ever having to meet him again stopped him from doing so. His mother, who he loved dearly was a silly woman. She was more a servant than a wife to her husband.

"You will write," she said, as she saw him off.

"Of course," said Reuters.

"You'll make us proud, Albert. I know it," she said, kissing him on the cheek before going back into the house. She had a cocktail party to organise after all.

Reuters grimaced at that memory. What would his mother say if she were to walk in here right now? What would his father say for that matter? He closed his eyes. His apprehension of the Academy had proved unfounded. He'd enjoyed his time there despite the hardships and regime. He had made good friends, mostly from his own background. Young men with the same upbringing and ideals as his own. He was no star pupil, but he'd held his own and had been accepted into his father's old regiment, the 112th Artillery. He and his fellow Cadets had graduated amid much pomp and ceremony and felt the world lay at their feet. They would secure a new German empire if asked to, why not? Nothing felt impossible or too far fetched. But that was all before his first posting to Stalingrad. A place that shattered illusions, hopes and lives. Reuters was beginning to accept his fate but regretted not being able to prove himself to his father, returning home perhaps with an Iron Cross. But then again, he thought, would that have satisfied him? Reuters doubted it. If I die here and lies are told of our 'Glorious Defeat', then maybe that will be just as well.

*

Benz and Huber Swap Stories

The cold bitter air seemed to creep around them and attach itself like a living being to their very bones. Wasn't it always so? Yes, but this day broke with a wind that drove it through every hole and crack in the depot they huddled in and frozen limbs were constantly moved with effort to escape the worst of it's affects. But there was no escape from it, and all that could be heard over the whisperings and mutterings were the wails of lost souls, many in tears, as they suffered the constant unrelenting torture of the cold.

Men formed into twos and threes in a parodic embrace to share bodily warmth but this too proved to be of little help as bodies that were bitterly cold to their cores could offer little respite to their neighbour. But still, most persisted though the dying went on as the lice and fleas thrived.

"Do you still believe, Padre?" Benz asked Huber, almost smothering him, so close they were to each other.

"B..Believe?" said Huber, his teeth chattering painfully.

"Yes, in your God."

"Wh..why does everyone consider God as mine alone? He is everyone's God Theo. Open your heart and he will embrace you in his love and salvation."

It was sincere but Huber sounded like it was said by rote. It was therefore unconvincing. Benz managed a brief but dismissive smile.

"So you believe," he said. "But don't you have doubts? Even sometimes?"

"Yes Theo, I have doubts. I struggle with them but they never last. All I have seen? All we have seen? Yes, I have doubts. God forgive me, yes."

"Why doesn't your God, full of love and salvation as you say, stop this? Stop all the suffering?"

"Whose Theo? Ours? The Russians? The civilians? Perhaps just the children?"

"All of it, Padre. Everyone's."

"And if He did so, which war? This one? The last one? The-."

"Alright Padre," said Benz, weary of Huber's reasoning.

"Theo, I'm just making the point that we have free will, that..Look, can God save every man from every bullet? Every shell? Even the unworthy?"

"Why not? Isn't it in his power to do so?"

"This life we lead is a test, Theo. At the end of that life we will be judged. And those judged worthy enough will join Him."

"That being the case, and the fact that the bad and unworthy outnumber the good, the Devil will reap a vast bounty," said Benz.

"How can you think the bad outnumber the good? God will always prevail-."

"Padre, there is no God. There never has been. It's a lie. All of it. I think deep down, you know that," said Benz harshly. "What did Voltaire say? If God didn't exist, we'd have had to invent Him? That it mattered little if He existed or not, as long as it was believed He did?"

"Well Theo, you hear me now! I believe in God, believe it all. I've seen wondrous things; beautiful things that could only come from him."

"Such as?"

"The birth of a child; The beauties of nature-."

"Those are wondrous things, Padre, but they are just...natural."

"And where does that come from? Out of thin air?" asked Huber. "Like a rabbit out of a hat perhaps?"

"What about evolution, Padre? Survival of the fittest? You've read Darwin?"

"When I was twelve Theo, there was a girl in our town, who was dying of some disease. A terrible disease that confined her to her bed. The Doctors were at a loss to help her. It was said that she had a blood cancer. There was nothing that could be done.

"We, her neighbours that is, gathered together and held a constant vigil by her bedside. We prayed for her salvation. We said rosaries. Priests from the local church came and blessed her. Well Theo, that girl made a complete recovery. It was a true miracle and made a great impression on me. I saw the power of God with my own eyes and it was what made me want to join the church," said Huber, the memory of that time coming back to him vividly.

"But that contradicts what you said earlier, Padre," said Benz. "About God saving or not saving everyone?"

Huber stayed silent. He knew they could talk like this until the end of time and not reach even common ground. He wearied of the men around him who had given up on God, if they had believed in Him in the first place. And who could blame them? Their experiences of the horrors of war had had it's effects. They had abandoned Him as He had forsaken them. But he believed, didn't he? Huber asked himself. Yes. I believe. Otherwise I am lost.

"I have seen things too, Padre," said Benz later. "There was a Russian peasant girl. I can still see her face. Her name was Svetlana and she was six years old. We were based in her village, near Riga, and the people couldn't have been more friendly. They took us in. Housed us; fed us. Well, you know how it was in the beginning.

"Svetlana used to pick us flowers everyday. Then one day, the village was shelled for hours on end. Svetlana's mother came to us afterwards. She was frantic. Svetlana was missing. Well, Padre, I looked for her. We found her head floating in a bucket of water. She was still smiling that beautiful smile of hers." Huber closed his eyes and cried silent tears.

"Another time," Benz went on, "we were part of a relief column and there was one kid, a Panzer Grenadier, who'd been badly injured. He was lying under a couple of greatcoats and a horse blanket that we'd thrown over him to keep him warm. His back had been broken during a Russian attack. A piece of shrapnel had carved a hole in his back the size of your outstretched hand and severed his spine. He could feel nothing below his ribcage. Anyway, there was little we could for him, except patch him up as best we could and send him home back west. Our Surgeon though, cut off all his frostbitten toes while the kid chatted with us, smoking a cigarette. He couldn't feel a thing. He was convinced he'd be patched up back home and couldn't believe his luck to get out of this mess.

"We let him believe it. Should we have told him the truth? Perhaps. But there were so many others..." Benz' voice drifted away. He and Huber stared vacantly into the distance. After a while, Benz continued.

"After a couple of days, it was time to get the wounded on to the trucks and get them to the trains. When we went to fetch the kid-."

"What was his name?" asked Huber.

"Ah now, let me think," said Benz. "His first name was Rolf, I think, yes, Rolf. He was eighteen. I can't remember his family name. Came from Munich as I recall. Anyway, we took the blankets off him so he could be moved, and..oh Jesus Christ.." said Benz, the memory coming back in a brutal rush. Huber looked at him piteously.

"He was covered in rats, Padre. Where others had swept them away or been able to fight them off, poor Rolf hadn't felt or noticed them crawling all over him. In the couple of days since we'd found him, they'd eaten the flesh off his legs, his genitals and there were some inside his stomach starting on his insides. How he was still alive is yet another mystery. Rolf lay on his back and looked at the sky as we replaced his blankets."

"What happened to him?" asked Huber, appalled.

"The Surgeon wanted to overdose Rolf with morphine. That would have been the humane way. He would have simply drifted off as if asleep. But there was limited amounts of morphine, and in the end the Surgeon couldn't justify it."

"You didn't leave him to die?" said Huber.

"No Padre, of course not. In the end, though no one wanted to, an old Sergeant put a pistol to his head and blew his brains out. Young Rolf wouldn't have felt that either."

Huber clenched his eyes shut, wiping frozen tears away then. He understood completely how men could abandon God under such circumstances. His life had become devoted to offering solace and spiritual care to those who had no need for it. Not any more. Not now or ever again. He wept once more.

"We came across a Panzer IV," Benz continued. "Took a direct hit by the look of it. Incredibly, when we opened the hatch, the Commander was still alive! He was however-."

"Theo, please. Enough," said Huber. He'd heard as much as he could take for one day.

"Alright Padre. Just as you like," said Benz. "Just remember, yours is a cruel and dispassionate God. So that being the case, how can He possibly exist?"

Huber stared into the distance, weeping as he did so and offering no reply.

*

A New Idea

Time wore on. Men arrived. Men left. Men died. The suffering continued for all. A veritable status quo. Someone, nobody knew his name, suddenly announced one early morning as he stood in front of the barn doors..."I've realised what's going on you dumb bastards!"

Morgenstern and the group opened their eyes to look at him, but no one moved further. It wasn't exactly a revelation. Eventually Morgenstern sat up. He looked across at a young man with ragged unkempt hair that covered his tunic collar. He wore a Leutnant's artillery tunic but an infantryman's field trousers. So what? There was nothing unusual about that. You took what you needed. A lot of the men here wore different items of uniform from different regiments or services. These days, identity was irrelevant.

"We're already dead! You stupid cocksuckers! We're already dead and this is hell!"

"Well that's all we need," said Voss, sighing heavily. "Another Einstein!"

There were various shuts of derision and..."Sit down and shut the fuck up, you arsehole!"..or.."Give it a rest you selfish bastard!"..

The young man cackled. "I'll prove it!" he said, producing a Luger pistol. He held it to his head. Benz made to stop him but Morgenstern grabbed his arm. "He'll shoot you, you idiot!"

It was too late anyway. The young man pulled the trigger. The top of his head with most of it's unkempt hair, flew across the barn, sending blood and brains on to another group, who howled in protest. "Fucking bastard!" said one. "Selfish arsehole!" said another.

"We're not ghosts then," said Voss drily, shutting his eyes once more.

Morgenstern got up and eventually dragged the young man's body outside. He came back and retook his place; back to the wall. Nobody had noticed him picking up the Luger pistol and secreting it in his greatcoat pocket. That was why he had got up at all. Usually only issued to Officers, and even before the madness, a 9mm Luger pistol was a prized possession. He didn't bother to think how the dead young man had it. Perhaps he was an Officer after all. So what? What mattered now was, now it was his and could prove useful.

Later in the morning, Jürgen came back to the group after looking around. It was something he did regularly for no apparent reason. Reuters noticed his look. "What is it?" he asked the Senior Sergeant. "What's wrong?" The rest of the group looked at him.

"I've just been out back," said Jürgen. "Spoke with a Chain Dog-."

"A fucking Chain Dog?! Here!" said Voss, sitting up. He glanced around nervously.

"Listen for fuck sake," Jürgen said vehemently. "He told me a story about the Reds capturing-."

"But a fucking Chain Dog! Here!" Voss was shaking. Chain Dog was Army slang for the dreaded Military Field Police, so called because they wore a silver gorget around their necks which signified their rank and authority. Chain Dogs were widely despised by all.

"Are you finished?!" said Morgenstern, looking at Voss with contempt, who now wept silently. "Go on," he added, looking at the old Veteran. Jürgen bit his lip, the blood freezing immediately.

"So as this Dog has it, the Reds captured 158 men near the Cauldron, few weeks back. These bastards were Siberians and well, you know them! Instead of the usual interrogations and delivering 'em to the rail yards across the river, they kept 'em. For their own amusement! The Dog said some of 'em were boiled alive, which took two days he says. Others were carved up, slowly, or forced to kill each other. Long story short, he said it went on for a couple of weeks."

Huber went a whiter shade of pale and buried his face in his hands. Voss started to shake uncontrollably. Everyone else felt a new kind of revulsion, but it passed quickly. Was it the worst story they'd heard? No, not really.

"Fucking animals!" said Benz, his stomach turning over.

"Jurgen, there's more isn't there?" said Morgenstern. "You wouldn't just-."

"The Dog reckons these Siberians are everywhere now. Says they're a Battalion of the Black Scouts? Anyone ever hear of 'em?" Nobody had. "Well they're a bunch of the craziest, bloodthirsty bastards you're ever likely to meet. If we had 'em at home, we'd keep 'em in a zoo! Seems they've been ordered to saturate this place and sow terror everywhere they go. The Dog thinks it's a matter of time before they show up here. That being the case, I think we should fuck off and sharpish!"

"Oh for Christ's sake!" said Morgenstern. "And where are we supposed to fucking go? There's no escape! And nowhere to go! How many times have we been through this?!"

"But Karl," said Stark. "What if it's true? What if those bastards show up here? They'd have a fucking field day!"

"How does the Chain Dog know this?" Morgenstern asked.

"Says he was one of the captured. Says he escaped," said Jürgen.

"Bullshit!" said Morgenstern. "Impossible!"

Stark relaxed, trusting the savvy veteran. Reuters wanted to say something, but stopped when he looked at Morgenstern. Everyone else stayed motionless and quiet. After a while, when everyone had a chance to digest this latest bit of gossip, Jürgen sat down beside Morgenstern and the two spoke quietly.

"Look, we're two old soaks, you and I. Think about it. I believe the Dog," said Jürgen.

"It's possible he heard a story."

"Nah, I believe he was there."

"Jurgen, come on for Christ's sake! How'd he escape then? Would have been a fucking miracle, sanctioned by the Chief Crow!" said Morgenstern, referring to Pope Pius XII.

"Well fuck off then! Think I'm an idiot do you?"

"And any fucking way, what are we supposed to do about it?"

"I say we take off! Get away!" said Jürgen. "I've had it with this damn place!"

"Don't be a fool! And don't mention it to this lot!"

"Look, you arsehole! Whether the story is true or not, doesn't mean shit! But if Siberian Black Scouts really are here, then we're fucked in the worst way possible! We're going to die. We all know that. But we can still decide how that happens!"

"You're dreaming," said Morgenstern, slumping down and closing his eyes. Here, he reasoned, they could stay alive. Outside, their chances were slim at best, with all it's dangers, the weather being the worst one.

He woke later, to the sound of hushed excited chattering. Jürgen had obviously told of his idea.

Morgenstern rolled his eyes, succumbing to the inevitable. He could of course, he told himself, let them go and die somewhere in the snow, and stay put here alone again. That would mean making new friends, reliable friends and the truth was, he didn't have the mental strength to do so.

"Karl! We're going to hike out of here!" said Stark, noticing he was awake.

"Keep your voice down!" Jürgen was saying. "Don't want the fucking world to know, do we?"

"I'm for it," said Voss, wondering if the Chain Dog here had a list with his name on it.

"Me too," said Benz. "Should have done it days ago."

Morgenstern didn't need to think what Reuters thought of the idea. It was obvious by the look on his face. "What do you think, Padre?" he asked Huber.

"If it means getting away from here, then so be it," he said. "What's out there that could possibly be worse?" Nobody had the heart to tell him. "Besides, most of us feel better now. Stronger. How long have we been here? Couple of weeks? At least we're rested. I say yes, let's move on. Better to die out there in the snow, than wait here for the Siberians to show up, or whatever worse fate has for us. Easiest thing in the world to die in the snow. Just sit down and sleep."

"We're not dead yet," said Reuters.

Everyone went quiet, finding a comfortable position to contemplate things. After a while, perhaps an hour or so, Morgenstern finally spoke. It was what everyone was waiting for after all.

"Alright," he said, coming to the obvious conclusion that they had nothing to lose. "We'll wait till it's dark. But everyone's responsible for themselves. Nobody helps anyone else. If you can't keep up, get injured or just keel over, then hard luck. You're on your own and you get left behind. Got it?" Everyone nodded or muttered so, even though no one was going to leave anyone stranded.

"First thing," Morgenstern went on, "everyone have a ramble around. Don't make it obvious. Take whatever you can find that might be useful, but do it without getting caught, or not at all. We'll leave separately in ones and twos and by different ways. We don't want any curious bastards following us. As it is, there are seven of us. Too many to be pissing about outside, but that's a damn sight better than twenty or thirty!" More nods and whispers. "Right. I suggest we get some sleep for now. We'll meet up outside at dusk behind the wrecked Panzer. When it gets dark, we'll move on. And we're not waiting for anyone. If you're not there, that's your problem."

*

A New Purpose

Huber and Reuters were the first to get up that evening and make a move. Their unsuccessful nonchalance amused the others who watched them disappear into the darkness beyond. But so what? thought Morgenstern. Nobody gives a shit anyway. Even if they'd noticed them. Still, when your very life depended on it, caution was always a good idea.

Reuters made Morgenstern think of all the poor young bastards he'd had to break in here over the last year or so. Kids mainly; Barely old enough or able to manage themselves without a mother or father to supervise them. He remembered one kid who was sixteen years old. Morgenstern had been wounded and after a cursory stay in hospital in Kiev, he was sent to a depot to help prepare a batch of new arrivals for life on the Russian front. It was a thankless task. He'd put in a request to return to his unit, where he'd be of greater use, which was true. But he knew from experience that this was a shit posting, and more importantly, a waste of time. Barely two percent of new arrivals would survive longer than six weeks. Anyway, a young Hauptmann told him to fuck off and get on with it.

So one morning, after what passed for breakfast at the depot, he stood in the square of a former Russian Guards barracks as the rain poured down. He watched a Corporal marching a squad of maybe twenty 'men' towards him. Eventually they formed up in neat rows and stood to attention while he looked them up and down. Most Senior Sergeants he knew would now be saying.. 'Jesus wept! What a sorry bunch of bastards you are!' or maybe,... 'Is someone taking the piss with you lot?! Go home to your fucking mothers!'.

But Morgenstern had mellowed quickly after arriving in Russia. This was not Poland or France. The horrors he'd experienced were catching up with him. All he felt now was pity for these kids who'd been dragged away from their family homes and anger and hatred for the scum back in Berlin who were happy to keep sending them here. Six months ago, new arrivals were averaging around eighteen or nineteen years of age. Now, they were sixteen or seventeen. How soon, he thought before we resort to fourteen year olds and old men?

Now sitting here in Stalingrad, the only kid he could remember properly was sixteen year old Schroeder. Morgenstern had walked up and down the ranks eyeing the lads for the sake of appearances. He stopped in front of Schroeder who was barely up to his chin. As he stared down at the youthful bespectacled face, Morgenstern wondered absently if the kid had even started shaving. For a millisecond, he wanted to run away from this madness.

"Name?!" he barked.

"Schroeder!"

"Schroeder what!?"

"Schroeder, Gerd!"

"Schroeder, Gerd, Herr Unteroffizier! Got it?!"

There were some sniggers from the others. Morgenstern told them to shut up. The Corporal, who was standing off to one side, smoking, cackled. Morgenstern told him to fuck off and report for latrine duty. He could manage this sorry lot on his own. Turning back to Schroeder, he asked the lad his age and where he was from.

"Eighteen, Herr Unteroffizier! Cologne, Herr Unteroffizier!"

"Eighteen? What weeks? Months maybe?" he finished with, before moving on. He picked out maybe another half dozen of the kids and asked them the same questions.

"Nineteen, Herr Unteroffizier!"

"Frankfurt, Herr Unteroffizier!"

"Wiesbaden, Herr Unteroffizier!"

"Eighteen, Herr Unteroffizier!"

And so on. He had them march up and down while he remembered the files he read briefly listing the new arrivals today, with their ages and home towns. He knew Schroeder was sixteen. Knew also the others would torment him later for being the youngest, so he let it go.

"You've had your basic training," Morgenstern said. "You've learnt how to march, fire a rifle, look after your uniforms and kit. What you haven't learnt is how to survive. This is the Eastern Front! Whatever you've heard or think you know, forget! Life here is tough and harsh. For some of you, it will also be short. Pay heed to what I tell you. Listen to those around you in your platoons. Learn from them. Keep your wits about you and maybe you will come through this. Right. Form up outside the armoury. Wait for me there. We'll see if you can shoot or not! Dismissed!"

Morgenstern told himself he'd done his best in the few weeks he had to educate these raw recruits beyond their basic training for what life was really like on the Russian Front, and how to survive. But all he'd done was to put off the inevitable. Most of those twenty or so young lads were now dead.

Later, back with his unit and while preparing to spearhead the drive south to Stalingrad, amazingly he bumped into Schroeder one day, who tramped past him with fifty or so other men, heading for a new emplacement up the line. Schroeder was struggling with his own kit, rifle, bi-pod and box of ammunition for a MG42 heavy machine gun. The kid looked tougher, meaner and more of a soldier than he had back at the depot. Maybe he'll do, Morgenstern had thought.

It wasn't to be of course. Eventually Schroeder had been wounded and ended up in a Field Hospital that the Russians later overran. They shot everyone able to stand, including the Spanish nurses and Russian Red Cross personnel. They dragged the wounded outside along with Schroeder on his stretcher, and drove a T34 tank over them; back and forth, back and forth. Morgenstern felt tears welling in his eyes.

Now someone was beside him, elbowing him in the side. He came out of his reverie. It was Jürgen. "Ready to move?" he was asking.

Morgenstern shook himself. "I'll take Voss. You go with Stark and Benz."

"I'll go alone, if its all the same to you," said Jürgen, his eyes darting about.

"Just as you like. Get them going then."

Voss followed Morgenstern while Stark and Benz went the opposite way. Jürgen slinked away on his own. There was a commotion as Stark tripped over somebody in the darkness, forcing the man to cry out in pain and alarm. "Bastard! Watch where you're going, you arsehole!"

Then later, everyone met up outside behind the wrecked tank and slumped to the ground. It was still dusk. Darkness was maybe an hour away. "Well, we're all here then," said Jürgen. "Any issues?" There weren't. They waited for darkness to fall.

"Anyone manage to get anything?" asked Huber.

"I've still got a loaf," said Morgenstern. He didn't mention the Luger pistol. Only Reuters had managed to grab a cloth bag of scraps. Potato peels and some rotten fruit among them. He also produced a huge collarless shirt that must have belonged to a giant of a man at one time.

"Great," said Voss. "We can cut that into seven. Have it later with the spuds and fruit cocktail!"

The group waited in the snow, freezing cold and anxious to move on. Morgenstern insisted they wait for nightfall. When it came, they trudged away silently into the darkness. Jürgen took the lead, telling everyone this way was North-West. No one argued. North-West meant the last known position of General Von Manstein's rumoured relief Army. They all agreed it was as good a place as any to aim for, even though they had little or no chance of getting anywhere near it. After all, it was fifty or so kilometres away, if it was still there. And that had been two weeks ago. If it had ever arrived in the first place, it had been forced to retreat to God knew where. But still, North-West it was. The little group trudged on through the snow into the freezing night but away at least from the Siberians for now.

*

The Hiwis

They tramped through the freezing night for maybe an hour; perhaps two. It was the Padre who gave up first. Huber cried out pitifully as he collapsed into a shell hole, breaking the ice around it's edge and disappearing into it's cavernous depths. Being out in the open and at the mercy of the savage weather with it's vicious wind chill, was one corner of hell they hadn't experienced for quite a while and it was taking a toll on all of them.

Despite Morgenstern's insistence earlier that nobody was to help anyone, everyone stopped.

"Huber!" said Reuters, looking down at the Padre. He was about to try and climb down after him.

Morgenstern shoved him out of the way. "Help me," he said to the others, climbing into the shell hole. Voss and Benz made ready to follow him. They watched as the Senior Sergeant stumbled over to Huber who had stopped moving now. "Padre!" Morgenstern hissed, his hands bleeding from his brief climb over the assorted rubble. The blood would freeze on his hands and every movement would open the cuts again. In the freezing temperature, it was agonising. "Huber! Come on man! Get up now!"

"Leave me," he mumbled, starting to shake. "I..can't..go on. Enough!" he said, wrapping his arms around him and moving into a foetal position.

Morgenstern beckoned the others for help. He grabbed the Padre's overcoat lapels and pulled him into a prone position. "Take his legs!" he told Voss. "Theo, here!" he added, nodding towards Huber's other arm and shoulder.

Together they carried Huber up and out of the shell hole and dropped him beside the others who'd been squatting in the snow in front of a large black shape that might have been an overturned cart. Huber resumed his foetal position while his rescuers, now on all fours, gasped for breath while recovering from their effort. The Padre was mumbling to himself again. "Yeah," said Jürgen, recognising the words. "You say your prayers Padre!" Reuters crawled over to him.

"We should get going," said Stark. Then there was a loud crack. Someone close by in the darkness away to their left, had stood on a branch or a plank of brittle wood.

"Move!" said Morgenstern under his breath, taking off into the night.

Everyone followed him in earnest; stumbling through the drifts, falling over but getting up again, getting away in their terror. The last to follow was Reuters and the Padre. Somehow Huber had been persuaded to run. Their fear and panic had kept them going for several minutes. They charged through the knee-high snow. Then they were in a field and everyone collapsed again, coughing and gasping for air as everyone fought to recover. Jürgen lay on his back, clutching his heart. The rest nursed various knocks and bruises from their bolt through the night.

"Are we safe? Are we clear?" asked Voss, coughing and spitting out some blood. He'd fallen and knocked out a couple of teeth.

"Dunno," said Morgenstern. "But there was definitely someone nearby! Probably Reds!"

"Oh Jesus!" said Reuters, rocking back and forth like a child. "Oh sweet Jesus!"

"My fucking heart," Jürgen was saying, crawling towards Morgenstern.

The rest followed him. They formed into a rough semi-circle looking back at their wake, several troughs gouged out of the white blanket that covered everything. The cold was unrelenting. "Hush!" someone whispered, pointing into the blackness. Then everyone could hear it. Movement in the darkness. All around them now.

"Ey Nemetskiy musor!"

"Fucking shit!" said Benz, rolling into a ball. The rest of the group tensed and clutching the ground with bleeding hands, stayed quite still.

"Vstan', kiski; Polozhi ruki na golovu!"

"What are they saying?" Reuters whispered, panic stricken. Then a dozen shapes were all around them. Most were holding makeshift clubs but one had a German rifle, which he kept slung over his shoulder.

He spoke in halting German. "Look with you! Great German soldiers! Hah! Move now! Up!"

The Russians beat everyone to their feet and made them go back the way they had come. After some time, they found themselves in a wood, walking into a clearing where other men were huddled in snow holes, covered in branches and foliage. They were beaten again and herded into a tighter group. They were searched and the apparent leader found Morgenstern's pistol. His eyes widened at the prize. "Good for me, bad for you," he said laughing into Morgenstern's face. He could see now they were German Army Auxiliaries, or Hilfswilleger; Hiwis for short.

"You look at my coat, Nemetskiy," the man with the rifle said. "And what? I am a friend? I am Russian! We, Russian! We take coat from you to stay with life, or we die. We take gun; we take money. Sure! No problem. Would you the same? Of that I know." The rest of his men laughed. "We lose everything. Family, woman, home. So we come with you. Fight Russian Army with you. Sure. But we live! Now, you are finished here! Stalingrad finished here! You forget us. Leave us to die! To die by Russian Army. Very bad!" The Hiwi leader squatted in front of Morgenstern, looking around at the disparate group, tied up as they were, helpless. "So now we kill you. First, we eat."

His men laughed again. Terror gripped Morgenstern and spread to the rest. They knew what the Hiwis meant. Reuters wept as he trembled uncontrollably. Stark and Benz went white. Jürgen stayed impassive though inwardly, he was horrified. Huber said a useless prayer to himself.

Voss' eyes widened. "No!" he screamed.

The Hiwi leader unslung his rifle and smashed the butt into his face, breaking his jaw. Voss passed out immediately. The Hiwis laughed some more. They spoke among themselves for a while. The group looked at each other. Nobody wanted to say anything. Nobody wanted a broken jaw like Voss.

Now some of the Hiwis were gathering bits of wood, branches and other detritus. It became obvious they intended to make a fire. Morgenstern's mind was racing. What could they do?

Nothing, he concluded. He resolved to fight to the death once he was untied. It would be better than being boiled alive. Better than being eaten by these animals. He whispered this to everyone. After a while, some of them nodded in agreement. Reuters had passed out; the terror overcoming him. Jürgen bit his lip as his eyes darted around. Stark and Benz, who were near each other, fought with their ties with bloodied fingers. It seemed useless. The Hiwis knew how to tie a man. Voss was out cold.

Then Huber cried out. "For the love of God!" he shouted. "Stop this now!"

The Hiwi leader turned to look at him with a pitiless expression on his face. He scratched his beard and turned back to his men, saying something. There was more laughter.

After a few more hours, with dawn struggling to appear, an oil-drum filled with snow that the Hiwis had placed on what was now a blazing camp fire, shifted slightly and one of them who went to look at it, declared it ready. Three others approached the group tied to the trees. One of them produced a huge kitchen knife. The other two carried clubs. The man with the knife spoke over his shoulder. "Kotoryy iz?"

The man with the rifle got up from where he'd been sitting near the fire and made a great show of looking at each member of the group in turn, adding to their terror. Eventually he gestured towards Reuters, who screamed as he was untied and dragged towards the oil-drum.

"Fight Albert!" Morgenstern shouted.

"Fight boy!" said Jürgen.

The Hiwis ignored them. They stripped Reuters naked in the snow. There was nothing he could do. One of them looked down at the teenager with a lascivious look. He said something to the Hiwi leader. There was a brief discussion. Then Reuters was being dragged to one side, where he was tied face down to four pegs already hammered into the frozen ground. Three of the Hiwis, despite the weather, took turns in raping Reuters there in the snow, who screamed in agony with a pain that felt like he was being cut open, which in a way he was. He was bleeding afterwards and when it was over, his three rapists carried him over to the oil-drum, shoving him into the boiling water head first. Reuters never made a sound. He was probably already dead.

Morgenstern and the rest hung their heads, their eyes squeezed shut. Some wept. Some joined the Padre in a silent prayer to a God they didn't believe in. Everyone felt lost. It went on for hours.

"Don't look!" Morgenstern said, as the Hiwis started to cut up Reuters' body, ready to eat. Blood and viscera seemed to be everywhere.

Two more dawns came and went. Other Hiwis arrived. Some left, including a few of the original men who had captured the group. Several remained, along with the leader still carrying his rifle.

Morgenstern felt he was dying. He knew it with a certainty. His hands and feet were frozen and he couldn't feel them any more. Everyone was the same. The Padre continued with his prayers. His eyes were squeezed shut. Stark kept trying his bonds. He'd lost most of his nails, but he persisted. Benz was in a kind of stupor, more dead than alive. Jürgen concentrated on his heart again. Had it stopped beating?

Then there was a commotion. The Hiwis sprang to their feet and hurriedly gathered their belongings. Ignoring the group tied to the trees, they took off through the woods, clubs in hand, eventually disappearing from sight. A dead silence fell.

Morgenstern looked at Jürgen. "Now or never," he said, struggling with his frozen hands. Everyone was the same. No one could move, let alone release themselves.

"What happened?" said Huber, after a while. "Why did they take off?"

"It's like they were fleeing," said Jürgen, his eyes darting around for a new danger.

"We must get away!" said Stark, struggling frantically.

"Voss is gone," said Benz, coming back to life. "He's dead."

And so it was. Voss was dead alright. His bloodied swollen head hung to one side. Blood red icicles had formed at his open mouth. No one spoke for a while. What was their to say? They sat for some more time.

"How quiet the wood is," Huber remarked. "Not even birdsong."

Then it was getting dark again. Their suffering seemed endless. Suddenly, Stark fell forward, free at last from the rope that bound him. He reached for a sharp stone and cut the rope around his chest. His hands were in an appalling state, but he was oblivious to them. Later, he had released all of them in turn.

"We should bury Voss?" asked Huber.

"No!" said Morgenstern. Everyone nodded in agreement. "There's no time. The Hiwis could come back, any time. Who knows? The Reds themselves might show up. What made those bastards fuck off anyway? We have to go, Now! Voss won't care anyhow. Nor will poor Albert come to that."

Once everyone had gathered themselves and restored some circulation to their frozen limbs, they had a quick look around for anything useful the Hiwis might have left behind. There was nothing. Everyone ignored the blood-stained snow.

"Let's move," said Jürgen, once more assuming point. "The Hiwis went that way," he gestured with his chin. "So we'll go this way," he added, taking off in the opposite direction. "Come on!"

The rest of the group followed him in silence. No on had time to marvel at their escape. That would come later.

*

The Woman in the Rail Yard

The five remaining members of the group made slow progress through the wood which seemed endless. Looking around them, they got the impression they were the first people to ever pass through here. It seemed nature itself ruled this land.

"We must be heading into the interior and away from everything," said Stark. "This fucking wood must go on forever!"

"And that's a bad thing?" said Benz. "You want to go back?"

"I don't want to die in a fucking forest in the middle of fucking nowhere!"

"As opposed to what? Dying somewhere you know?"

"Fuck off Theo," said Stark in disgust.

Benz laughed, sounding like a madman. Back in the days before Stalingrad, he knew the two of them would probably be rolling around on the ground by now, beating each other senseless. But neither of them had the strength or will now. It took all their strength just to keep standing and staying alive.

They kept going. At one time through a freezing sleet that seemed to stab them all over. In fact, everyone's face was bleeding and the blood froze quickly, matting their beards into a macabre mask. Then Jürgen collapsed into a hollow half full of thick exposed tree roots. He leant back against an earth wall to one side.

"Fuck sake! I'm done," he said, breathing hard. He began coughing, at first normally then violently, finally spitting out a glob of phlegm clotted with blood.

Benz slumped down beside him. "That's bad, Jürgen," he said. "The blood I mean. Any pain? In your chest?"

"I don't need a fucking Medic to tell me what I already know, kiddo!"

Benz sighed and leant back, closing his eyes. There was a time he would have felt anxious and worried about someone like Jürgen. Now all he felt was useless and frustrated. But so did everyone in the end. For different reasons.

Morgenstern produced a heel of bread from his pocket. He held it out under the easing rain to soften it a little before breaking it into five pieces and handing it round. "That's the last of it," he said.

"Let's say a prayer," said Huber. "God has watched over us so far. Let's give thanks," he said, looking at his piece of bread. Nobody had the heart to mention Voss or poor young Reuters. But nobody bit into their bread either. They waited for the Padre to begin.

"Dear God who watches over us. Thank you for this bread. Thank you for our lives. Thank you for our friends and comrades, who give us strength in these dark times. May we be worthy of your faith in us. May we give thanks through our actions and daily struggles. May we live to see a better future with our families, and with our friends. May we find piece. May we die one day waiting for your embrace."

Huber bit into his bread and quickly spat out a rotten tooth. Morgenstern felt tears streaming down his face. "That was very good, Eduard," he said, and began to break his bread into smaller pieces. He only had four teeth left at the back of his mouth. He wanted to keep them. Jürgen and Benz chewed in silence, moved by Huber's prayer. Stark finished his bread quickly and watched everyone else as they ate in silence. Then he spoke, reciting a poem he knew by heart.

> "You, who never arrived in my arms, beloved,
> Who were lost from the start,
> I don't even know what songs would please you.
> I have given up trying to recognise you in the surge of the next moment.
> All the immense images in me-The far off deeply felt landscape, cities, towers and bridges,
> And unsuspected turns in the path, and those powerful lands that were once pulsing
> With the life of the Gods-All rise within me to mean you, who forever elude me.

> "You, beloved, who are all the gardens I have stared at, longing.
> An open window in a country house-And you almost stepped out, pensive, to meet me.
> Streets that I chanced upon-You had already walked through them and vanished.

And sometimes the mirrors were still dizzy with your presence and startled,

Gave back my too sudden image.

Who knows? Perhaps the same bird echoed through both of us,

Yesterday, separate, in the evening."

"Jesus, Wilhelm," said Benz. "Where did that come from?"

"Another time, another life," said Stark.

"Who wrote it?" asked Morgenstern. "It's quite beautiful."

"Rainer Maria Rilke. It's a favourite of mine. My mother used to read his poetry to me after my father died. I was thinking of her just now, and Greta, my wife."

"Well," said Jürgen, breaking the spell. "We should move on," he said, getting to his feet. He clutched his chest, wincing with pain.

"You should rest," said Benz. "We could wait. We could all rest-."

"Don't bother me boy!" said Jürgen. "I'll rest when I'm dead! Let's go!" he said loudly over his shoulder and began to climb out of the hollow. The rest followed wearily.

"Can I help you?" Huber asked Jürgen, meaning it. "Perhaps-."

"Why don't you say a prayer for me," said Jürgen unkindly. "For all I've done, I'm going to need it where I'm going!" he finished with, chuckling inanely.

The day wore on. The rain that had followed the sleet finally took pity on them and stopped. Morgenstern looked up to find the sun, trying to guess what time it might be. It was late afternoon; that was all he could be sure of. Above them was a grey expanse that hung over them like a bleak, stone blanket. Everyone was in pain of one kind or another. Jürgen because he was dying. The rest from various knocks and injuries together with sheer exhaustion. Then a shout broke the silence and Jürgen was coming back towards them. "You won't believe it till you fucking see it!" he said excitedly, wheezing like a fire bellows. "Come on!" he added, disappearing through the thick undergrowth.

The rest followed, catching up with him eventually. They were on top of a small rise looking down at what appeared to be a rail yard. There were some tracks that disappeared into the snow, a couple of wooden shacks and an assortment of train wheels on their side that looked like they'd fallen off the back of a nearby wagon that had lost an axle and was tipped over to one side.

"My God," said Morgenstern. "Are we dreaming?"

"Can you believe it?" said Jürgen. "Out here! In the middle of nowhere!"

Stark and Benz gave a collective whoop as they began to start down the hill. Huber was going to follow them.

"Wait!" said Jürgen, pointing. "Look!"

Everyone followed his gaze. "Smoke!" said Huber, a familiar fear returning.

"Reds?" said Morgenstern, while looking around and beyond the yard.

"Got to be," said Jürgen. "Though there can't be many and they're on foot. No transport around."

"Let's go then," said Morgenstern. "Single file behind me. No talking and keep your eyes peeled!" He wished he had the Luger pistol he'd lost to the Hiwis.

Leaving the rest huddled by the overturned wagon, Morgenstern carefully and slowly approached one of the shacks. He didn't risk opening the door which would probably creak loudly, but instead peered through a hole where a knot of wood was missing from a thin plank. He reckoned a strong persistent wind would blow the whole flimsy structure away. It was dark inside, but he could make out familiar shapes. A crate here; A drum of grease there. He turned and made his way towards the larger shack and as he did so, a woman suddenly stepped out of it, the door swinging shut behind her as she prepared to empty some dirty water from a large steel pot. Morgenstern froze. The woman froze also. Then she let out a cry, dropping the pot and retreating back inside the shack. Morgenstern crept closer. He had to be sure she was alone or if she had company. A quick look through some gaps in the planks satisfied him that she was. He whistled to the others who came trudging through the snow towards him.

"There's a woman inside. She's alone. I'll go in first. You follow when I call you!"

Everyone nodded anxiously. Could she really be alone? Out here? Then Morgenstern was inside. The woman yelped again. "Pozhaluysta! Ne Volnuysya! Ya ne prichinyutebe vreda!" Morgenstern said in broken Russian. The woman, who was around sixty or so, reached for a club nonetheless. "Nyet! Nyet" said Morgenstern, slowly sitting down on a box, his hands outstretched to show he was unarmed.

The woman relaxed slightly, but still brandished the club. She spat on the floor. "Nemetskiy!" she said, with disgust.

"Yes, Nemetskiy," said Morgenstern. "But friend. Drug!" he said, remembering the word. "More friend. Here," he said, gesturing towards the door. He called out and everyone came inside, slumping to the floor. "Okay now," he said. "Okay." The woman was wide-eyed and clearly terrified.

Everyone sat till for some time, looking at each other. Eventually the woman spoke in fluent German. The group were taken aback, their mouths open in disbelief.

"Yes, I speak good German," she started with. She'd decided these five men were no threat, to anyone by the look of them. "I went to school in Germany a long time ago. I trained there as a Radiographer in Wuerzburg. I had a good job here. A good life. In Kiev, then later in Stalingrad. But that was all before you bastards showed up!"

"Are you alone?" asked Morgenstern.

"Yes, I am alone. Who would want to join me here?"

"How long have you been here?" This time from Jürgen.

"Oh how long?" said the woman. "Who knows? Some months perhaps?"

"What is your name?" asked Huber.

"Anya. My name is Anya," she said.

"Do you have any food?" asked Stark. "Anything at all?"

"No!" the woman lied. "You are joking?"

"Then how did you survive here?" said Benz. "For months!"

"I did have some, that I brought with me. A few turnips, some potatoes. But they ran out some days ago."

"You're lying!" said Jürgen.

"No, I am not," said Anya. "It's true, I'm telling you."

They sat in silence for some more time.

"Where are we?" Morgenstern asked later.

"About twelve miles north of Stalingrad. I don't know exactly. I can't give you the name of any town, because there isn't one. Not one that I know of anyway."

"What about you?" asked Huber. "Do you have family somewhere?"

"Not any more," was all Anya would say.

*

Goodbye Anya

There had been a stove in the shack at one stage, the men noticed. But not any more. The remains of a chimney was lying in one corner; A hole in the roof where it would have been now stuffed with old newspaper. There was a rusted five gallon pot where the woman had lit a fire once, it's blackened lower half stuck to the scorched floorboards beneath it. Everyone knew it would be virtually impossible to light a fire even if they had the materials to do so. The most likely outcome of having maybe an hour's warmth would be asphyxiation if the shack didn't burn down first.

"What were you doing with the pot Anya? When you came out and saw me?" Morgenstern asked, remembering. He wondered where she had stashed her food. He knew she had some.

"I was washing," she said. "Myself. I was washing myself."

"But the snow had melted. It was water you threw out."

"You don't know how to melt snow without a fire?" he said, sardonically.

"Okay Anya," said Morgenstern, trying to smile. He couldn't though. "We're not going to hang around. We need to keep moving but not yet. We need to rest. We need to heal. But what we really need is food."

"I told you, I have nothing," she repeated.

The others were listening once more. "You must have some!" said Stark. "If we weren't here, what would you do for food today?"

"Same as the last few days! Do without!"

"Anya," said Jürgen, sounding very weak. "Me, I don't want anything. This time tomorrow or sooner, I'll be dead. My insides." He gestured. "I'm finished. But these men here," he went on, waving a hand towards the rest of the group, "they need something to keep them going, else they will be dead too. Anyone can tell by looking at you, you're not starving. Please, help them and then they will leave you alone once more." With that, Jürgen lay back down. He was coughing again. He spat into a corner and wrapped his arms around him, breathing hard as he looked at the woman.

Anya was crying. Her tears slowly froze and stuck to her puffy cheeks. She knew well the men would turn the shack upside down to look for her food. She reckoned she had enough to feed herself for another month. Then what? She'd have to leave here? Move on somewhere? Where could she go in God's name!? If she left, and she'd have to, she knew, would it matter if it was three weeks or a month? Besides, a lot could happen in those three weeks. A lot that might change her circumstances. A practical woman, she came to the conclusion that all things being equal, she'd probably be dead in a month anyway. From one reason or another. Especially if the Russian Army showed up. She'd long thought that though this horror might end one day, the only people who would be left alive would be the soldiers who won the war. Everyone else and every living thing must surely die before that day came. She thought of her food and what she could afford to give up.

Then she got up. Kicking the blackened pot to one side, she knelt and took up two of the scorched floorboards. Reaching down into a hole in the ground, she brought up a filthy sack with some Cyrillic letters stamped on it; SzhD.

The men, apart from Jürgen, sat forward in anticipation. Opening the sack with her back turned, she took out four turnips and two loaves of black bread about the size of a house brick. Stark lunged forward, followed by Benz. "Stop!" Morgenstern shouted, grabbing Benz' arm.

"This is half of what I have," said Anya, lying, though there was little more. "Please," she added, pleading with the men to accept her offer.

"We're grateful," said Huber.

"Thank you Anya," said Morgenstern, getting up. He threw a turnip each to the others and picked up the two loaves, before retaking his seat on the box. Those three started to gnaw at the vegetables while they eyed the bread Morgenstern had placed at his feet. Looking at them, he reached down and put them in his greatcoat pockets. "For later," he said. Then he looked to his left, where Jürgen lay, his eyes shut. The man was in great pain, he could see. "Jurgen?" he said, offering the man a piece of turnip. Jürgen opened his eyes briefly and shook his head.

They ate in silence for a time while Anya replaced her sack. She watched them eat. It was a veritable feast these days. She remembered her days in Germany. Youthful days. She remembered the men she'd known there as she looked at this pitiful group. She sighed heavily.

Then Benz wiped his mouth on a sleeve and put half of his turnip in a pocket. "Don't eat it all," he said. "You'll feel terribly sick otherwise. Besides, think of tomorrow." The rest took his advice. Sitting back and with something at last in their stomachs to ease the hunger pains, everyone drew breath. Jürgen was now in a foetal position, though nobody noticed.

"Tell us Anya," asked Huber. "How did you end up here?"

She sighed again, looking at everyone in turn. She couldn't however, look at Jürgen. His intermittent laboured breathing was an uncomfortable sound that filled the shack unless someone spoke. Morgenstern looked back from the old soldier to this old woman.

"What happened to me belongs to me," Anya said finally. "If I told you my story it would just add to the many stories you have already heard. Add to your own. It is no more important than any other story. No better or worse. But it is mine, and will remain so. I don't want to hear any of your stories either. I have enough to deal with without taking on any more.

"What happened to me is not your fault. I know that. More importantly, it is not *my* fault. You as individuals here today are not responsible for it or any of this. We each have little choice in what befalls us. Life," she said, waving a hand to all that was outside the shack, "is just a series of events that we have little control over. I used to believe in God. A God I could turn to in moments of anguish or despair." She thought for a moment.

"God is always with you," said Huber.

"No, I don't think so," said Anya. "I don't believe in God any more. With all that has happened? No, He can't possibly exist." Huber sighed, but said nothing. "So I live from day to day like you, and I cling to life with white knuckles, not really knowing why. Perhaps we are like the wolf or wild pig. We simply exist."

Anya sighed again and began picking at her blackened nails. Everyone looked at each other as they thought about what she had said. Then after some time, Benz, who was nearest to Jürgen, pronounced him dead. "He's gone," he said. "At least he went peacefully," he added, thinking briefly of the myriad of other possibilities. "Come on," he said to Stark. "Help me."

Together, the two men picked up the 47 year old former Alpine Regiment Unterfeldwebel, and carried him outside and some distance away from the shack. They returned after a short while.

No one had moved or spoke since they'd left. Benz shut the door, wrapping a rope around a nine-inch nail which secured it.

"Did he have a family?" asked Huber.

"I don't know," said Morgenstern, feeling guilty about knowing so little about the dead man. Then he stood up. "We should go," he said. "We've been here too long."

"Can't we wait a little longer?" asked Huber.

"You can, by all means," said Morgenstern, nodding to Stark and Benz who followed him to the door.

Huber reluctantly got up. "Goodbye Anya," he said. "And thank you."

The rest said the same, thanking the woman in turn. Then they were gone.

Anya watched them from the open doorway, trudging away and looking like ghosts floating heavily across the white landscape. When she could no longer see them, she shut the door and slumped to the floor. She wept.

*

The Two Red Scouts

"Might be wolves," Morgenstern was saying. If it is, he thought, we're in big trouble. He kept it to himself though.

"Wolves?" asked Huber. Knowing little about them, he didn't recognise the situation as a threat.

They were resting in a wooded area about six hours from Anya's shack. It was mid-afternoon. The wood was sparse, more spread out than before and it left them feeling terribly exposed. But there was little to be done because it spread for miles in every direction. There were some mountains in the distance but these were very far away and there was nothing that even slightly resembled a track or path as far as the eye could see.

Stark sat on a fallen tree trunk that was covered in moss. He remembered tales from his grandfather in the Harz mountains. Tales of packs of wolves coming down to his grandfather's farm and taking sheep or goats, even chickens, from time to time. He never thought too much about them, perhaps placing them alongside foxes when it came to how dangerous they could be to people.

Benz however, was horrified anew at the prospect of wolves following them. As a Medic, he'd seen most things, including what wolves could do to a man in the Ardennes Forest in the summer of 1940.

Their trek from Anya's shack had been the usual arduous slog through deep snow mostly that reached their knees. They would stop every hour or so, simply falling down where they stood, exhausted and spent. They would rest for maybe another hour and resume their journey with no idea where they were or where they were going. All that drove them was the desperate need to keep moving away from where they had been. Lately, it had become obvious that someone or something, was following them. But whoever or whatever it was, kept their distance. It seemed there was no hurry as if their fate had long been decided and that it was simply just a matter of time. Every time the group stopped and took shelter, looking back to see whatever it might be that was pursuing them, there was no sign of anything or anyone.

"There's nothing," said Stark, one time. "It's our imagination playing tricks. If there was something, we'd have seen it by now."

"Wolves will follow you for days, even weeks," Morgenstern said then. "They'll wait for one of us to drop first. Why waste energy hunting you down when all they have to do is wait? They're very intelligent and have infinite patience."

"How do you know so much about them?" asked Huber, fascinated.

"Saw them in Berlin Zoo when I was a kid. Read a lot of books over the years. They're remarkable animals."

"Could be Reds," said Benz. He was concerned about wolves. He was terrified about the prospect of capture. Their encounter with the Hiwis was still fresh in his mind. Even if their lives were spared and they ended up prisoners in some camp, it was a dreadful prospect.

Stark straddled his tree and dug out the remains of his turnip from a pocket. He bit off a piece with difficulty and let it warm on his tongue. The Reds or wolves? he thought. What a choice. Wolves then, he decided. At least you had a chance there.

"It'll be dark soon," said Morgenstern, scanning the heavens. "We should look for cover."

But there wasn't any. All around them was flat ground covered in snow. Trees were scattered across the landscape. Turning full circle several times, he scanned the horizon until he felt dizzy.

"We should dig a hollow in the snow at least," he said then. "We can't just stay in the open."

"I'll look for some branches to dig with," said Stark.

"I'll help you," said Benz.

Morgenstern sat in the snow with Huber who looked like a ghost he thought now. The Padre was not a big man, but he looked like a child in his greatcoat which seemed ridiculously big for him. He got up and started to scrape away the snow with his boots, making out a rough square in the ground. Huber got up to help him.

"Stay put Eduard," Morgenstern told him. "I'm just restless," he added. "Why don't you eat something?"

"I finished my turnip the last time we stopped," said Huber forlornly.

"I'll share out some bread later," said the Veteran. "When we get settled."

Stark and Benz returned with some thick branches which they tossed on the ground. Everyone shoved the snow out of the way and began to hack into the frozen ground to make a hollow. They looked like sailors rowing on an imaginary raft. The earth was giving way but it was a slow, arduous and tedious effort. When they felt they'd done enough, they collapsed, exhausted.

Now it was dark. They huddled together, lost in their thoughts. Huber fell asleep first, followed in turn by the rest, one by one. Morgenstern had shared out half of one of the loaves earlier and it had been enough to leave them contented and able to sleep at least fitfully.

Then it was daylight. Morgenstern woke to noises. Shouting, followed by a panicked movement and a confused commotion all around him.

"Vstat' Ruki na golovu!" a voice screamed over and over.

Morgenstern could make out two figures in dirty white clothing looking down at them. One held a PPSH sub-machine gun. The other held two ski poles in a gloved hand. His other hand was by his side, holding a pistol. Both men were on skis. The man with the pistol also had a rifle slung across his back.

So we had been followed, thought Morgenstern, getting to his feet. He put his hands on his head and stood up, looking at the two Mongol type faces. Siberian Scouts, he knew and his heart sank. Their only hope was that these two would sell them on to a regular army unit as prisoners. That of course, would depend on their being one nearby. If there wasn't, they would be stripped of anything of value and shot dead right here and now.

"Dvigat'sya davay poydem seychas!"

With that, the two Siberian Scouts moved the group out back from where they'd come from, but not in the same direction. Morgenstern was surprised they hadn't been searched. They would be later though. He was grateful he didn't have the Luger pistol now. Otherwise, when they found it, they would have shot him out of hand. Morgenstern could detect a certain feeling of resignation from Stark and Benz, though Huber was plainly terrified. Memories of the Hiwis flooded his mind. Now what? he thought. This is the end, surely. It has to be.

*

Death March

They had walked for miles. If one of them fell, they were beaten till they got up again and continued. One of the Siberian scouts would do the beating while the other held the rest at bay by gunpoint. If one of them fell and couldn't get up again, the rest would gesture and shout that they would help and after a time, the Siberians would relent. Whoever of the four it might be, he would be dragged to his feet and helped on his way by the other three. And so it went on. No one spoke. If they did, they would be beaten.

Morgenstern determined what everyone else knew. That is, if they didn't rest soon, they were going to die. He wished he had the Luger pistol. He was sure he could have killed one of these bastards before he himself was probably killed. That would have given the remaining three a chance. Very hard for one man to watch and control three prisoners on his own. Perhaps he might have been able to kill both of them, but that was unlikely. Still, he thought he could have got one of them. That would have meant his being killed also but it would have been better than this slow march to what must be certain death if something didn't change soon.

Anyway, it was useless to think on that now. The Siberians were having an easy time of it on their skis. Morgenstern had heard many stories of their endurance and knew they could keep going like this, unburdened by prisoners, from sunrise till sunset. There was one story of how they covered 120km in one day. They had caught up with a motorised regiment and then staged an assault against them. He couldn't decide if that could be true or not but he knew the Siberian regiments had a well earned reputation. But right now, he thought of their cruelty and concentrated on surviving this march. Where it lead to, well, that was for another day.

The Padre was mumbling some prayers to himself. Was he mumbling aloud? he asked himself. Or was it all in his head? No matter. At least he was praying one way or another. The truth was though, he was struggling. His back was sore but it was his legs that worried him most. Sharp pains shot up and down each leg intermittently. Then there would be a short respite before the pains started up again. He wished he could ask Benz, the Medic, what was wrong. These Russian soldiers terrified him and he asked himself for the umpteenth time, why had he joined the Army instead of taking a parish in somewhere like Freiburg. A place that he had sought out and asked for. Had he taken his time, he might have been offered such a place, but instead he had got caught up like so many others, in the mass hysteria of the thirties. The Master Race might conquer the world but they would still need their God to watch over them.

It was so utterly ridiculous to look back on it now, but that's how it was. It could be argued how naive or impressionable people could be but Germany at the time had been sold a huge lie that had seemed to be the only truth worth considering. Huber struggled with how his faith was linked to such a corrupt and immoral regime as those in charge back in Berlin. How could the murderers of women and children still attend a church service on a Sunday? And how could he administer such a service? A scream cut through his thoughts.

"Dvigat'sya seychas!" Huber turned to look. He quickly turned to look ahead again. Stark was on his knees and the Siberian with the pistol, weary of having to beat these prisoners so often, got in front of Stark and pointed his pistol at his head, shouting at him to get up and keep moving. Morgenstern held out two hands and slowly going over, with Benz joining him, pulled Stark to his feet and dragged him along until he stood on his own.

Stark trudged on but he was losing direction and bumping into his comrades until Morgenstern and Benz took turns shoving him forward in the right direction. He was hallucinating now; his eyes shut. The expanse of snow was hurting his eyes and he kept getting stabbing pains in his head. Images he didn't recognise danced across his mind. He kept moving though; every so often feeling a shove from behind from someone. A mechanical, automatic movement that would have looked comical under any other circumstances.

Stark was now seeing images of his childhood. These would flash before him like pictures on a

Viewmaster he'd seen once. Then he would see Greta; smiling at him as she came into a room with yellow wallpaper. Then came images of war. Horrible images. Men stumbling around on fire, screaming. Men disappearing in front of him in a red mist. Men crushed by tanks. Men-. He was down again on his knees. This time he was roughly pulled back to his feet and he felt something tear in his shoulder, but he forgot about it instantly as he saw Greta again. Now she was standing across a vast room, perhaps a ballroom, at one end, looking at him. She was dressed in black and holding a handkerchief to her face. He tried to move towards her, but couldn't.

Benz had an arm around Stark now and was more or less pulling him along. If he let go, he thought, Stark would just collapse again. Of the four of them, he was in the worst shape and Benz reckoned the Field Cook would not survive this day unless they stopped soon. Looking skyward, he thought it must be getting close to dusk now. For his own part, he was in pain all over. Every joint seemed to hurt. He thought it could be scurvy due to his poor diet, being half starved, but then they all were. Were the others in similar pain? Probably. What ever it was or it's cause, it was getting worse. Oh Jesus Christ, he cried to himself, let this end now.

He thought of his mother, who when he was a child, taught him to nurse a blackbird that had flown into a window of their small apartment and lay on the sill, gasping and struggling to get up. It was flapping one wing as it lay with it's head down and going around in circles. His mother had gone to the window and picked up the bird with cupped hands, bringing it inside. She determined that nothing was broken, but one wing was damaged in some way. "Why don't we find a box to put it in?" she said to a young Theo. "We can put some absorbent cotton in it to keep it snug."

Benz remembered caring for the bird for over a week. He'd fed it worms from the garden until eventually it flew away one day while they were outside in the back yard. It had pleased him greatly to help another living thing recover and get well and as he grew older, sparked a desire in him to become a Doctor. The war intervened however, and he was called up, opting to join the Sanitatswesen, or Army Medical Service. Did he still want to become a Doctor if he survived this madness? No, truth be told. His experiences had snuffed out that desire a long time ago. Any thoughts of clean hospitals filled with pretty nurses and grateful patients that he had helped to heal, were blocked out with violent memories of the battle wounded or general horrors of war.

Now it was getting dark and they were heading down a slope that led to a depot maybe? Perhaps a small village? It was hard to tell in the fading light. Then they were on flat ground and others were coming towards them. "Stoi!" one of the Siberians shouted. The four men swayed as they stood still, fighting to stay up right. The Siberians chatted with who appeared to be regular Russian soldiers for a time. Vodka was exchanged. Cigarettes were lit.

Then the four prisoners were shoved along a wet, muddy track. One of the Russians, an officer, slapped them repeatedly around the head as they trudged on. Then they halted again. The Siberians had vanished and another group of soldiers appeared out of the darkness. They were kicking the four men now and beating them with fists; later with makeshift clubs and sticks. When they tired of that and the four prisoners were curled up on the ground, there was much shouting and a general commotion until finally, Morgenstern, Stark, Benz and Huber, were bundled into the back of a truck which took off into the night at a crazy breakneck speed. The driver and his companion sang as they smoked and shared a bottle of vodka.

*

Camp 47

Huber couldn't feel anything. No pain. No sense of reality nor awareness of being alive or dead. But he was alive and the first to come to. Dark shapes surrounded him and ghoulish voices mocked him and the others as his memory of the last few hours swam around in his head. "Am I dead?" he said aloud and a terror gripped him that he was. He wept with the fear that he was in hell or purgatory and he instinctively prayed for his soul's salvation. "Deum oro hac hora tormentorum.."

After some time, he was once again racked with pain and cried out in anguish before covering his face with his hands as he wept uncontrollably.

Next was Morgenstern who jolted awake as if prodded with a live wire and he too cried out as he fought to raise himself up on his elbows. Then he was checking himself for broken bones and in the end decided he could well have a couple of fractured ribs. Slowly he glanced about. There they all were and everyone was breathing. Huber's hands were across his face. Was he awake? Stark and Benz were still out cold and he tried to sit up but the truck hit a pothole and he was tossed to the side of the Gaz, smashing his head off the solid wooden side of the cargo area, coming to a jolting halt with a gash in his right ear. He felt the blood trickle down his face and blinked.

Huber was mumbling now while Stark and Benz remained out cold on the other side of the truck in a heap and bizarre embrace.

"Huber!" said Morgenstern, but it sounded like a whisper. There was no reply. "Huber!" this time louder. The Padre looked up at him through wet eyes. "Check the others! You're nearest."

Huber came out of his despair and self-pity and slowly ran his hands over Stark and Benz. Then he was dragging himself closer and determined that they were both alive.

"How is their breathing?" asked Morgenstern.

"They seem to be just sleeping," said the Padre. "I think they're alright."

Morgenstern eventually sat up with his back to the cabin. He winced. "We're finished," he said quietly, closing his eyes. He couldn't remember ever feeling so bad.

"Where are they taking us?" asked Huber. He tried to sit up, but failed. He slumped back down, staring at the fabric roof, which was billowing in the wind.

"Who knows? A camp? If we're lucky, they'll tire of us somewhere and kill us."

"A prison camp? In the east?"

"If we live that long."

Huber wept again. Then a thought gripped him. "We could jump out of here! Escape!"

Morgenstern looked at him. "Go ahead," he said. "It'd be the quickest way to finish yourself."

"But Karl," Huber pleaded. "There's a chance-."

"At the speed these bastards are going? You'd be dead the instant you hit the road! If you're really meant to suffer, you might not die immediately and linger in a ditch with two broken legs while the local dogs-."

"Stop! Stop!" Huber cried.

Morgenstern spat to one side and wiped his face with a sleeve. Then there was a groan across from them and Benz stirred, rolling off Stark who hadn't moved. In time he was fully awake and lay on his back beside Huber. He said nothing.

"Stark?" was all Morgenstern could say.

Benz rolled his head to look up and across at the Field Cook. "He's..breathing. Where are we going?"

"To hell," said Morgenstern, believing it.

*

After about an hour, the Gaz truck finally screeched to a halt. The three men who were awake in the back saw someone fleetingly lift up the tarpaulin covering and peer inside. They heard footsteps walking away and then silence.

"Are we at the camp?" asked Huber.

"Camp?" said Benz. "What camp?"

"Prison camp," said Morgenstern. "What do you fucking think? Holiday camp? Try and wake Willi. If he can't get out of here on his own, they'll kill him for sure!"

Benz tried, slapping Stark's face and shaking him with the little strength he had left. It was no good. He didn't respond. Morgenstern thought of water, but of course they didn't have any. Desperate now and with footsteps once again coming their way, Morgenstern undid his flies and pissed on to Stark's face. It worked. He came to slowly; coughing and spluttering and the three of them fought to bring him to his senses. They were lucky. An argument seemed to be brewing outside, which gave them precious time. When the tarpaulin was thrown back, the four men looked out at two others they hadn't seen before, each carrying a club.

They were shouting now, beckoning the prisoners out of the truck. As they climbed down, a pack of dogs were suddenly running over to them, growling and barking viciously, their teeth bared. The two camp guards laughed as one of the dogs reached Benz, grabbing his arm and threatening to pull it off his body. He fell to his knees, screaming in pain. The force of the dog's bite was incredible and amid more laughter, other camp guards appeared and finally the dogs were called off.

Then more shouting. More clubs hitting them. But as everything has to come to an end, so too did the prisoner's torment and they were pushed through a gate and into a fenced yard crowded with others. The gate was now clanged loudly shut behind them and what seemed like hundreds of ghost-like figures were shuffling towards them. One muttered something in Romanian; another in Croatian. Morgenstern instinctively pushed the other three to one side, sensing the danger around them. Then a shout from afar in German stopped everything in an instant.

"Stop!" cried the voice. "Get back you trash! Leave them be!"

*

The four men collapsed in a heap where they were. The German voice was standing over them now. Morgenstern looked up and was about to say something but the voice spoke again.

"Shut up and listen!" the man said. "Name's Krandt! I'm one of the big men here. These scum around you are our glorious Romanian comrades who fucked off and left us in the shit!" he went on, spitting in their direction. "You're in a holding camp. Rumour has it, we'll be transported east soon, but well, fuck if I haven't been here for weeks I think.

"There's about fifty of us and hundreds of these scum bastards!" Krandt spat again. "There's no food but some days the locals from somewhere nearby, will toss a cabbage over the fence or even a loaf of bread, but that hasn't happened lately. But look out for it and be prepared to fight for your life if you get something. There are no Officers here. They were taken to a separate camp of their own. We're all from Stalingrad but I did see someone here before who came out of Kharkov, believe it or not. God knows how he ended up here. Anyway he died."

As Krandt seemed to pause to catch his breath, Morgenstern made to speak while the rest of them came to terms with this new horror. A holding camp! Transported east! No food! And for how long? Weeks?

"Morgenstern," said the Veteran. "Benz, Stark and Huber," he added, by way of an introduction. "We walked out of Stalingrad some days ago. A week maybe? More or less. There were seven of us at the start."

"Anything new?" asked Krandt. "Any sign of Von Manstein's lot?"

"Not when we left," said Morgenstern. "He's not coming. If he ever was!"

Krandt spat again. "I used to be a fucking Sergeant Major once," he said then.

Morgenstern and the others lay down and stared up at the grey sky, which seemed oblivious to them. They all knew what was coming and some closed their eyes, leaving Krandt to tell his story.

*

Hauptscharfuhrer Krandt's Fall from Grace

"We, that is, the 14th Panzer Grenadiers, came to this shithole in the summer of '41, fresh from Poland and France. I've been a soldier since I was 18 and this fucking place is the fucking limit, I can tell you!"

The four newcomers to Camp 47 listened to Krandt despite themselves. Morgenstern knew well it was a story that had been told over and over; a purging if you like.

"We swept across the border in the first week of July. We were part of Army Group Centre. Our lot was attached to the 4th Army. Back then, well, you must remember, we felt we could take on

God and his Angels if they asked us to. Within days, half of the Reds we came up against were either dead or captured and it was like France all over again, but better! But then we outran ourselves. Supply chain couldn't keep up, could it? Okay, you say, bide your time. Dig in and rest up. The bastards back home had other ideas of course. Wanted the whole lot done with before winter. Their fucking fault leaving it so late at the start, but anyway, on we went.

"I was Hauptscharfuhrer Krandt! I was fucking someone back then. I had a great bunch of lads under me too. They made those Waffen SS bastards look like a bunch of pussies! We ended up on the Volga like you lot and waited to cross the river while Goering's boys pounded Stalingrad to dust. Eventually, we crowded on to some barges and made our way over.

"Well, you know what happened next! We were shelled every inch of the way by the Reds who the fly boys were supposed to have wiped out! Once ashore and settled, I found out just over half of us had made it across! It was a proper balls-up right from the start. Anyway, I was like a fucking bear you've just kicked in the nuts for days! Just as we were about to get going, I ran into an SS bastard Colonel. Standartenfuhrer Lange his name was. He commandeered some of our trucks and our boss let him apparently.

"I wasn't going to take it lying down, I can tell you! Why should my boys have to walk while this bastard's gang travelled in style? Long story short, we came to blows and I was charged with hitting an Officer, by my own boss!"

"What happened?" asked Morgenstern, remembering the SS Colonel. He hadn't had any dealings with him, but he knew of his reputation. It was said that he was a rising star; a Colonel at the age of 34? It was unheard of. Others said he was reckless. But whatever he was, he's dead now, Morgenstern knew. He and his Battalion had been wiped out near the tractor factory last November.

"I ended up on a fucking train going home and stripped back down to Private! Jesus Christ Almighty!" Krandt shook his head at the injustice of it, as he saw it. "I spent three months in Torgau."

"You were in Torgau?" said Morgenstern in disbelief as he sat up. Torgau was the notorious brutal military prison from that town on the Elbe river.

"Yeah, Fort Zinna," said Krandt, sounding like it was a badge of honour.

"And you survived? Three months!"

"I was a proper tough bastard back then! And they knew it! Made me a Corporal in a Penal Battalion. The 17th. Here I stand in front of you arseholes and I've come through every sort of shit job they gave us when we were sent back out here!"

"Keep you voice down!" said Morgenstern. "If the Reds find out who you are-."

"Do I look like fucking stupid to you?" said Krandt, chuckling.

"Do the rest of our boys here know?"

"Yeah, some of 'em at least. I'm not the only one. There's a few of us here from the 17th. Our boys, like you, know we didn't have a say in it. Know we did what we were told because the alternative was death. But I have to say, I wish I'd died long ago. Don't have a clue how I'm still alive. It's sheer obstinacy that keeps me going. That and the hope that one day I'll get home and find some of the bastards responsible for this mess!"

*

Time passed and was judged by when the sun rose or when daylight started to fade and darkness fell. It wasn't easy judging how many days had gone by but it was generally agreed that it had to be double figures by now; perhaps ten or twelve?

Morgenstern and the rest of the little group of four were feeling better since when they'd arrived here. But better insofar as they weren't in pain or suffering from the results of the beatings they'd taken. There were of course the usual discomforts; Aches, joint pain, and the agonies of slow starvation on top of the unrelenting cold. But you could get used to anything over time, couldn't you?

So far, they'd shared a cabbage one day they'd managed to get after some locals threw a couple over the fence as well as a loaf of black bread. Another day, a small sack of fish heads had appeared in the early morning light. Benz had been the first to see it and had scrambled away to retrieve it. But so far, that was the only food they'd had. It seemed most food was thrown over the fence at night. It was assumed that obviously the locals were afraid of tossing their leftovers over the fence during daylight in case they were seen and punished by the camp guards for doing so. Everyone was amazed they even bothered to in the first place considering how they had been treated, especially by the SS since the German invasion.

But there it was; a small candle in the darkness and it was keeping them alive but at a terrible cost. On the days food, such as it was, did appear in the yard, at least one, maybe two men would die in the mad frenzy to get it. Morgenstern and the group would only consider retrieving something that no one had noticed. Most fights over food were among the Romanians or Croats. On the rare day a German prisoner died, Krandt and his ilk would later exact a terrible vengeance for it.

It was well known that the camp guards were obviously keeping whatever food was meant for the prisoners for themselves. Perhaps they too were short of what they needed to survive. Everyone knew of the stories early in the campaign where Russian Army prisoners were allowed to starve to death. One camp near Kiev had held around 250,000 prisoners. It had been run initially by the SS Liebstandarte Division and then later by the SS Viking or *Wiking* Division. This Division was made up of mainly Scandinavian volunteers but also counted many Estonians among it's ranks, who had an axe to grind against their Soviet oppressors. And grind their axes they did in the most dreadful way; Less than 4,000 prisoners survived the war from that camp.

Morgenstern looked across the fenced yard. It was raining now and had been for most of the day. A bitter, ice-cold rain that saturated everything you were wearing and if it stopped or eased, your clothes froze around you. If you didn't get up from where you lay or sat and moved around, thrashing your arms around you, then you would simply freeze to death in minutes. But for now, the freezing drizzle persisted, a mixture of snow and rain or sleet and looking up at the sky that was always grey here, Morgenstern was content to sit and wait while he watched a group of Romanians huddle near a corner of the yard. Stark, Benz and Huber were to his right, but not close. Nobody spoke. There was little to say any more.

Morgenstern knew the Romanians were up to something. One kept looking at the dense wood beyond that part of the fence. Three or was it four of them were facing in his direction. Another three had their backs to him. Every thirty or so minutes, one would move around to lean back against the fence while another would shuffle around to face it. They were taking turns going around in a loose circle. Morgenstern couldn't see what they were doing of course, but he was sure they were doing something. Could they possibly be working on the thick wire strands of the fence? And if so, with what? Before being tossed inside here, everyone was searched and stripped of anything they possessed. Huber for instance had had his wooden spoon taken off him this way but remarkably, he told himself, you still have Marta's little toy drum. The guards had missed that so it's possible one of the Romanians managed to smuggle something in here that enabled them to work on the fence.

Morgenstern thought of going over there but that would be a waste of time and effort. They would see him coming and simply stop what they were doing. If he tried to speak to them, they'd just tell him to fuck off, if they said anything at all. So he stayed put and watched through the rain, constantly shaking with the cold as everyone did.

"Lads," he said eventually. "Look to the corner on your left. See the group there? They're up to something. Working on the fence I think."

"How can you tell?" asked Huber, wincing as he shifted position.

"Because they're moving around in a circle, swapping places and taking turns."

"If the guards notice," said Stark, sitting up, "they'll come in here and kill 'em all in a quick minute!"

"What guards?" said Benz, glancing over his shoulder to the hut outside. "Not going to come out are they in the pissing rain, if they can help it. Far as they're concerned, we've nowhere to go."

"Still, they're taking a big risk," said Morgenstern. "The guards will notice some time."

"What have they got to lose?" said Stark then. "What have any of us got to lose?"

"Our lives?" said Huber.

"We're going to die, Padre," said Benz. "If not today, then some other day."

"Please Theo," said Huber, looking mournfully at the Medic. "Please."

Suddenly Morgenstern sat forward. "I don't believe it!" he said. "One of them has got through! Look! There's another one gone! Sit still!" he snapped at the others. "We don't want the world to know, do we!"

The four men watched in stupefied silence as one by one, the seven Romanian prisoners crawled on their bellies or went out backwards through a hole in the fence they'd taken weeks to work on that was perhaps eighteen inches wide and maybe eight inches high.

Morgenstern looked around the yard. No one seemed aware of what had happened. He glanced back quickly to the hole in the fence. The last of the Romanians was out and crawling towards the treeline. Then he jumped up and was running after his fellow escapees.

"Come on," said Morgenstern, getting up. The four men shuffled over to the hole in the fence as casually as they could, thrashing their arms around them so it looked like they were just trying to stave off the worst effects of the cold. The freezing drizzle continued and kept the rest of the prisoners in the yard where they were, huddled in small groups and oblivious to what was going on. Looking over to his right at the opposite diagonal corner, Morgenstern noticed out of the corner of his eye, two men throwing another dead body on top of the heap there that grew bigger everyday. It made him think.

He sat with his back to the fence, covering the hole behind him. Huber, Stark and Benz sat down also in front of him. Once enough time had passed, they spoke in hushed tones. Morgenstern first.

"I say we wait till it's dark, then wait some more. But before those bastards bed down for the night," he said, looking out at the guard's hut. "They'll leave the dogs out as usual and we don't want them on our tail! We wouldn't last a minute once the guards catch up with them!"

"You're saying we should escape!" said Huber. "But where in God's name do we go, Karl!" He was in tears but no one noticed in the rain.

"Where do we go?" said Morgenstern, exasperated. "Where were we fucking going before we ended up here? If you don't want to come, then fucking stay put! Here, we're dead men! It's just a matter of time. Outside, well, we have a chance. A small one but it's better than nothing."

"Agreed," said Stark. Benz nodded.

"But Karl..." said Huber, his voice trailing off. He was shaking violently now. With the cold but also with this new fear which gripped him.

"Look at me Eduard," said Morgenstern now. "Get a grip of yourself, or so help me, I'll kill you myself! Shit! Some of Krandt's mob are already looking this way!"

"Calm yourself, Eduard," said Benz quietly. "We'll make it out and then, well, who knows?"

"Ask your God for help," said Stark unkindly.

Huber looked at him through his tears and the rain. My God? he thought again.

And so they sat. The rain persisted. The light grew dim. No guards left their hut. No dogs as yet were let out. No one in the yard moved from where they'd been since the Romanians had escaped. Morgenstern acknowledged that it was a small miracle only he had noticed what had happened. But there it was. And soon he and the others would make their escape too, or die trying to.

He thought through where they should go; what they should do. For a start, they'd go in the same direction the Romanians took through the trees. Perhaps they know this area and where they should head to. It didn't really matter though. One direction was as good as another. After that? Well, there wasn't much to think about, was there? All you could do was lie low during daylight hours and move at night. You scavenged for food as you went along, if there was any. You stayed off the roads and tracks and kept away from any village you came across, except maybe to steal some food, which you would do at night. But only if you were as sure as you could be that it would be low risk and there wasn't a dog tied up somewhere outside. The dog would pick up your scent and bark, alerting the whole damn place and you'd have to high tail it fast.

If you got really lucky, you might find yourself in a field of cabbages or turnips one night. Potatoes perhaps? Then in the darkness you could all fill your pockets with as much as you could carry away into the night. Then you holed up somewhere, in a barn or a shed and rested and ate and rested some more. Then you moved on another night, all the time heading west.

It sounded simple enough to Morgenstern sitting in the rain now. He knew it wasn't of course. It was stupidly dangerous. They had no idea where they were. They were in the middle of enemy occupied territory. They would probably be hunted down and if caught, probably killed. They might go for days without finding food and could end up holed up somewhere too weak to carry on. There was also the prospect of running into partisans, who if they caught you, would make the Hiwis look like a bunch of girl scouts! And how far can we possibly get anyway? Morgenstern considered. 50 kilometres? 100? 200? The more time he spent thinking about it, the more impossible it seemed that they would reach their own people. But he was determined to try. Better to die out there somewhere having tried than to die for sure in this squalid shithole, he told himself.

"Right, listen up!" he said after a while. It was getting dark. "I'm first. The rest of you as you like. It'll take me two or three minutes to crawl to the trees. Wait till I do, then follow one by one. I'll wait for you lot and once we're all out, we run for lives through the trees there," Morgenstern said, jabbing a thumb in that direction. "Okay? Right then, huddle closer. I'll lie down and go out head first."

*

Freedom?

Morgenstern lay down and put his arms out through the hole in the fence first, using them to prise himself out slowly whilst also using his legs bent at the knee and pushing with his feet. The others watched his technique while keeping an eye out for onlookers or any potential trouble.

Once fully out, Morgenstern crawled a short distance and lay still, counting to thirty. Then he was up on his feet and crouching low, made for the treeline. Stark went next, followed by Benz, both of whom got out with no problems. Benz' coat pocket lapel did snag on some of the wire strands but he was able to tear it off without any difficulty and after that was soon away. When he found Morgenstern and Stark among the trees, the three of them watched anxiously and waited for Huber.

The Padre lay down and started to get through the hole, using the same technique as before. As he did so, light flooded out of the guard's hut and two huge Caucasian Shepherd dogs came tearing out. They ran around barking and sniffing the ground, one of them making for the pile of prisoner corpses that was piled high in a grotesque heap on the opposite side of the fence.

Huber, aware of what had happened, froze, panic stricken. He looked to the trees but could see nothing in the darkness. Half in and half out of the fence, he had to decide quickly whether to keep going or get back inside the yard. Now the other dog, not interested in the fresh dead bodies, was sniffing around the yard entrance and making it's way to the corner, which if it followed the fence around, would lead it straight to Huber.

Over in the trees, Morgenstern, Stark and Benz looked on in silence. Together they urged the Padre to move. They all wanted him out but if he decided to retreat back inside the yard, well, that would be alright too. It would be his choice and he would still be alive. Then they could get away and convince themselves that that was the case and that he might somehow survive whatever fate befell him.

"Come on Eduard!" Benz muttered under his breath. "One way or another damn you! Move man!"

"If he doesn't get going, he's a dead man," Stark whispered.

Morgenstern looked on without saying anything at first. He thought this had to end badly. Now someone in the yard was on their feet and going over to Huber. Others joined him.

"Shit!" said the Veteran. "Someone in the yard has seen him! The fucking dog has turned the corner too! If it picks up Huber's scent, it'll pick up ours! We have to go!" Morgenstern turned and made ready to go.

"Wait! Goddamn it!" said Benz, grabbing Morgenstern's arm. "We can't just fuck off and leave him!"

Morgenstern pulled his arm away from Benz' grip. He looked one more time in Huber's direction. Then he was gone. Benz and Stark waited and watched. Huber still hadn't moved.

"We can't outrun the fucking dogs!" Stark hissed through gritted teeth. "Come on Theo!"

Then Benz was alone. He watched helplessly. It was too late. There was no more time. The dog had seen Huber. Benz turned and ran, taking off after his two comrades.

Back inside the yard, the Padre had looked to his left, seeing the giant dog coming for him. He let out a shriek and desperately tried to get himself back through the hole. But he wasn't moving. He pushed with his arms; pulled with his legs bent at the knee, but it was no good. He was stuck. Two other prisoners inside the yard now had hold of Huber's legs and were pulling him for all they were worth, which wasn't much. But the dog was on him in seconds and it became a grotesque tug of war between the dog, who had it's jaws embedded in Huber's neck and shoulder and the two prisoners, who pulled and tugged ferociously, one of them calling over his shoulder for others to help. Huber's legs felt like they were dislocating at the hip. Then the dog let go, snarling and trying to get inside the hole through the fence, but it wasn't big enough. Now some guards were running towards the scene, shouting and promising awful menace. The other dog had joined in by now but it didn't matter. Huber was already dead.

*

The Legend of the Weisse Tod

Morgenstern, Stark and Benz ran for their lives. Blindly, and with only one purpose, to get away. Morgenstern, who'd gone first, was heading in one direction while Stark and Benz went in another; Benz tearing after Stark, who had maybe twenty metres on him. But after just a few minutes and having only covered perhaps 300 metres, they all collapsed in the snow, lungs bursting and gasping for breath. Fortunately, they were also within a short distance of each other and when he recovered from their mad sprint, Morgenstern could hear the other two talking to each other.

He hadn't the strength to get up yet, but he crawled over to them slowly, still fearful of any pursuers who might be on their trail. With that in mind, he paused briefly to listen. Above Stark and Benz' chattering, he could just make out a dog barking. Poor Huber, he thought absently. Where was his God when he needed him?

He whistled softly as he got nearer to the two men. Benz stopped talking and looked over Stark's shoulder. He held a finger to his mouth. Quiet! he was saying to Stark, who froze and went pale. The two of them crouched low and faced the direction of the whistle. Stark pointed. "There! By the tree! That's-."

"Yes, I see him," said Benz. He knew who it was. "It's Karl!"

Then the three of them were reunited and squatted on the ground. "We should get going!" said Morgenstern with urgency. "We're not far enough away. I heard the dogs just now!" Benz and Stark stood up, looking fearfully in the direction from where had just come. "Who was last to see the camp?" the Veteran asked, standing also.

"I was," said Benz. "Huber didn't make it. The dogs were on him while some men tried to get him back inside the yard. He was probably already dead when they managed it."

"Shit!" said Stark. "Poor Eduard!"

"That's too bad," said Morgenstern, who'd wanted the Padre to make it. Wanted the boy to live.

"Any sign of those Gypsy bastards? Even what direction they took?" He was thinking of the Romanians who'd escaped before them.

"Nah," said Stark. "No way of knowing which way they went. Anyway, we don't need to follow them, right?"

"Right," said Morgenstern. "But it might have helped if they'd known where we are. But it doesn't matter really. We're out and we're alive, eh boys?!"

"Yeah," said Benz. "Fucking right! Another bloody miracle! Know how many that is now?"

"We're three lucky bastards!" Stark marvelled, leaning back against a tree. He stared up at the grey sky.

"For Christ's sake!" said Morgenstern. "It's not about luck, sodding miracles or anything fucking else! It simply is what it is!"

"Which is what?" said Benz, frowning. "Fate?"

"It's not that either!"

"Well what is it then?" asked Stark.

"Jesus!" said Morgenstern, rolling his eyes. "There doesn't have to be a reason for everything. There's no luck in this shitty world! No fate! No God, for sure. No any fucking thing! Things happen or they don't. It's all chaos! We might live to be a hundred or we might die today!"

"That's a bleak way to look at life," said Benz.

"Fatalistic, you might say," said Stark, chuckling.

Morgenstern looked at him, frowning. Then he smiled. Looking back at Benz, he said, "after all you've been through and all that you've seen, you're going to tell me there's another way?"

"There's hope Karl," said Benz.

"Hope? Hah! Fine okay, you keep hoping."

"Yeah, I fucking will!"

"Fine!" said Morgenstern. "Now can we get going?"

Later, towards dawn and perhaps three or four kilometres further away from the camp, they huddled together for warmth in a ditch. They were still in the wood and had no clue where they were. They talked about the possibility of being pursued, but Morgenstern thought that the Russians weren't going to commit to a sweeping search for a few missing prisoners that would be considered of little importance. Let them die in the snow was the probable attitude.

"Let's try and sleep," said Morgenstern, closing his eyes. It was hard though. He tried to stop shaking from the cold, but soon gave up. He had no control over it. His body continued to tremble. Stark and Benz tried too. It was no good. And anyway, sleep these days came when it wanted to. You couldn't just lie down and sleep any more. You just waited till it overtook you. You could be talking to someone and in mid-sentence, just keel over. Whoever you were talking to might wonder briefly if you'd just died. They might check you were still alive and then leave you to it. So many men had died like that, no one thought it odd any more.

"Ever hear about the Sniper they used to call 'White Death'?" Stark asked after a while.

"Sleep!" said Morgenstern.

"Can't say I have, no" said Benz. "White Death? What was he? A fucking snowman?" he added, chuckling.

"He was a Danish soldier," said Stark. "Fought back in the early days. Europe somewhere."

"And?" said Benz.

"Well, they called him White Death because he always wore white fatigues, so you couldn't see him in the snow, could you? Like the Siberians here. Anyway, they say he killed over a thousand men and-."

"For fuck sake!" said Morgenstern, breaking away from the huddle and sitting up once more.

"Jesus Karl!" said Stark. "Give it a fucking rest, can't you?! We're just talking."

"Fucking talk then," said Morgenstern irritably. "We'll sleep when we die, eh?"

"Yeah, probably," said Benz, looking over at the Veteran. "Go on Wilhelm," he said to Stark. "A thousand kills? Were they verified? That has to be exaggerated."

"Course it fucking is!" said Morgenstern. "Any, he was Finnish, not Danish."

"So you know the story then," said Stark. "Let's have it then."

The three of them tried to make themselves comfortable. Morgenstern sighed and forgetting his irritableness, began.

"White Death was what the Reds called him. His own boys called him the 'Magic Shooter'. I heard it all from an Infantry Corporal who'd actually served in Finland in '41, when we sent some boys over there to help out with their fight against the Reds. This Corporal was from the 6th Mountain Regiment, an Alpine Division, Bavarian I think."

"Did he meet this Magic Shooter?" asked Benz.

"No," said Morgenstern. "He'd been wounded and had gone back to his farm. Used to keep Reindeer apparently. Probably still does."

"So he survived!" said Benz. "Incredible!"

"That's just the half of it. The Reds invaded Finland in '39. This chap-."

"What was his name?" Stark cut in, fascinated.

"I dunno, can't remember," said Morgenstern. He thought for a moment. "Hang on. Samo? Simo? Something like that. Yeah, that was his first name. Don't know his family name. Anyway, he was a Laplander. Like I said, a reindeer herder. Used to follow his herd across the northern wastes throughout the seasons. When he'd heard the Reds had invaded, he joined up, aggrieved at the bastards, like most were. He thought himself handy with a rifle on account of all the wolves he'd shot looking after his reindeer."

Just then, a twig snapped somewhere. The three men froze and looked around anxiously. When they were satisfied it was nothing, they relaxed, breathing out slowly.

"Go on," Benz said to Morgenstern.

"Where was I?"

"He used to shoot wolves," said Stark. "Looking after his reindeer."

"Yeah, well, he was a competition shooter too, in the Civil Guard. Before the war. Won a trophy once for hitting the same target sixteen times in under a minute from 300 metres!"

"Ah that's balls!" said Benz, shaking his head.

"As true as I'm sitting here," said Morgenstern. "Another time, he hit a target five times but left only two holes in it!"

"Impossible!" said Stark, looking at Benz. Both men chuckled.

"Yeah well, whatever," said Morgenstern. "But when it came to shooting, he was a force of nature. He had over 500 confirmed kills by the end of it. Weighed down with medals he was."

"Fucking hell!" said Stark. "500 kills? That's a helluva lot more than Zaitsev will ever manage!" he said, referring to the infamous Russian Sniper.

"If he exists at all," said Benz. "Red propaganda, isn't it?"

"Oh he's real alright," said Morgenstern, speaking from experience.

"But Karl, 500 kills? Really?" said Stark.

"Well over 500 apparently. Nobody knows the exact number, not even Simo I'll bet. And remember, that was just over the course of one winter. A matter of months. He'd get at least a half dozen every day. Often more, but never less."

"Jesus Christ!" said Benz, whistling softly. "Jesus Christ!" he repeated, raising himself up on his elbows.

"They say one day he killed 24 Reds by midday."

"What?!"

"The Reds back then were even more stupid and badly led than they are now," said Morgenstern. "What they have in their favour, as we all know, are numbers."

"Oh yeah," said Stark. "That they have!"

"And their bosses don't mind wasting 10,000 men just to stop us taking a piss!" said Benz. As a

Medic, he thought about the Soviet ruling mentality that included whole NKVD regiments whose sole task was to cut down their own soldiers who dared to retreat when ordered otherwise.

"Lots of numbers," said Morgenstern. "And all dressed in bright green back then in Finland in '39. Stood out like sore thumbs, didn't they? But the best part is, Simo was using an old bolt-action rifle without telescopic sights that he'd brought with him. Had it at home for years. It was said he routinely shot from 500 metres. They offered him the best rifle they had with the best sights, but he refused, saying he was used to the one he had. Stands to reason I suppose."

"Ah come on Karl," said Benz. "An old rifle? With iron sights?"

"Yep! He said a scope would glint in the sun. Give away his position."

"Christ Almighty!" said Stark. "Didn't we have a chap? What was his sodding name? Back in Poland in 1940?"

"You don't mean that chap from Hamburg?" said Benz. "The one they used to call William Tell?"

"That's the one," said Stark.

"He's only managed a hundred so far, last I heard," said Benz. "But don't forget, he was using a crossbow!"

Morgenstern closed his eyes and left them to it. He was desperately tired. The last thing he thought of was Benz saying, 'only a hundred', as if killing a hundred men was a matter of routine.

*

<u>Not Among Friends-The Black Hunters</u>

Morgenstern grabbed Stark's arm, pulling him back and down roughly. "Where the fuck are you going?" he said harshly. Stark looked at him menacingly, his eyes wild. He was about to say something but Morgenstern clamped a hand over his mouth. Stark made an effort to struggle but couldn't find the strength. Benz ignored them and continued to look across the small clearing from where they were among the trees.

They had struggled on through the wood soon after dawn and had stopped here after being alerted by the sound of men talking. They had assumed they were Russian soldiers but there seemed to be a mixture of languages and pretty soon, the three men could hear someone speaking German. That was when poor, half-starved Stark, who of the three of them was in the weakest shape, suddenly got up from where they were crouching and made to go over to what he thought was a regular German Army unit. Morgenstern still had a hold of him when Benz turned to look at them.

"SS maybe?" offered the Medic.

"Can you make out any insignia?" Morgenstern asked him. He let Stark go, who frowned and then closed his eyes, slouching back down on the cold frozen ground.

If it was an SS unit, then it wasn't good news. If this was France, then yes, maybe you could saunter over to them and explain yourselves. They might tell you to fuck off but usually, you could expect to be fed and maybe taken somewhere safe before being brought to German occupied territory. But this wasn't France, or anywhere else. This was the apex of the Eastern Front where you took nothing for granted.

Benz squinted and spent some minutes looking at the group in the clearing. Eventually he turned to face his two companions. He rubbed some snow over his eyes before wiping a sleeve over them.

"All I could see was a crest on a helmet," said Benz then. "Crossed grenades, like this," he added, crossing his arms in front of him.

"Ah you're fucking joking!" said Morgenstern bitterly. "Shit!"

"What?" said Stark. "Who are they then?" He and Benz waited for Morgenstern to answer.

"They're SS alright," he said. "But the worst kind! Dirlewanger's lot!"

"The 36th!" said Benz, going pale.

"Who?" asked Stark. What the hell now? he thought.

"You've never heard of 'em?" said Morgenstern through gritted teeth.

"No, should I?" said Stark, frowning.

"Yeah, you should!" said the Veteran. He was angry at this new bad card they had been dealt. No, there was no luck in this world. Not any more.

"The Black Hunters?" said Benz. "Surely Wilhelm, you've heard of them?"

"Oh my God!" said Stark, shaking now. "Are you sure it's them?"

"That's their fucking crest!" said Morgenstern. "No one else in their right mind would think of using it. If they were caught, they'd be shot in a quick second!"

"They're fucking crazy!" said Benz quietly.

"Dirlewanger is the worst kind of bastard I've ever heard of," said Morgenstern. "His mob make the Einsatzgruppe look like boy scouts! These lot are a rag-tag bunch of psychos. They're the worst type of scum; ex-cons and God knows what. Rumour has it, they even took prisoners from Landsberg," he said, referring to the notorious prison in Bavaria that housed the criminally insane.

"But why use those bastards?" asked Stark. "Are things that bad back home?"

"I remember reading somewhere the idea was to sow fear and terror," said Benz.

"It's Himmler's gang back in Berlin who are criminally insane," said Stark, shaking his head in dismay. "Who else would think of using trash like that?"

"And think about it," said Morgenstern. "Who actually controls them, in the field? Some bastard sitting at a desk down the corridor from Himmler? No, out here, they can do what they fucking like! With no one to answer to. Only consolation I can think of is the casualty rate in the 36th, which is around 80%. Life expectancy is measured in weeks."

"Did you hear the story about the kindergarten in Warsaw, Karl?" asked Benz.

"What was that?" asked Stark in dread.

"Yeah, I heard it," said Morgenstern. He said no more though.

Stark looked at him, then at Benz. "Well?"

Benz sighed heavily. "During the uprising," he said, looking over at the group of SS men in the clearing. "Dirlewanger himself led a group of these bastards into a kid's school. Think about it, a fucking kid's school! Anyway, I say led, he was actually at the rear. Pistol in one hand, bottle of booze in the other. They say he drank at least three bottles a day. So, he told his mob to shoot everyone inside, no matter what their age. By the time they'd got to the top floors, they'd ran out of bullets. Dirlewanger had some left though. Ordered his men to use rifle butts and clubs. Anyone who protested, he shot. An Engineer Regiment who passed by later, told tales of blood running down the fucking stairs!"

"My God!" said Stark, thinking it was the worst atrocity he'd ever heard of in his life.

"So Wilhelm," said Morgenstern. "Next time you go running towards what you think are our lads, think again!"

"What do we do, Karl?" asked Benz. Morgenstern looked at him as if he was an idiot. "But for fuck sake! They have food!"

"Jesus Christ!" said Morgenstern. He crawled over to get a better look at the clearing. He counted eight men. No campfire though. They were a lot of things, but they weren't stupid. A campfire in the open would be seen for miles around. And yes, they had food. They were eating sausage by the look of it. Bread, for sure. His stomach rebelled at the thought. They were all armed with rifles and you could bet most had pistols too. He marvelled absently at the chance they were taking. Sitting there in the open, eating sausage without a care in the world. But they were crazy, weren't they? If the Russians came across them and knew who they were, these SS men would wish they'd never been born.

They were all roughly his age; early to mid-thirties with one or two maybe older. But there was one who looked much younger though. He wore a cheap pair of spectacles and looked frail and weak. Morgenstern thought he could almost pass for Himmler himself.

"I don't know really," he said, turning back to Stark and Benz. "There's no way of knowing how they'll react. If they don't shoot us straight away, what will they make of us? Deserters?"

"But we could tell our story! How we escaped and-."

"And what about are trek from Stalingrad? What if they ask us why we fucked off? Despite the order to hold out?"

Benz thought it over while he chewed his lip. He couldn't stop thinking about the food though. That's what it came down to in the end. It was all about the food really.

"What have got to lose?" asked Stark then.

"Remember the Hiwis?" said Morgenstern.

"But their on our side! For Christ's sake, Karl!" Stark protested.

"The only side their on is their fucking side! If you walked into Landsberg last year, two years ago, would you mix with 'em in the exercise yard? Unarmed?"

"Shit no!" said Benz. And here now? he thought, shaking his head. Better to stay hungry and alive, he decided.

"Come on then," said Morgenstern, slowly backing up. "Let's get out of here!"

"Wilhelm!" said Benz, following the Veteran. "Fucking come on!"

But suddenly, as the Medic turned to follow Morgenstern, he was looking at a rifle muzzle. Looking up, he saw one of two men who for all intents and purposes appeared to be a couple of German Army Corporals. The only thing that gave them away was their unit badge; the dreaded crossed grenades.

Benz froze and looked to the ground. He squeezed his eyes shut, expecting to be shot out of hand. He heard a whimper from Stark and Morgenstern saying quietly, "Shit!"

"Up you get lads," said one of the SS men. "Off you go then," he added, gesturing towards the clearing and the rest of his unit.

"What have we got 'ere then, eh Otto?" said the other SS man.

"I don't rightly know, Johann. They're our lot alright. Question is though, what the fuck are they doing out here in the middle of nowhere?"

"Well, we'll soon find out!" said Johann. Both men chuckled.

Tall Tales

"Look what we come across!" said Otto, stepping into the clearing.

The young SS man with the spectacles suddenly shot up from he had been sitting and aimed his rifle at Morgenstern, who ducked instinctively. He was the nearest of the three strangers.

"Erik!" someone bellowed. A tall Hauptscharfuhrer stood up, looking like he was ready to pounce on the younger man. 'Erik' then stood to attention and shouldered his rifle, as if he was on a parade ground. Then he sat back down on a box of ammunition. The Hauptscharfuhrer looked down at him as he approached the group.

Morgenstern stood up straight once more and looked around at the group before him. Am I dreaming this, he wondered. Most of the SS men didn't even look up from what they were doing. He glanced at Benz, who caught his eye. For fuck sake, play along, Morgenstern's look was saying. Our lives depend on it. Stark, for his part, was trembling, expecting a battalion of Russians to come charging through the woods alerted by the noise they were making.

"Alright Otto," said the Hauptscharfuhrer. "Sit down lads," he added, addressing the three newcomers.

Morgenstern, Stark and Benz slowly sat on the frozen ground while their two captors, Otto and another Corporal named Johann, sat on some sacking under a tree. Morgenstern relaxed a little. At least this Sergeant he sat before seemed amiable and appeared to have control over his unit.

"Schultz!" said the Sergeant now. One of the group looked over at him. "You're nearest. Give 'em something to eat!"

Schultz, who had been cleaning a pistol, sighed heavily and got up, walking over to a sack of food wedged between a boulder covered in moss and a box of rifle ammunition. He rummaged through the sack and then stopped to look back at the three strangers in his midst. Using a pointed finger, he counted them like a child would before returning his attention to the sack.

Meanwhile, the SS Hauptscharfuhrer sat and faced Morgenstern. He'd already looked Stark and Benz over. A Cook and a fucking Medic! They weren't worthy of his attention. But this one? Yes. This one was a survivor.

"From one Sergeant to another," said the Hauptscharfuhrer, leaning forward and offering his hand. "Name's Adler."

"Morgenstern," he said, shaking his hand. He was struck by the irony. Adler was a German Jewish surname. "This is Stark and Benz."

Adler ignored them and kept his eyes on Morgenstern. He said nothing more though. The Veteran glanced around the clearing. Some of the men were asleep; some were cleaning weapons and one was sharpening a combat knife. Others smoked and chatted among themselves. Morgenstern counted ten in all, with Adler making it eleven. Schultz was still rummaging through the sack of food. Adler followed Morgenstern's eyes.

"Otto," he said then. "Give 'im a hand, would you?"

Otto sighed and got up. He went over to Schultz, a certifiable retarded Austrian recruited from Landsberg prison and shoved him out of the way. Schultz picked himself up and retook his seat, where he continued to clean his pistol as if nothing had happened. Otto came back quickly with a whole Bratwurst sausage which he broke into three, tossing the pieces on the ground in front of the three newcomers. Then miraculously, he also produced three quarter kilo loaves of wholemeal bread from his pockets. He threw these down also before sitting back down beside Johann under the tree.

Morgenstern looked at the food in disbelief before slowly reaching out a hand. Benz picked up his ration and ate without a word. Stark initially stared at the food; tears coming to his eyes as if it represented salvation.

"Where have you lot come from then?" asked Adler now.

"Stalingrad," said Morgenstern, taking a bite of his sausage. It was so delicious compared to what they were used to.

"Oh really?" said Adler. He couldn't care less really but knew well he had some power here, considering the circumstances. His whole adult life was about instilling fear in others. That was why he ended up in Landsberg prison at the age of seventeen.

"Yeah. We escaped from the Reds and ended up here. Been trekking for days."

"How many days?"

"Fuck if I know," said Morgenstern, thinking fast. "Couple of weeks maybe? It's hard to-."

"Stalingrad fallen then?"

"Well, the bit of it we were in, yeah. The airfield is overrun. Won't be long before the Reds take the whole city."

"Bastards!" said Adler, spitting on the ground. "You take something, then you give it away," he said, shaking his head. "Still, what do you expect, when the Reds have got a steady supply of farm boys to feed the grinder, eh? Be a different fucking story if they were facing our lot, wouldn't it?" Adler asked, looking at the three men before him. He wanted to see their reaction. Nobody spoke though.

Later, Morgenstern said, "Yeah, maybe, sure." He didn't mention the two SS Regiments that had been wiped out already in Stalingrad.

"Maybe?!" Adler roared, standing up. He reached into a pocket, taking out a packet of cigarettes. He sat back down and after he lit up, said, "There's no fucking maybe about it mate! The Waffen SS are the finest soldiers the world has ever seen! We are warriors! Servants of death! With a hundred men, I could wipe out a whole Red Division!"

Now Morgenstern could see who and what he was dealing with here. He silently wished Stark and Benz kept their mouths shut. "Yes, of course," he said, hoping it was enough.

"I was in Kharkov," said Adler, drawing on his cigarette. "May last year it was."

"It was June," said Otto, suddenly interrupting. Adler looked at him. There was a sudden tension in the air.

"So as I was saying," said Adler, turning his attention back to Morgenstern. "I was in Kharkov, in fucking May, last year!" he said, raising his voice as he glanced at Otto. "There was what, 200 of us?"

"Three," said Otto.

Adler closed his eyes and sighed heavily. He took his pistol out of it's holster and pointed it at Otto. "Open you're fucking mouth again! I dare you!"

Otto stopped what he was doing and looked at Adler. He opened his mouth to say something but stopped when Adler cocked his pistol, ready to fire. He knew the other man would do it. He'd seen him do it before for less. Otto looked down at the ground. Adler replaced his pistol in it's holster.

"We were up against what we'd been told were about 2,000 Reds," Adler continued. No one in the clearing seemed to notice the Sergeant's exchange with Otto. It appeared to be normal behaviour. Morgenstern was quietly horrified.

"Sitting on their arseholes near a farm, weren't they? Morgenstern, we're a couple of Old Hares, aren't we?" said Adler, using the army slang for combat Veterans. "See what happens when the Itchy Neck bastards want a job done properly?"

Morgenstern nodded, smiling. 'Itchy Neck' referred to a Commander in the field who wanted an Iron Cross, or similar decoration. "What happened?" he asked.

"Well, the 2,000 Reds turned out to be five or six, didn't they? Anyway, we got the job done," said Adler, ending the story quickly. He might have told a longer version, but lost interest. Otto had spoiled it for him after all.

The truth of it was, 287 SS Grenadiers or heavy infantry, had taken the Russian position north of Kharkov that day in June 1942, killing over 4,000 Russian soldiers. Around 1,800 Russian prisoners were captured by the 103 surviving SS men. It wasn't unusual. It happened many times in many places. Unbelievable heroism and impossible victories that gave the Waffen SS their reputation of being invincible. It was of course borne from a creed of madness and fanaticism.

Morgenstern had finished his sausage. The bread he put in a pocket, for later. Stark and Benz had done the same. "Got a spare smoke?" he asked Adler. He couldn't help himself. How long had it been since he'd had a whole cigarette to himself? Months?

"Course, here," said the SS Sergeant, offering the pack. He didn't offer Stark or Benz a cigarette. They may as well have not been present at all.

Morgenstern took the Juno out of the pack. It was like his birthday had come early. He held it under his nose and smelt the tobacco. It was glorious. Then Adler was holding an IMCO lighter in front of him. He took a light and inhaled, coughing quickly. But he was touching heaven.

Adler chuckled. "Been a while, eh?" he said knowingly. "Here, keep 'em," he added, holding the closed pack out for Morgenstern to take. "I got more."

Morgenstern took the pack of cigarettes in a daze, mumbling his thanks. He couldn't help opening them to count how many there were. Twelve! Jesus Sweet Christ!

"Got any matches?" asked Adler. "Course you don't! Stupid bloody question! Johann, matches!" he barked, looking back at Morgenstern. He was clearly amused. Johann threw a box of matches that landed in front of Morgenstern.

"Thanks," he managed to say, shaking the box and putting them in a pocket with the cigarettes. He'd count them later.

Adler finished his own cigarette while he contemplated the situation, glancing briefly at Stark and Benz. What now? he asked himself. Can't hang on to them. This one maybe, but all they really want is to be on their way. I could use this Morgenstern though. I'll bet he knows what he's doing. But these other two? he pondered, looking again at Stark and Benz. Waste of fucking space. If it had been just these two that Otto had found, well, I would have shot them myself straight away.

But Morgenstern won't stay, will he? Nah. As much as he wouldn't leave without these two useless bastards! Do I let them go then? Adler thought. Send 'em on their way with some grub? Point 'em in the right direction, as it were. Let's test 'em first, eh? Adler smiled inwardly.

"So, mate, what are your plans then?"

"What? Apart from getting through tomorrow?" said Morgenstern, forcing a laugh.

Adler wasn't laughing. He sat forward, close to Morgenstern now. "No mate," he said, his tone different. "What are you going to do? Once we go our separate ways," he said slowly.

"Er, dunno really," said Morgenstern, trying to think. They're going to let us go then? "Keep trekking west, I suppose. Look for more of our lot," he said, hoping Adler would relent. "What about you? Where are you headed?"

Adler sat back. "We're staying put. Least for now. These woods are crawling with fucking partisans. That's why we're here, isn't it? Perhaps you'd like to join us?" he finished with, letting the question hang.

Morgenstern finished his cigarette, revelling in the luxury of it. He reconsidered his views on luck and then thought about what he was going to say. He could ask Adler to hang around for a couple of days, to try and regain a bit of strength but he'd want a lot in return, even for feeding them. But if he did allow them to stay, a lot could happen in those couple of days. The last thing on this earth anyone would want would be to end up captured by Russian partisans, and mistaken for SS men. No amount of protestations would help you. The Virgin Mary might appear and appeal on your behalf. It would do no good. Morgenstern remembered stories he'd heard about partisans skinning SS men alive and shuddered at the thought.

"Thanks mate," he said finally. "But as you can see, we're in pretty bad shape. Wouldn't be much use to you. If it's all the same, I reckon we'll just be on our way."

Adler flicked his cigarette away. Good answer, he decided. Alright then. That's settled. "Well, take your time. But it's us who'll be on our way," he said, standing up and stretching. "Right!" he said loudly to his men. "Let's get going!"

Perhaps ten minutes later, Morgenstern, Stark and Benz watched the SS Dirlewanger unit of men trudge off into the trees going God knows where. Morgenstern couldn't help marvelling at their courage. They had to know their chances were slim at best, and if they were captured alive? Jesus Christ! Another story he'd heard came into his head. The one about the Russian regiment of women and what they did to captured prisoners. He winced inwardly, as a shiver ran down his spine. Were people like Adler and Otto courageous? Or so fucking crazy not to realise the danger they were in? He finished his cigarette deciding it was probably a bit of both.

Then Benz spoke. "What now?" he asked. He didn't mention the SS unit. What was there to say? He couldn't think of the right words.

Stark stood up and looked through the trees. He felt for his loaf of bread in one of his pockets. "Craziest bastards I ever met! They'll be dead in a week or so. Did you see, what was his name, Schultz? Jesus Christ!"

"What about the kid, standing to attention? Not to mention the fact that Adler nearly shot that Corporal!" said Benz, shaking his head.

"Let's go," said Morgenstern, standing up. He looked up at the sky. Forever grey. "I'm guessing it's near enough to noon. We should at least get cover somewhere. Think about our next move."

He didn't mention the fact that their chances were even slimmer than Adler's. Their whole situation was impossible really, he thought again, trudging through the trees. Stark and Benz followed him. We're in the middle of fucking nowhere! Morgenstern thought. We could just as easily run into a Red Division as a Panzer Regiment of our own lot! And then get a ride all the way home! He laughed out loud.

"What's so funny?" Benz asked him.

"Oh I dunno. The fact that we're still alive? With food in our belly and headed in the right direction, or so our friend Adler says. Shit, if that isn't funny, I don't know what is!"

*

The River

Morgenstern could hear the river Adler had told them to listen for. The three men had been walking for more than three hours. The light was fading and it was becoming important to find some shelter before they stopped for the night.

"Well, he was right about the river," said Stark. "It's got to be over that rise."

"What about the peasant's hut?" asked Benz, grabbing a tree branch to help him up the incline.

"Hope he was right about that too."

Adler had said that once they heard the river, to follow it west and eventually they would come across a peasant's hut used in the past by locals for fishing. "Bastards would sit there all day long," Adler had mentioned. He never called them Russians, Reds or anything else. "And for fucking what?!" he'd added, laughing. "A fucking fish about the size of a sodding sardine!"

"If he led us to the river, why wouldn't the hut be where he said it was?" said Morgenstern. "But that's for tomorrow."

"Why not keep going?" asked Benz. "How far did he say it was?"

"He didn't," said Morgenstern. "Besides, I've seen these huts before. They're only the size of a field shit house. What are we supposed to do? Take fucking turns in it? Anyway, I'm spent. Let's call it a day."

But where? he thought. He crested the rise. Stark and Benz appeared beside him. There was the river below them. It was perhaps thirty or forty metres wide and fast flowing. They could see chunks of ice moving with the flow, swept down the river from it's source miles upstream. Across the far side and it's bank, there was open scrub and seemingly endless steppe with mountains in the distance. It looked harsh and heavy going and it was.

Benz was disappointed. He wanted the hut to magically appear down there on the river bank. Adler had said that when he and his unit had come across it, it was full of frozen fish, all filleted and piled a metre high on one side. If the three men could rest there for a few days, they would be on their way back to feeling healthy and well.

Morgenstern looked around them in frustration. There wasn't even a tree to shelter under. They'd left the wood behind and now were out in the open without any shelter. If there was a snowstorm or blizzard, they would all die in less than an hour.

"That will have to do us," he said, pointing to a spot. Down by the bank was a few square metres of ground covered with pebbles. It looked like a giant had bitten a chunk of the river bank away. A ridge above it would protect them from behind but they'd be exposed to the river's far bank, but it'll have to do, the Veteran decided.

Morgenstern was exhausted. He thought briefly about lighting a fire, fingering his box of matches. It was too risky out here in the open. Besides, there was little or no wood nearby and even if there was, everything was wet and damp from the snow. He dropped to the ground and tried to make himself comfortable. It wasn't easy, lying on the pebbles. Stark and Benz joined him, Stark leaning up against the earth bank behind them.

Will we ever feel the warmth of a fire again? thought Morgenstern, taking out his matches to light a cigarette. The luxury of it swamped him. He counted them again. Ten! He thought back to his late teenage years, when he and Elke would get together with some friends on some waste ground during the summer nights in Berlin. They would light a small campfire and share a bottle of cheap booze one of them had pinched from a store earlier.

He could see beautiful Elke, seventeen back then, take a half litre bottle of the new liqueur, Jagermeister, and swallow a mouthful. She would cough and gasp, holding her throat in alarm. Everyone would laugh as she complained it tasted like bad vinegar and that her insides were on fire. Then he and his friends would smoke and talk about this new chap called Hitler and his cronies. No one at the time could imagine what lay ahead for them in such a short time.

"This is fine," said Stark, interrupting Morgenstern's memories. He began nibbling his loaf of bread. "We're in good shape. Yes sir, we're not doing too badly at all."

"Yeah," said Benz. "We're alright."

"Still think we haven't been lucky?" Stark asked no one in particular.

Morgenstern stayed silent. He was lost in the reverie of his Juno. His head spun lightly with the nicotine he wasn't used to these last few months.

Benz broke off a piece of his bread and let it melt on his tongue. He hadn't felt so good in a long time. After a while, he said, "How far do you think it is Karl? I mean, really?"

Morgenstern leant up on an elbow. "Adler said they're in that direction," he said, pointing across the river to the far bank. "Reckons may ten kilometres? And that's if they're still there. What did he say, three weeks ago? But fuck it, ten, twenty or a hundred and twenty, what difference does it make? It'll take us forever, if we're not caught by the Reds first. Don't get your hopes up. And," he added, "don't forget, we still have to cross the sodding river! I don't want to wade across, what can it be? Fifty metres? And freeze to death before I get there!"

"Would it be that bad?" asked Stark.

"What are you? Blind?" said Morgenstern. "See the fucking ice? Only reason it's not completely frozen, is because it's fast flowing. We need a boat or some other way across."

Adler had said there should be a German Infantry Battalion camped in a village called Marinovka, or what was left of it. Morgenstern pondered the reality of it. What was an Infantry Battalion doing so close to Stalingrad in the first place? Depends what direction they're heading in, he decided. They must be heading west. Clearing out like the rest of us. But why are they only, what? Forty kilometres away? What are they waiting for in Marinovka? He tried to think. Even if they left the same time as we did, they should be well out of it by now. And would a whole Battalion just scarper like that anyway?

Perhaps they were involved in some sort of plan; Maybe even part of Manstein's great relief of Stalingrad and what was left of the 6th Army. They had holed up in Marinovka and were waiting for others to catch up with them? Everyone knew Manstein's plan had gone awry and that he wasn't coming after all. This Battalion was probably stuck in this village then, deciding what to do next. Morgenstern gave up thinking about it. Could be a thousand reasons they stopped in Marinovka. The most likely being the Reds had them surrounded and pinned down. Whatever the reason, he didn't expect to find them there, alive or dead.

But he wasn't going to fret about that now. He closed his eyes and finished smoking, seeing Elke again with her long black hair and-. He was asleep in seconds. Stark and Benz soon joined him, lying either side of him as had become their habit, so all three could benefit from each other's warmth.

*

Among 'Friends' - But With Consequences

Around 5am, as dawn was struggling to appear, Benz woke to sounds of activity on the far bank. Shit! he said to himself, getting into a crouch. He shook Morgenstern and Stark awake and once everyone had gathered themselves, he held a finger to his mouth. "Shush!" he whispered, pointing.

Stark started trembling involuntarily again, the blood draining from his face. Morgenstern rubbed his eyes and tried to look across the river to see what had alerted Benz. There was hardly any light yet but he heard scratching and could just make out some dark shapes against the dim, grey background.

"Wolves?" he said quietly. "Or boars maybe? Anyway, whatever they are, they're not going to brave the water, even if they're aware of us."

Morgenstern lay back down and pulled out his cigarettes. Lighting one, he stared up at the ever grey morning sky and picked up his thoughts of Elke where he'd left them the night before. For the first time in almost a year, he contemplated the possibility of surviving this nightmare and finally getting home to see her and little Marta again. Tears welled in his eyes at the thought of them and he wiped them away and sniffed heavily. He drew on his Juno and swore to his non-existent God that if he ever saw them again, even for just one day, that he would settle for that and never complain about anything else in his life again.

If, and it was a big if, they found their own side again, they'd most likely be sent west somewhere to a larger Divisional stronghold, and be allowed to recuperate and receive medical attention. Then the three of them would be interrogated for a couple of days, alone or together, probably both, before being granted some duration of leave. Perhaps a whole week or even two! Afterwards they would almost certainly be sent back to the cauldron that was the Eastern Front, assuming they got any leave at all. Of course, there was always the slim possibility of being posted to Western Europe again; Italy perhaps? Or even France once more!

That was when he decided it was all too fanciful and he gave up such foolish thoughts. But the thought struck him suddenly that wherever he and the others ended up, they would not be going back to Stalingrad and that gave him some comfort at least. He also decided that he could die happy if he could just have that day with his family first.

Once he finished smoking, he opened his eyes to see Stark and Benz looking down at him. They seemed to be waiting for him. "Help an old man," Morgenstern said, grinning and holding up a hand.

"Should we make for this town?" Benz asked, pulling him up, "or try for this fishing hut?"

"I say let's keep going," said Stark. "Our bellies are full and we don't even know if this sodding hut is still going to be there. Imagine looking for it all day to find it empty! No fish, no sod all!"

"Wilhelm, you took the words right out of my mouth," said Morgenstern. He looked at Benz who was obviously disappointed. "Theo, he's right. It's better we keep going," he added, pointing. "Think of the grub we'll have once we get back. That and clean sheets somewhere with Spanish nurses to wait on us!"

"The nurses don't have to be Spanish!" said Stark, chuckling.

"There you go," said Morgenstern, grinning.

Benz couldn't help grinning either. The prospect of a proper bed with clean white sheets was enough on it's own. But the thought of adding a pretty nurse and maybe a bottle of Schnapps to that dream was, well, enough to lift his spirits and he relented gracefully.

"Okay," he said, still grinning. Looking at Morgenstern, he asked, "How do we get across?"

"Fuck knows," he said, biting his lower lip. "If we had a boat..." He found himself clutching his cigarettes in his coat pocket. "Help out! Use your brains! Don't wait for me to know!"

The three men stood on the riverbank and stared across it. Whatever animals had been there were now gone. They could see where they had disturbed the ground looking for God knows what. It was brighter now, after sunrise, but they were each bent over with the cold. Looking down at the moving water full of chunks of ice made them feel even colder.

"Let's go back up," said Morgenstern, jerking a thumb over his shoulder. "Head that way," he added, vaguely pointing west. "Who knows? Maybe we'll find a boat or even a bridge. But at least we'll be heading in the right direction."

They walked for a couple of hours without seeing anybody or anything. Now they were back in woods and Morgenstern took on the responsibility for keeping his eyes open for danger; either from the Russian Army or local civilians. He knew Stark and Benz would only be thinking of boats and bridges. He didn't blame them. They weren't front-line men after all.

"First thing I'm going to do if we get back is cook the biggest fucking duck I can find," said Stark, as they tramped along up to their knees in snow. All the world's snow seemed to be in Russia, he thought briefly.

"Or a pheasant!" said Benz.

"What about venison? Or a nice beef joint?" said Morgenstern, joining in. "Or hell, why not a giant bowl of spaghetti Bolognese? With a couple of bottles of Chianti to wash it down with?" His stomach rumbled in protest.

"For fuck sake," said Benz. "Right now I'd settle for anything you put in front of me as long as it was hot!"

"Look," said Stark, knowingly. "Beef and pheasant are all very well, but duck it has to be! I cooked in a depot back home before this shit. We had a load of bastard Generals in for dinner once. We cooked them Breast of Duck with Savoy cabbage! Fucking beautiful! Best meal I ever had!"

"Oh yeah," said Morgenstern, salivating.

"Actually, can we stop talking about fucking food!" said Benz. "My stomach is in mourning!" he added, clutching the last of his bread they'd got from Adler's SS Platoon.

They all laughed, despite the miserable conditions they endured. Then suddenly, they heard voices. The three of them ducked to their knees instinctively. Morgenstern strained to hear. What was that? A woman speaking? Now a man. Then a third voice, higher, less harsh. A child?

"Locals," he whispered, pointing to where they should go and look. "Not one sound!" he added, getting up and making for some bushes that were scattered among the trees. Sure enough, when they were together again and skulking behind some briar, they could hear what sounded like a family chattering among themselves. Morgenstern raised himself up slowly. A man, a woman and a girl of maybe twelve or thirteen. Beyond them, an older woman sitting on a neatly cut tree stump, holding a baby.

Morgenstern crouched back down. "Peasant family by the look of it. Cutting wood?" he whispered. "We'll go back the way we came."

"Can't we go around them?" asked Benz.

"Too risky. One of us will step on a branch and they'll hear us."

"But Karl,-." whispered Benz, starting to protest.

"The man has a fucking axe in his hands that's bigger than his daughter! They'll have hatchets and knives too. We're in no shape to take them on if they start something!"

"But fuck it-." Benz began.

"I saw a peasant woman once," said Morgenstern. "An old dear, like that one holding the baby, take on a Grenadier twice her size. She gutted him with a hand scythe. These people know how to fight!"

"Come on Theo," said Stark, following Morgenstern, who had already backtracked slowly and quietly.

Benz sighed heavily. Something has got to happen today. A boat. A bridge, some fucking thing. He got up and followed his two companions. His luck held. By dusk, they had found the remains of a footbridge by continuing down the river bank in the opposite direction. It wasn't lost on any of them that if they had gone that way in the first place, they'd be across the river and God knows where by now. With the Infantry Battalion? Enjoying a bowl of stew in front of a fire? But such was life. They'd wasted another day. So what.

The bridge, such as it was, was a flimsy structure that like most things in Russia now, had seen better days. It looked like someone had tried to drive over it once. What appeared to be the rusted remains of a truck's rear axle was sticking out of the river about half way across. The rest of the truck had probably long since washed away downstream. But after careful consideration and much discussion, while looking across it, it seemed the bridge's foot way was intact, albeit under water except for a small section either side that led to the riverbanks. Crucially however, was a rope fastened to a post on either side that served as a handrail, at least on one side. The rope on the other side had long gone too.

"I'll go first then," said Morgenstern. "Should be easy enough. Remember, don't let go of the rope or you're dead! We'll light a fire later somewhere to warm up and dry off, okay?"

Stark and Benz nodded without saying anything. They had all been overjoyed at finding the remains of the bridge. The rope handrail was the best part of it. Without it, the foot way was useless on it's own. The river would simply wash you away. But the joy soon turned to dread, when they realised how cold and wet they'd be once they'd got across to the other side.

The light was fading fast. Morgenstern grabbed the rope and started to wade across. The shock of the cold water took his breath away. As soon as he stepped onto the wooden foot way under the water, it gave way under him and he struggled to maintain his balance. He held on, though it was like standing in the middle of a see-saw. The flow of the river was also stronger than it looked from the bank and he was hit repeatedly by chunks of ice that felt like rocks and threatened to sweep him away. Half way over, he suddenly remembered his last few remaining cigarettes, now soaking wet in the bottom half of his greatcoat. "Shit!" he said aloud. Then he was across and pulling himself up the bank. Breathless and shivering badly, he staggered a few more steps and collapsed on the ground. His hands were bright red from the cold and very painful.

Morgenstern whistled for the next man to come across, as he placed both hands under his arms in an effort to warm them up. It didn't help really. He watched helplessly as Stark made his way over. He slipped once or twice and struggled to hang on to the rope, but eventually, he made it to the other side.

"Oh my sweet Jesus!" he said, collapsing near Morgenstern. "My fucking hands!" He was shaking severely too, so much, that he strained a muscle under his ribs. He winced in pain as he sank to the ground.

Morgenstern ignored him and took a couple of steps towards the river. "Come on Theo!" he called, his teeth chattering madly.

Benz started out. He'd watched the other two make their way over. It seemed easy enough. Foolproof even. Just before he got half way across though, he slipped badly. Somehow however, in his panic, he'd managed to keep hold of the rope with both hands and pulled himself upright. It had saved his life, though he was now facing the wrong way, toward the bank from where he'd come from. The river had tried to wash him away but only succeeded in turning him around. Benz cried out in pain as he turned himself around to face Morgenstern, who now stood in the water up to his shins on the far bank, urging him on. Would you have tried to rescue Benz if he'd lost his grip? he asked himself. No, you wouldn't, he knew, because then you'd have both died. He held out both his hands. Benz grabbed them and he pulled him across the last metre or so.

The two men sank to the ground beside Stark. Morgenstern wondered briefly if it had been worth it. Yes, they'd crossed the river, but they'd paid a high price for it. Remembering his cigarettes again, he reached into a pocket and pulled them out. Soaking wet and mostly covered in ice already. The matches too. He shoved the lot back into a pocket. His hands were on fire! My God, he gasped, closing his eyes. When all three of them had recovered somewhat, they staggered up the bank, cresting the rise on that side, before being forced to run down the steep decline and back on to flat ground once more. They dropped to the ground again, breathing hard and in pain. Benz almost passed out.

Several minutes later, Morgenstern opened his eyes and fought with himself to get up. We're dead otherwise, he knew. Hypothermia would kill them all.

"Come on!" he shouted, struggling to stand. "Up with you now! You'll die here otherwise!"

Stark and Benz helped each other up. It was almost comical. They were like a couple of drunks trying to stand on an ice rink. Benz sank to the ground again though, once Stark let go of him and he and Morgenstern had to help him to his feet once more.

Then a shot suddenly rang out and all three of them dropped to the ground this time. Stark yelped and Benz passed out. "Shut the fuck up!" Morgenstern hissed at Stark. Reds!? he thought, shaking uncontrollably with the cold. He rolled over and looked around him, peering into the darkness. He could see nothing though except for the outline of some trees near them. Then somebody, no! A group! Six men? It was hard to tell. Coming through the trees towards them and Morgenstern couldn't believe his eyes! The uniforms! The colour! Salvation!

*

Nacht Jagers

Standing over Morgenstern, Stark and Benz in a rough semi-circle was a German Infantry patrol of seven 'Nacht Jagers' or Night Hunters. Benz had come to again to the sound of harsh, loud voices that told them to stand up and raise their arms. The atmosphere was electric and filled to the brim with tension. Stark started to speak, slowly and quietly, trying to tell the patrol who they were. Immediately, he received a rifle butt to the stomach, which left him gasping in pain and back down on the ground. Morgenstern, who knew better than to open his mouth, bent down help Stark, but flinched back upright when another member of the patrol spat the word 'Nicht!' at him. Don't!

An NCO type approached Morgenstern, though he wore no rank badges. He looked him up and down and grunted. "Take these two," he said to the Nacht Jager closest to him, referring to Stark and Benz. "I'll walk with this one," he added, turning back to Morgenstern.

The NCO let the patrol lead them out, slowly following with Morgenstern beside him. "You can drop your arms," he said after a couple of minutes. Up ahead the two Veterans heard the sounds of Stark and Benz stumbling in the dark and being punched and slapped by the patrol as they all made their way through dense vegetation and eventually onto a sort of dirt track that was really just a gap in some tall grass where others had come or gone before.

"Name's Dekker. Yours?" said the NCO then.

"Morgenstern. From the Cauldron."

"You came out of Stalingrad!? With these two clowns?"

"Yeah," said Morgenstern. He sighed heavily. "Had no choice really. But they're good sorts. There were seven of us when we left."

"Fucking hell! One man alone? Maybe. But seven!?" Dekker shook his head. "And you made it this far? Unbelievable. Course they won't believe you. You'll be shot most likely as deserters." He couldn't believe Morgenstern's claim. If it was true, it was a story worth hearing.

"Look, you're best chance is to come up with another story," said Dekker later, looking down at the ground as they walked. "I dunno. You got lost or-."

"If they know anything about Stalingrad, they'll believe us. Intelligence has to know what happened. Think we're the first to get out? There must be hundreds, thousands even."

"Of course, but I heard about a couple of fly-boys who were shot down while dropping supplies at Gumrak airfield. They made it out to some place near Kiev believe it or not. 'Stapo had some Chain Dogs shoot 'em for cowardice and desertion! So don't get your hopes up," said Dekker, chuckling.

Morgenstern looked sideways at him. Could that be true? "Must be more to that," he said.

"Mate, we got a full house at our place. Chain-Dogs, some SS, and a couple of 'Stapo bastards! All I'm saying is, be prepared for the worse."

Morgenstern's heart sank. Gestapo? Here? "What the fuck are Himmler's boys doing this far east?"

"Interrogatin' prisoners I 'spose," said Dekker, spitting to his right. "Must have some good reason. Course, no one tells us shit!"

Morgenstern bit his lip. Military Police? SS? And even the Gestapo! All attached to a regular Infantry Battalion? It could only mean one thing.

"It's got to be about Stalingrad. That damned place!" he said, looking at Dekker. "Has to be! What the fuck else are they all doing out here?! Damage limitation!"

"Salvage more like," said Dekker.

"One and the same really," said Morgenstern. "For the benefit of the poor sods back home. Victory from defeat?"

"Word'll get out," said Dekker. "Always does. Some loudmouth somewhere in a bar is all it takes."

"Not this time," said Morgenstern. "At least, not in the same way. It's too much of a fuck up!"

They walked, stumbled and at times, crawled on their hands and knees. But Dekker said they were about half-way home and that they would stop soon.

"Got a smoke, mate?" Morgenstern asked him. He was thinking of Stark and Benz who would be terrified if they knew what was waiting for them.

"When we stop," said Dekker, looking straight ahead. "Soon," he added.

*

The group of ten men were resting in a ditch that was perhaps a metre below the dirt track it ran beside. They formed a neat queue as if waiting for a shop to open. Stark and Benz with three of the patrol in front and behind them; Morgenstern and Dekker a couple of metres to their rear.

"Here," said Dekker, taking a Juno out of a pack and passing to Morgenstern. He lit it first before his own.

"Thanks," said Morgenstern.

They smoked in silence. Eyes peeled against any danger that might be around them. Morgenstern wallowed in his cigarette. It was almost joyous.

"Any Reds around?" he asked Dekker eventually.

"A sniper here, a sniper there," said the other man, clutching the drum of his captured Russian sub-machine gun. "Sometimes we'll come across a patrol. They know we're in this area. Probably know all there is about our little lot, right down to the colour of the eagle on our bog roll! But they're leaving us be for now. You know how it is."

"Yeah," said Morgenstern. "Especially after Stalingrad. They've got a fire under them now. They can play the waiting game. Wish some of our lot had had their patience. Bit late now."

"Or their fucking resources!" said Dekker. "Ever see the dumb bastards charging a heavy emplacement?"

"Well of course," said Morgenstern.

"I was in Kiev, mate. It was in the early days. Good group of lads under me back then. Most of 'em gone now," said Dekker, flicking some ash away. He was silent for a few minutes. "Anyway," he said, beginning again. "We were in the city centre. Holed up nicely at the top of this wide thoroughfare. Can't remember it's fucking name! Big statue of Lenin outside a-."

"I know it," said Morgenstern, biting his lip. Careful, he told himself.

"Really? When were you there then?" asked Dekker, studying him.

"After your lot I suppose. Just drove through on our way to Moscow, before we got diverted here."

"Okay," said Dekker, trying to work out dates and times. Something bothered him, but he let it go. "So, eventually the Reds put together a half-arsed counter attack. Mate, we had two 88's, mortars, the fucking lot. There were 300 of us at the top of that sodding road. "And," said Dekker, sounding excited, "best of all, we had close to three dozen Bone-Saws!" he finished with, referring to the MG34, a deadly, lethal machine-gun in professional hands.

"It started with a couple of fucking Shermans rolling towards us like their drivers were pissed out of their minds, which they probably were!" Dekker chuckled. "Swerving all over the fucking place they were. Like they were on a glacier or something. Anyway, they didn't make a hundred metres. Our 88's saw to that! Then it goes quiet, see? Like the Reds were thinking about what they were gonna do next. Fucking hopeless lot! Then after an hour or so, a fucking hour, mind you, the far end of the road starts heaving with these farm boys charging towards us with their rifles and bayonets!" Dekker chuckled again.

Morgenstern looked at him, listening impassively. He'd seen it all before in different places and heard many similar stories. Some involving NKVD platoons who would cut down their own side for retreating in panic and terror under similar German onslaughts. He didn't like the way though Dekker seemed to revel in the carnage. By now, someone like him shouldn't feel that way any more.

"Well, you can guess," the Nacht Jager NCO went on. "We cut 'em down like a field of wheat at harvest time! Must have been three or four thousand by the end. Can't think of how many 'Saw barrels we got through. Took us days to clear that sodding road."

Dekker looked sideways at Morgenstern. He'd expected more of a reaction from him than a simple shrug. He made up his mind about these three stragglers. Especially this one. He got to his feet. One of his Corporals stood with him, turning to look at him.

"Right," he said. "Move out!"

A couple of hours later, they were approaching Marinovka. It was almost dawn; perhaps around 5am. Out of the darkness came a low, guttural warning. "Halt!" Everyone did so. Morgenstern, Stark and Benz looked around them in alarm. Dark shapes were everywhere. The Nacht Jagers didn't seem concerned though. Nobody moved a muscle.

"Alright," said the NCO. "It's Dekker. We just got back. Got three stragglers with us."

A Sergeant in charge of the sentries stepped out of the darkness. "Right," he said, after looking everyone over. "Bring 'em in then."

An hour later, Morgenstern and his two companions were huddled over mess-tins of Erzatz coffee, which were luxurious in themselves, not least for the warmth they provided. They were in what appeared to be someone's living-room but was in fact a small hotel or guest house, the original occupants long gone. Two guards sat across the room, weapons to hand. They were playing cards.

The three 'stragglers' sat on broken wooden chairs or boxes. Morgenstern had been holding his mess-tin in cupped hands for maybe fifteen minutes now. He couldn't feel any warmth in his hands though. Perhaps those particular nerves have long died, he thought, frowning.

"What'll happen now Karl?" asked Stark then. He was sipping his scalding coffee, which was the only way it ever came. Benz was still huddled over his mess tin, half dazed.

"They'll grill us for sure," said Morgenstern. "Got a smoke?" he asked their guards. The two young men across the room playing cards ignored him. Turning back to Stark, he said, "They'll want to know what we know about the Reds first. Especially where we've seen them on our travels. Numbers and so on. Then I'm guessing they'll pass us on to the Dogs. They'll quiz us on how we got out. More importantly, from their point of view, *why* we got out. In the end, it's their decision to call us deserters or not. After all that, maybe the 'Stapo will want a word. If we get that far, they're the bastards I'd be most afraid of!"

"Should we come up with a story? So that it rings true, coming from each of us in turn?" asked Stark, obviously anxious, especially at the thought of being 'interviewed' by the most ruthless of Secret State Police, the Geheime Staats Polizei, or Gestapo for short.

"Another time I might have said yes," said Morgenstern. "But fuck it, Wilhelm, the more I think about it, the better I think that we should just tell the truth. What happened to us before we met up. What forced us to leave what we were doing and so on. If we start lying, they'll trip us up and then we're dead. Besides," said Morgenstern, leaning forward and whispering now, "I hate to say it, but I don't think we can rely on Benz right now. Look at him, he's somewhere else, far away."

Stark glanced at the Medic. He did seem lost in a world of his own. "Well we'll be alright," he said after a long silence, trying to convince himself. "We've done nothing wrong except survive."

"That in itself could be a crime these days," said Morgenstern. "Look," he went on, shuffling forward and bending towards Stark. "We're...an inconvenience, at best. Think about it."

"What the hell does that mean, for Christ's sake!" said Stark, frowning heavily.

"How many of us do you think there are? Scattered all over this region? It'll be in the thousands for sure. Not huge numbers, maybe five or so. That's five thousand men with stories to tell, everywhere they show up. Stories of betrayal, incompetence and so on. Enough to give those arseholes back in Berlin a headache, as to what to do with us. So what'll they do? Shoot us for desertion? Like the old days? They'd never get away with it; the numbers are too big. What then? Torgau maybe? I doubt it. The way this war is going already, my best guess is they'll probably fix us up, maybe send us back home for a bit and then we'll find ourselves right back here where we started."

"Back?!" said Stark, appalled. "Here? Oh no, no, no. That can't happen Karl!"

"Well, there's a slim chance we could end up somewhere else. Depends I suppose what's happening in other places. But my guess is Wilhelm, it'll be straight back here," said Morgenstern, draining the last of his coffee. He wished there was more.

"But Jesus Christ-." Stark began.

"Just calm down," said Morgenstern gently. "There's nothing we can do about it. If our luck holds, we'll be on our way home, at least for a bit."

Stark was suddenly horrified. He stayed silent, sipping his coffee. If they got home, and deep down, he knew it was a big if, and if they sent him back to Russia, he'd desert, he decided quickly. Try and get to Sweden like a friend of his did back in 1940. That friend, another Cook he worked with, could see the writing on the wall early and had tried to persuade Stark to come with him.

"Bring Greta," Stark's friend had said one night in a Hamburg bar. "I know someone right here who can get us aboard the ferry. We'd be part of the crew! It's a piece of piss!"

Stark had thought his friend, Hans, a younger man, mad in those days. He was a Communist, but he didn't shout about it. If it was well known, he could end up in a concentration camp somewhere. He'd decided that Germany was not for him and might have gone to Russia but Sweden was a much safer bet and easier to get to. Anyway, he thought, Hans was probably a Chef now in some fancy Stockholm hotel, having side stepped this mess. Or he was dead, having been caught and shot as a deserter. Stark sighed and closed his eyes, trying to bring himself back to this new reality.

"I won't make it Karl," he said now. "Not if that's how we end up; back here!"

"Course you will," said Morgenstern, trying to offer him some encouragement. "You'll end up cooking in some depot somewhere just over the Polish border. You'll get home to Greta every six months and see out your time. You'll weigh three times what you are now by then!"

Morgenstern forced a chuckle. He couldn't bring himself to mention the most likely outcome. That they would be shot as deserters. It was as clear as day to him.

"Well, that would be something," said Stark with little enthusiasm. He didn't really believe it. He closed his eyes and thought of Greta and Sweden.

Then Benz suddenly came to life. Sipping his coffee, he said, "We're dead men Wilhelm. They'll shoot us for sure!"

*

Ordeal by Fire and Water

Sure enough, the next day it began. The three men were taken, after a meagre breakfast, to a large shed that served as a general storeroom. A short, fat Quartermaster Sergeant with a monocle, smoking a short fat cigar, looked them up and down and began throwing bits of uniform at them with the practised skill of a professional tailor or outfitter.

"Take those rags off!" said the Quartermaster. "Have yourselves a wash! Jan will take you," he went on, referring to one of their guards. "You fucking stink!"

Outside at the rear of the shed, they were forced to strip naked and told to burn their old uniforms in a huge open pit fire near a transport shed. Morgenstern handed his only possession, Marta's little toy drum, to Jan. "Look after this for me," he said. "I'll get it off you later. If you lose it, I'll kill you." Jan blanched and swallowed at the threat. He took the toy though, carefully putting it in a tunic pocket.

Mechanics watched impassively as the three newcomers tossed their old clothes into the fire that was being used to heat bars of steel for the blacksmiths to work into spare parts for their tanks and trucks and so on. Morgenstern, Stark and Benz shivered uncontrollably. Nobody present was laughing at their predicament. Worse was yet to come after all.

Next, they were taken to a shower block near the field latrines. A Medic sat nearby on a crate of grenades, smoking. Seeing the group approach, he flicked his cigarette away and stood up, sighing heavily. "Drop your uniforms there," he said, pointing to a traffic barrier that served as a bench.

Then the Medic produced a 5kg tin. He dug a hand into it. "Quickly now!" he shouted, lighting another cigarette. "I'm freezing my nuts off too! Into the showers with you!"

The shock of the cold water, coming from twenty gallon drums slung above the roped off cubicles, felt lethal. Stark couldn't help shrieking in agony. Benz yelped like an injured puppy over and over again. Morgenstern, more conscious of their audience, gritted his teeth, but couldn't help crying out several times. The drums above their heads were old catering drums of vegetable oil, with around twenty holes drilled into their base. A stopper in their centre served as a plug. The idea was, you stood under the drum, which was insulated to stop the water freezing, together with the dregs of the vegetable oil that served as a sort of antifreeze, pulled out the stopper and washed under the holes which acted like a giant shower head. There was enough water for maybe three or four minutes. Afterwards, though cleaner, your skin felt greasy from the vegetable oil, but it wasn't a bad idea for a makeshift shower. It was wonderful in the deserts of North Africa. The Afrika Korps swore testimony to that.

But here in this frozen wasteland of a country, it was absolutely torturous. In fact, the SS were known to use these showers when interrogating prisoners, though for a lot longer than four minutes. The Medic was present lest one of the three men collapse and die of shock from the cold.

Once moderately clean, Stark and Benz left their cubicles trembling violently. Morgenstern quickly followed. "Here!" said the Medic, tossing them some sheet towels. Once they were dry, he walked around them in a circle, covering them with handfuls of delousing powder from his tin. "Grab your clothes; then back to the fire with you," he said. He waited while he watched them go. They were like wild animals that had just been pulled from a hole in a frozen lake. They jerked involuntarily or trembled and shook violently.

The fire pit by the transport shed was of little help. One of the younger guards sniggered. A grizzled old mechanic shot him a look. Taking a pipe out of his mouth, he spat in the guard's direction. "Think it's funny boy!?" he said. The guard, who was still a teenager, glowered at the older man.

Eventually, Morgenstern, Stark and Benz were dressed. They were still freezing cold, but the new uniforms felt good. All three were wearing the basic field-grey of an infantry private. Suits me fine, Morgenstern said to himself as buttoned up his new greatcoat. The less attention the better. It was too big for him, like everything else he wore. Stark and Benz were the same. Maybe we'll live long enough to fill them out, he thought.

Their ordeal over for now, their two guards walked them back to where they'd come from; the dilapidated guest house. On their way, a Hauptmann suddenly appeared, walking up a small rise in the road towards them. Looking them over as he approached, he seemed to take pity on them. He waved a ream of papers towards the two guards.

"Take them to the barber first, then the field kitchen. Tell Gerd I sent them. He's to give them a proper fucking feed, with bread and coffee. A *proper feed,* got it? When they're done, and let them take their time, bring them back to me there," he finished with, jabbing a thumb over his shoulder towards the guest house.

"Jawohl! Herr Hauptmann," said Jan, the guard, clicking his heels. "Right," he said, addressing his three charges. "This way." The group marched away in the direction of the canteen and field kitchens.

The Hauptmann watched them go. What have they not been through? he wondered in awe. But more importantly, what can they tell me?

*

The Beginning of the End

Morgenstern sat outside the main field kitchen. He'd eaten his fill and was smoking a cigarette from a drum of 120 in a box on his lap that a young lad from the stores had left with them earlier.

That had been the Hauptmann's doing as well.

The three men, feeling almost human again and much better psychologically, especially Morgenstern, had been brought to the mess hall where they'd been told to wait at one of the tables. They'd had a haircut and a shave and were all looking like German soldiers again. One of their guards, who kept a respectful distance, stayed with them while Jan went through the back into the kitchen. Chaotic voices could be heard as he went through the double doors. The sounds and smells of the kitchen made Morgenstern think of a restaurant in Paris not so long ago. That seemed like a world away now, but maybe not as distant as it was.

While they had waited in anticipation for their expected food, a young Gefreiter walked in and approached their table. He looked terribly young and taking a cigarette out of his mouth, he announced, "With the compliments of Oberwachtmeister Vogel," before leaving a box in front of them.

Stark opened it excitedly as the stores man left. "Jesus, what now?" he said.

Morgenstern watched him opening the box. Even Benz seemed interested, now much improved in his general mood. They were like kids on Christmas morning.

"Ah shit!" said Stark, pushing the box away.

"For fuck sake!" said Benz, equally disappointed.

Morgenstern pulled the box towards him. His eyes widened as he saw the contents. Six drums of military issue Juno cigarettes, 120 in each drum! He beamed. "Well, you're loss is my gain!" he said in delight.

"If you have the time left to smoke them," said Benz, a little cruelly.

"Good for you Karl," said Stark, frowning at Benz. "Are we home and dry then?"

"Don't count on it," said Morgenstern. "But shit, things are definitely looking up. The way they're treating us? All depends on how much influence the Colonel in charge here has on the cops and spooks," he said, referring to the Military Police and the Gestapo personnel stationed here with the

Infantry Battalion.

Now sitting on a wooden cask at the rear of the field kitchen, Morgenstern pondered their situation while at the same time trying to come to terms with how improved it was compared to a day or two ago. It was a lot to take in so quickly. But he was dealing with it; At least better than Stark and Benz. They'll come round, he thought. Especially Stark. Benz had been close to collapse, both physically and mentally. Where his body was starting to heal, his mind lagged behind. But overall, they were all going through a head-spinning experience. It'll settle down, he told himself.

The swing-doors to the kitchen opened and a Cook came out with a massive pot of vegetable peelings that he tossed into a corner of the yard with others from days gone by. Immediately, some dogs that had been resting there, came over and sniffed the pile, before voraciously attacking it and each other for the privilege. Morgenstern suddenly wept at the sight. He flicked his cigarette away and buried his face in his hands. After a while, he looked up, still sobbing. A week ago, the three of them would have rejoiced at finding that pile of peelings. Had they been no better than dogs then? Reduced to scavenging left overs in order to survive?

Yet here they were, in a garrisoned town where everything seemed normal; At least, how it was. How it should be. And how it had been in the thousand towns he'd passed through since 1939. But we're still in fucking Russia, he told himself. And every day we're here, the odds of us surviving this damned place get slimmer and slimmer. Surrounded by an enemy of overwhelming numbers that, as they had proved at Stalingrad, mean to wipe us from the face of the earth. And they will, he knew. Or they'll come close to it. There's no one to tell them any different. No one who'll mourn us. They'll wipe us out for sure. Next week. Next month. Next year. Sometime. He dismissed the thought. No point going down that hill, he thought. All you can do is concentrate on now and how to come out of it.

He lit another Juno. He had pains in his stomach from the food he'd just eaten. He wasn't used to it. Stark and Benz were still inside the mess hall, as if leaving it meant they would never eat again.

They'll pay for it later, he chuckled. A dose of the shits for sure! he reckoned. He laughed out loud. There had been proper brown bread, with actual margarine! Even honey to spread over that! Cheese, salami and fried eggs for Christ's sake! And real coffee, with milk! Well, it was a feast. Out of all proportion to their expectations.

He belched again and rubbed his stomach. Then Stark and Benz came out with their two guards, who were now treating them all differently, even allowing Morgenstern to wander off earlier for a smoke. He put that down to the Hauptmann. As they made their way back to the guest house, he asked the guard, Jan, about him.

"He's not the worst," came the reply. "Decent enough really. Not like some of the other bastard officers!"

"What is he? Intelligence?" asked Morgenstern.

"Well, that's where he finds himself these days. Used to be in the Judiciary back home in some officer school. Before this mess. Staff Officer now, isn't he? Close to the Colonel too, by all accounts."

The Hauptmann in question was waiting for them when they got back. He smoked as he watched them approaching from the front porch. He watched Morgenstern in particular.

"Feeling better lads?" he asked with a smile. "You look like new men!"

"Much better Herr Hauptmann," said Morgenstern, smiling back.

"Please, sir will do you," said the Hauptmann, wanting the two guards to hear him. Word would then get around that these men were his charges and were to be left alone. "You can go," he told the guards, who promptly left, looking relieved. "Let's sit inside," he said to Morgenstern. They all followed him in. "Sit," he added, waving a hand towards the two armchairs. Sitting on a box himself, he said to Stark, who'd missed out on a chair, "look, over there," as he pointed to a stool that may at one time, have accompanied a piano now long gone.

"First things first," the Hauptmann began, when everyone was settled. He handed out some paper and pencils. "Write your full name and number as it would appear in your Soldier Book. Then your rank and who you belonged to, sorry lads, *belong* to. Where exactly you were stationed in Stalingrad and with who and finally, where you were *before* Stalingrad and with who. Give as much detail as you can and feel free to write down anything about your circumstances in Stalingrad before you left and your subsequent journey here. Then we can talk." The Hauptmann then lit a cigarette, leaning back against an empty bookcase which rocked gently; a cloud of dust gathering around him.

It took them a long time to think of those details. Some things were easier to remember than others. Morgenstern finished first, keeping what he wrote to a minimum. Stark wrote of the Bone Road and his friend, Hugo Wagner. Benz wrote of Russian prisoners who'd become cannibals; eating the flesh off severed limbs from the sick and wounded. They handed their sheets of paper over one by one. Morgenstern lit a Juno and wondered if they had signed their own death warrants.

"Keep the pencils," said the Hauptmann. "There might be more paperwork for you to sign," he went on, scanning the sheets quickly. He folded them neatly and put them in a file. "My name is Dieter, by the way. You must be Karl Morgenstern? Which of you is Stark and Benz?" They introduced themselves.

"What'll happen to us?" asked Stark.

"I'll get to that...Wilhelm, isn't it?" Stark nodded. "Okay then, right," said Dieter. "First, can I ask you, do you know or have you heard of, a Leutnant Willi Eggar?" None of them had.

"Why do ask?" said Morgenstern, frowning slightly.

"He is my brother," said Dieter. "He was posted to Stalingrad last October. I have not heard from him since early November."

"I'm sorry," said Morgenstern. Stark and Benz shifted uncomfortably.

"Don't be," said Dieter. "He may yet show up somewhere. He was in the 24th Panzer Division. A tank commander. I'm hopeful," said Dieter, sounding like a man who knew there wasn't any reason to be.

Don't be, thought Morgenstern. He's dead. They were all wiped out before December. Before things really started to fall apart. He said nothing though. He looked at this army lawyer, or whatever he was, in a new light. His empathy and apparent sympathy could prove useful. But it all felt a bit too good to be true.

"Let's get started then," said Dieter. "Listen closely. None of you are in any big trouble. Or any trouble really. A month ago, it might have been different, but we know a lot more about what happened than we did. Questions will undoubtedly be asked as to why you didn't stay put and follow the Fuhrer's orders but allowances *will* be made. *Are* being made. There'll be considerations given to help you too. At the end of the day, you made a wise choice coming here. You were looking, weren't you?" Dieter said as a prompt. Everyone nodded. "Tell the Field Police that, if they want to talk to you. The Gestapo too. I know of others who unwisely tried to just get away. Desert. They were found and summarily shot.

"I can't imagine what you've been through. It's a miracle you're sitting here with me now. Back home, in Berlin especially, things are spiralling out of control, but there's a slow progression on squashing what happened and putting it too bed. On the streets I hear, they are in shock. Before Stalingrad, everyone felt we would conquer the world."

"What about the British?" asked Morgenstern, lighting a cigarette from a tin he pulled from his cavernous greatcoat pocket. He flicked a match away. "The Air War in '41? Or Rommel's men in Africa?"

"How the Air War finished was blamed on Goering, at least by the German public. And despite Goebbel's lies. As for Africa?" Dieter shrugged. "Well, Sergeant Morgenstern, that's not over yet."

But it will soon be, Morgenstern thought. He didn't blame the Hauptmann really. He'd probably never been near any front line. All he knew what was he had been told.

"You can all understand at the very least," Dieter continued. "Moral has to be maintained. Both here and at home, but especially here."

"Naturally," said Morgenstern. "And if anyone had any sense, they'd leave this fucking country in a quick minute! Even *Grofaz* has to know we're finished here!" Grofaz was the common soldier's term for Hitler. It was a sarcastic abbreviation of *'Grosster Feldherr Aller Zeiten',* Greatest Commander-in-Chief of all time, which in itself, was meant as an insult.

"Careful Sergeant," said Dieter. "People are being pulled out of bars back home and shot for using that term."

"I'm sorry, Herr Hauptmann," said Morgenstern. You have to be more careful, he told himself.

"It's Dieter, remember? That's what I mean about allowances being made. You're not, any of you, going to get too many of them though. So be careful what you say from now on. Words and phrases can be interpreted in different ways."

"Will we be sent home, Herr Hauptmann...Er, Dieter?" asked Stark. It was all he could think of. The thought of seeing his wife again, Greta, consumed him.

"At least for some leave?" asked Benz.

"Maybe," said the army lawyer. "What's in your favour is supply and demand. Men and equipment continue to pour into Russia. For how long though is anyone's guess."

"Not long, judging by the age and quality I saw last," said Morgenstern.

Dieter sighed heavily. Lighting another Juno, he looked up to face the three men. "So, you'll be allowed a day or two here first to recover and settle down. Mind you, we were supposed to head north a week ago."

"Not south then?" said Morgenstern.

"No Karl, not south."

That was that then. Stalingrad was forsaken. Forgotten already. Lost. 300,000 men abandoned.

"It may interest you to know," Dieter added. "General Paulus surrendered to the Russians."

"When?!" asked Morgenstern, shocked at the news.

"I can't tell you," said Dieter. "We've only just heard."

"But that means..." Morgenstern's words trailed off. Was there hope then? For the 300,000 left behind? Stark and Benz looked at each other; exchanging looks of surprise. They said nothing though.

"Look," said Dieter, feeling the time was right to wrap this up. "Sooner or later, the MP's will want to talk to you, but consider that a formality. Unless you're on any of their lists. We'll do our best for you with the Gestapo as well, but they're not the worst I've come across. Far from it actually. My guess is they'll want to cast an eye over you for appearances and to satisfy themselves that you are who you say you are. Don't worry about their theatrics. It's all show mostly."

"What are they doing here?" asked Morgenstern. "So far from home?"

"Your guess is as good as mine," was all Dieter would say, whether he knew or not. "Okay then, that's enough for now," he said, standing up. "Anything you want to ask me? Anything I can do for you?"

"No, thank you, Herr Hauptmann," the three men said in turn, standing also.

"Feel free to visit the Medics. Even the Junior Surgeon if something really ails you. Give it a while though and eat well. That's maybe all you need. You can rest up. I'll show you where. Sleep, whatever. But take my advice. Don't mix with the men here. At least, not too much. And don't talk too much, got it?" Everyone nodded. It was common sense after all. "Come on, I'll show you where you can rest up."

With that, Dieter walked with them to a small cottage that seemed to have been prepared for them. Three bunks were new additions to the place. Three small tables as well. Apart from those, the single room dwelling was empty. A small fireplace full of ashes was at one end, but they all knew it would be forbidden to light a fire. Morgenstern glanced out one of the two small windows. There was little to tell him where they were in relation to everyone else, but he did see a bespectacled clerk come out of what might have been a sort of HQ across the narrow road. Two Chain-Dogs stood outside it, he saw now. Okay. Fine, he thought. Away from the men? And near the HQ where they can keep an eye on us. He flopped down on one of the bunks. Can we trust this Dieter character? Time will tell, he thought, ever practically.

*

A Chat with the Gestapo

Morgenstern lay on his bed smoking. It was around 2am and he couldn't get back to sleep, having woken with a full bladder. He'd braved the temperature outside to relieve himself in some bushes to the side of their cottage and hurried back inside to return under his blanket, still wearing his uniform and greatcoat. The only concession he made was to kick off his boots first. They were new and pinched his toes, otherwise he might have left them on.

Stark and Benz had hardly stirred and snored loudly in alternate rumblings that sounded like a comical siren. Morgenstern drew deeply on his Juno, lighting a new one from it's stub, as had become his recent habit. He was making hay and why not? he asked himself. He thought then about the resigned attitude that he and most combat Veterans seemed to adopt after spending years living in constant perpetual lethal danger.

When he was younger, he'd lived in fear all the time, especially of course in combat. But as his skill and confidence grew, the fear subsided. One seemed to negate the other. And now, when not in combat, or at least when not in danger, he didn't think about dying at all, except maybe when he thought of home and his family. The constant longing to see Elke and little Marta again, always brought with it the fear of dying before that could happen. But Elke and Marta seemed to exist in an alternate reality somehow that he never fully understood. Perhaps because spending time with them was the polar opposite of being here on the Eastern Front. There was too much of a difference between the two. Even in combat, being killed was the last thing on your mind as you fought your enemy with ferocious violence. It was as if your body took over; wanting to survive at any cost. You became a spectator. The possibility of a serious injury or wound was a far more terrifying prospect.

He lay on his back and smoked, staring at the ceiling. Images ran through his mind like a motion picture in a cinema. In 1940, he'd been part of 'Fall Rot' or 'Case Red'; the invasion of France. It was June 7 and within the last few days, the combined German Blitzkrieg had swept the French and British aside. It was a matter of time before they would sweep into Paris, victorious. He'd been a Corporal in those days and he and his platoon had their tails up, bursting with almost superhuman confidence.

Morgenstern rubbed his eyes. He'd been a different person in those days. He and his men had just finished taking a series of three pillboxes near the outskirts of a small town near the Somme. Had it been Abbeville? he wondered. There had been so many towns. As usual, the exertion, the adrenaline rush, and the withdrawal from the amphetamines they were all issued with, took it's toll. Everyone fell to the ground when the fighting was over, gasping for breath and coming to terms with the fact that they were still alive. The younger soldiers pulled out cigarettes and eventually talked loudly amongst themselves about their recent exploits as if they'd just taken part in a wonderful game.

Morgenstern had carried a Schmeisser machine pistol back then and had the presence of mind to check it's magazine. It was empty and throwing it away, he reached to his belt for a new one. All gone. No matter. He'd get new magazines later. There was no rush. He had his pistol after all. Feeling safe, he lay back down, lit a cigarette and listened to the chatter of the men around him. Closing his eyes, he drifted off.

Then, amid screams and shouts, suddenly dozens of French soldiers were running towards them. Morgenstern shot to his feet, barking orders at his small group of six men. It was too late. Two of them were dead in seconds, dropping to the ground in what seemed like slow motion. While another turned tail and ran, Morgenstern recalled reaching for his pistol, which was immediately swept from his hand. How? He couldn't remember, but it felt as if his whole arm had come away too.

That was as far as his memories took him. He woke up later in a Field Hospital, recovering from a bullet wound to his leg and a dislocated shoulder. The sole survivor of that particular skirmish. It was one of a series of enduring mysteries that stayed with him over time. How had he survived? He had no idea. He became a firm believer in fate; at least in those days. He didn't understand it but he did believe in it. He hadn't yet come to terms with the idea that all was chaos and what happened to you was pure chance.

Stark turned over in his sleep. One of his arms fell out from under his blanket, swinging momentarily over the side of his bunk. Benz didn't stir. Then Morgenstern could hear footsteps outside and the door of the cottage door suddenly flew open. Two Chain Dogs, complete with gorgets, stood over the three men.

"Wake up!" one of them barked. "Quickly now! Move! Let's go!"

A few minutes later, they were sitting alone, but for one Chain Dog, in a sparse room in the building across the road from their cottage. Morgenstern was fully awake but Stark and Benz were still half asleep, slumped on their chairs, yawning. Now they could all hear hurried footsteps coming up the corridor outside.

The door opened and two men, one in his thirties, the other in his forties, entered the room and sat down behind a small table perhaps two metres from them. The Chain Dog left them all alone, presumably having been told to get out.

Morgenstern cast an eye over the two men behind the table. Dressed in ill-fitting suits and open overcoats, it was obvious who they were. Gestapo. Secret Police. He frowned. Dieter had told them the Feldgendarmerie, or Military Police, didn't want to speak to them. If that was the case, what interest did the Gestapo have in them? The two of them looked purposeful and able enough, but Morgenstern frowned again at their dead expressions which gave nothing away and told him less than nothing. Were they taught that somewhere? he wondered.

He'd heard some grim stories about these types. They were fanatics, all of them. Devoted to the

Reich. Most were recruited from the various police forces in Germany after 1933 and their power was enormous. They had a free hand to act without judicial review, therefore putting them above the law. In effect, they could do what they liked; how they liked. This made them tremendously dangerous.

Opening a paper file now, one of them read some papers while the other one lit a thin cigar as he surveyed the three men before him. It seemed tiresome to him.

"Gentlemen," said the younger man who'd been reading. "Do you know who we are?"

Morgenstern nodded, followed by Stark and Benz.

"Smoke if you wish," said the older man, ignoring the ashtray in front of him and flicking ash on the floor. Morgenstern reached for his cigarettes.

"I am Kriminalinspektor Lotz. This is Kriminalkommissar Kruger. We wish to talk to you about your recent exploits."

"Yes, of course, Herr Kriminalinspektor," said Morgenstern. He cleared his throat and sat up on his chair. Drawing on his Juno, he eyed the file in front of the man. Where did all those sheets of paper come from? What information did they contain? Had these two been in touch with Berlin? Out here? Surely not.

"Theodore Benz?" said Lotz.

Benz looked up and across at him. "Yes, Herr Kriminalinspektor?" He was now wide awake.

"You are a Combat Medic? It says here you were a Krankentrager?"

"A simple stretcher bearer?" asked Kruger, smirking.

"No. Well, yes-."

"No what?" said Lotz flatly.

"No, Herr Kriminalinspektor," said Benz. His stomach turned over.

"Well, what is it? No? Yes?"

"That was my rank, Herr Kriminalinspektor. But it is just that, a rank. My duties-."

"Wilhelm Stark?" said Lotz, moving on. He had no interest in Benz' duties.

"Yes, Herr Kriminalinspektor."

"Who were you with?" Kruger interrupted, addressing Benz once more.

"30th Division; 17th Army; Attached to the 1st Panzer Division," Herr Kriminalinspektor."

"It's Kriminalkommissar," said Kruger, his eyes boring into Benz, who swallowed.

"Yes, er, Herr Kriminalkommissar."

Morgenstern sighed inwardly. These two were in love with themselves alright. He probably would have felt the same, he told himself. The power they wielded. The authority. The fear they instilled that preceded them everywhere. That had to affect your ego. But still, he knew, when this bullshit war is over and there's a reckoning, all their power will mean nothing, he was damn sure.

"Wilhelm Stark," Lotz continued, in his tired monotone. "You are a Cook?"

"Yes, Herr Kriminalkommissar," said Stark. He found himself very nervous.

"No, not yet," said Lotz, chuckling. Kruger smiled. "Herr Kriminalinspektor will do for now."

Jesus Christ, thought Morgenstern, closing his eyes. He finished his cigarette and lit another one.

"What is your rank?"

"Obergefreiter, Herr Kriminalinspektor," said Stark, shifting in his chair.

"And who were you attached to?"

"Originally, the 12th Panzer Grenadiers, Herr Kriminalinspektor. But I ended up in Staff HQ. The 12th didn't exist by then."

"Mmmm," said Lotz. "And Unteroffizier Karl Morgenstern? 21st Infantry. 6th Army?"

"Yes, Herr Kriminalinspektor."

"Says here, you were awarded the Iron Cross, 2nd Class. In France."

"Yes, Herr Kriminalinspektor," said Morgenstern. He hadn't written that down on his sheet. They had to have gotten that from Army HQ in Berlin. "In 1940,-."

"Yes, yes," said Lotz. He was tired and wanted to get back to his bottle of brandy. It had been

Kruger's idea to wake these men in the middle of the night. So as to add to the...drama. That was the word he'd used. It was completely unnecessary of course, but Kruger always liked to set the tone.

"Gentlemen," said Kruger now, leaning forward and steepling his hands. "Do you understand the gravity of your situation?"

"Gravity, Herr Kriminalkommissar?" asked Morgenstern, frowning. His mouth was dry.

"Yes, gravity. Why, after all, did you all desert your posts? Hike across enemy territory, unscathed? And then present yourselves here? Looking for salvation?"

"It wasn't like that, Herr Kriminalkommissar," said Morgenstern.

"Oh? How was it then?"

"I can speak for all of us?"

"Go on," said Kruger, sighing.

"There were seven of us who walked out in the end. We-."

"Seven!" said Lotz, almost shouting. Now it was Morgenstern's turn to sigh. He said nothing though. "Then we will want to know their names and whereabouts!"

"They're dead, Herr Kriminalinspektor," said Morgenstern. "They died along the way."

"Died along the way? That is most convenient," said Kruger. "You're lying!"

"It's the truth."

"It's the truth fucking what!?" Lotz shouted.

"It's the truth, Herr Kriminalinspektor," said Morgenstern calmly.

"The fact remains," said Kruger. "You deserted your posts. Disobeyed the Fuhrer's directive. Took the easy way out!" Morgenstern looked as if he might protest, but stayed silent. "Yes? Something to say?" asked Kruger, daring him to speak.

"It was hopeless, Herr Kriminalkommissar," Benz interjected. Morgenstern looked at him. Shut up boy! he thought. Waste of time anyway! You'll only make it worse! Shut up!

"Oh really?" This time from Lotz.

"Yes, Herr Kriminalinspektor, really," said Benz. Morgenstern closed his eyes. Shut up!

"In what way?"

"Stalingrad had become a wasteland. Of death. We all made up what amounted to hundreds of stragglers. No two people you met belonged to the same Regiment. Everyone they knew was dead. By a miracle we were left alive. How, I don't know. Will never know. The horror of it was-."

"Not one of you," said Lotz. "Not one of you hundreds thought to form a defensive group of some kind? Hold your ground? FULFILL YOUR ORDERS?!" he shouted.

"With what?" said Morgenstern, quickly adding, "Herr Kriminalinspektor. We had no weapons; No ammunition anyway, if we did. What were we supposed to fight with? Sticks and clubs? The airdrops had ceased. We had no food; no supplies of any kind."

"Bullshit!" said Lotz, looking at Kruger. "You're lying! All of you!"

"Benz?" said Kruger. "You were stationed in Field Hospital IV/2A?"

"Yes, Herr Kriminalkommissar."

"Where exactly was that located?"

"Near the tractor factory, Herr Kriminalkommissar. North of the city centre."

"Who was the Senior Surgeon there?"

"Oberstarzt Kalb," said Benz. "But he died, Herr Kriminalkommissar. I worked under Stabsarzt Miller in the end."

"And what of him?"

"Herr Kriminalkommissar?"

"Was he alive? Was he dead, when you left?"

"I, er, I don't know," Herr Kriminalkommissar. He was an opium addict. But we ran out of medicines before Christmas."

"And you left him on his own to tend the remaining sick and wounded? Abandoned him to his fate, as it were?"

"He used to amputate men's healthy limbs, Herr Kriminalkommissar. I couldn't-."

"Really?" said Kruger. His expression didn't change or show any reaction to what Benz had said.

"And Obergefreiter Stark. You mention burying a Gefreiter Hugo Wagner? A Signaller, you say?"

"Er, yes, Herr Kriminalkommissar."

"Where did you two meet?"

"He was also at Staff HQ, Herr Kriminalkommissar."

"How did he die?" asked Kruger, lighting another cigar.

"Badly, Herr Kriminalkommissar," said Stark, the memory of the Bone Road coming back to him.

"Badly?"

"Well quietly really. But he died of starvation, Herr Kriminalkommissar. He weighed no more than a child in the end."

"I see," said Kruger, who clearly didn't. "Morgenstern. What happened to you? You give no detail in your submission."

"Yes, Herr Kriminalkommissar. Well, my unit was overrun, but we managed to get back to our dugout. Everyone was dead though. The Reds, er, the Russians had swept through our positions. I stayed in our dugout with my men. There were four of us. We ran out of ammunition the following day. We left, trying to find some of our boys near the bus station. We knew there should be some of our people there."

"And? What happened?" asked Lotz.

"I was the only one to make it to the bus station. When I got there, Herr Kriminalinspektor, it was deserted. I kept looking for our lads."

"Mmmm," said Lotz again.

Then the two Gestapo Officers seemed to give up and leant back in their chairs, whispering to each other in hushed tones. Morgenstern, Stark and Benz, looked at each other, exchanging anxious looks.

"Herein!" Kruger suddenly roared. Come in!

The door opened immediately and the same Chain Dog entered the room. He looked at Kruger, standing to attention.

"Take these two back," said the Kriminalkommissar, waving a hand towards Morgenstern and Stark.

The MP clicked his heels. "Jawohl, Herr Kriminalkommissar. Right! Come on! Move! Let's go!" he barked at the two men. They stood up and were hustled out of the room, leaving poor Benz to look anxiously after them. He was terrified now. What does this mean? he wondered. Am I to live or die? And what of Karl and Wilhelm?

Minutes later, Morgenstern and Stark were back in their cottage. The Chain Dog abruptly left them to it, slamming the door after him.

"What the fuck is going on?" asked Stark, collapsing on his bunk.

"I have no idea," said Morgenstern, lighting a Juno as he stared out a window.

Then he lay down, throwing his blanket around him. He noticed there were only two bunks in the room; Benz' had been taken out. It became obvious. He leant on an elbow, facing Stark.

"Wilhelm," he said gravely. "Listen to me now."

"What? What is it?"said Stark, struck by the other man's gravitas.

"Theo is finished. As good as dead."

"How can you fucking know that?!" Stark shouted, sitting on the edge of his bunk now.

"His bunk is gone. This show was all planned beforehand."

"But why Theo? Why-."

"Could just as easily have been me or you," said Morgenstern, lying back down and staring at the ceiling.

"I don't get it," said Stark, suddenly very weary as he looked towards where Benz' bunk used to be.

"Nor do I really," said Morgenstern. "Maybe they just picked on Theo before. Maybe it's just a coincidence his bunk is gone. I don't know. But they must have wanted to make some kind of example. These bastards have to make their presence felt. Have to have a scapegoat perhaps. They don't want any of this lot fucking off when they feel like it, do they?"

"Are you serious? Theo has to die to set an example?"

"That, and maybe because he said too much in there. Should have kept his mouth shut."

"Well fuck you Karl!" Stark was angry now. It was a cruel twist of fate, after everything Benz had been through. Everything he suffered. "Kept his mouth shut?!" Stark wept for his friend. "He was 22 years old, Karl!"

"I know Wilhelm," said Morgenstern. It was outrageous. "I know."

The two men lay there wide awake for some time. Eventually Stark asked, "What'll happen to us Karl?"

"I don't know," said Morgenstern. He was shocked at what had happened to Benz. Why him? He couldn't think of a good reason. But he was thankful that it hadn't been him. "Maybe they'll let us go? Who knows? I'll try and speak to Eggar tomorrow. See what can be done about Theo. Get some sleep now. It'll be dawn soon."

*

Lonely but not Alone

Benz sat on the cobbled stone floor of what had been a storeroom in the same building across the road from the cottage. With his arms wrapped around his knees, he looked up at three quite large circular holes in the outer wall to his right that served as ventilation for the room which was two or three times the size of an average prison cell. The place still stank of vegetables though there hadn't been any stored here since the early days of the German invasion.

But it was Benz' prison cell now. Two Chain Dogs stood outside the thick wooden door. He could see them clearly through large gaps in the wood that were a result of the door being forced open at one time with tremendous force. The door wasn't locked. Why should it be? With the two guards outside, he wasn't going anywhere. When they shoved him in here early this morning, throwing an empty bucket after him and slamming the door, his first reaction was to open the door and bolt down the short corridor, in the sure knowledge that he'd probably be shot dead before he got to the end. If he managed to get away, well, that was another matter. He just felt at that moment that he couldn't take this any more.

To have come come this far against all the odds? To have survived, first the horrors of Stalingrad and then the trek of the last couple of weeks and all that he'd been through during that? Only to be dealt this worst of all cards? It was too much. He decided that had he been a braver man, he would have ran; Could still run. But he slowly convinced himself that there was still hope. Still a chance. They couldn't possibly shoot him, could they? And for what? Desertion? How can you desert something that doesn't exist any more? If a sailor jumps off a sinking ship that is aflame and dying, is he guilty of desertion or is he abandoning ship in order to survive?

Perhaps they just want to grill me again, he thought. Talk about the casualties; on both sides. God knows, he'd treated many Russian soldiers as well as his own side of course. At least in the field. He remembered spending hours in a shell-hole with two badly wounded Russian soldiers that were bleeding profusely. He'd patched them up as best he could. One had a stomach wound; his stomach contents mixing with the blood that seeped out of him. But remarkably, after Benz' efforts, he seemed to gain some strength and stabilized after a couple of hours. The other Russian had a hole in his throat the size of his fist and Benz could see that his larynx had been shot away. But he was breathing, albeit with a raspy sound and remarkably again, after Benz had done his best for him, he stabilised in time. Both men would have survived if they could have been taken to a field hospital.

The Russian with the stomach wound had grabbed Benz' arm at one time, begging him for morphine. "Morfiy!" he'd said, over and over. "Preparat!" I have none, Benz had told him, recognising the word. Hold on! Tears streamed down the Russian's face. The man was in agony.

Benz had waited six hours in the shell-hole with the two wounded Russians. The man with the neck wound had died towards the end, but he'd put up a remarkable fight. The other wounded man had lingered on and when help finally arrived, it was in the form of a Ukrainian SS patrol. Benz' mood had lifted as he peered across the brim of the crater at the approaching half-track. He waved like a lunatic; his white helmet with it's red cross clearly visible. A Feldwebel and a Corporal got out of the vehicle and approached him. The Corporal had got there first and reached out a hand to pull Benz up. He hadn't noticed the two Russians below. Before Benz could explain he had a wounded prisoner to evacuate, the Feldwebel appeared and unslung his machine-pistol, shooting the two Russians and killing Benz' patient for the last six hours immediately.

"NO!" Benz screamed in anguish. He sank to his knees, wailing in despair. The SS men looked down at him, puzzled.

"You want to come?" the Corporal had asked in poor German.

Benz wept. The two SS men shrugged and returned to their truck, cursing Benz in Ukrainian for wasting their time.

Another time, he'd met a crazy Doctor who thought Medics in the field, at least in combat zones, should just carry large amounts of morphine to administer to the badly wounded, thus overdosing them and letting them die peacefully and in no pain. "Saves everyone's time," said the Doctor. "What's the fucking point otherwise?"

If you sat and thought about the madness and futility of war for any length of time, it could drive you insane, Benz realised. He had seen his share of madness. A lot of it came from despair, he knew. All types of men across all ranks. He remembered the Brigadier General who shot all of his Staff Officers and then himself, because he had learnt that he was to be replaced for some failed strategy or other. He couldn't face the disgrace it would bring.

The solution to dwelling on madness and despair was to not think about it, but that was easier said than done. If you were lucky, you became tolerant of it but Benz was thinking about it now and tried to concentrate on his prospects instead.

But poor Benz, a sensitive soul to start with, couldn't concentrate on that either and found himself drifting back to the small flat in Stuttgart he'd shared with his mother. He'd never known his father and was thus as devoted to her as she was to him. His memories of his childhood were joyous and filled with happy times.

After caring for the injured bird and bringing it back to health, eventually releasing it, Benz would spend time roaming the streets and parks, looking for injured animals and birds to rescue and care for. His mother would offer great encouragement and helped with the variety of city wildlife he would sometimes appear with. Their flat became the talk of their neighbours and other children would bring them animals or birds they had found also.

But in 1939, Benz was called up, much to his mother's despair. She was distraught at the prospect of losing her son, her only child, but overcame the worst of her anxiety by encouraging Benz to join the Army Veterinary Service, thinking it safe. Benz however, explained that what he really wanted to do was to become a Doctor and that he would apply to join the Army Medical Service. His mother was content with that. She didn't realise that apart from hospitals, it involved following soldiers into battle and treating them where they fell in lethally dangerous situations and, unarmed. It just didn't occur to her and no one ever told her otherwise.

"You will care for our brave lads that have fallen, Theo," she told him. "That's worthwhile, isn't it?"

"Yes mother," he'd said. "It'll be worthwhile, and when this is all over, it'll help me greatly to get into Medical School."

So the next day, Benz went along to the recruiting station with his call up papers and joined the

Medical Corps. He never told his mother the reality of it. How could he? He let her think he would be working in some grand hospital somewhere, treating heroes and so on.

Sitting here now in this dank room that stank of vegetables, he wondered what she would make of places like Stalingrad. It would be beyond her. Benz thought for a moment. She would be 47 this year. He wished from the bottom of his heart to see her again, because of the joy it would bring her. Bring them both. He hadn't heard from her in 16 months. Letters from home were hardly a priority this last while. And you could write as many letters as you liked and hand them in to the clerks to be sent home, but they were simply tossed away out of sight like so much trash.

Footsteps outside his door brought him back from his thoughts. The door opened and a young cook slid a tin plate across the floor towards him. Being cobbled and uneven, most of the food ended up scattered across the floor and as Benz went to retrieve it, he heard a spoon clatter on the floor behind him. Then the door was slammed shut again.

He ate in silence. There was nothing to do but wait.

*

After a hurried breakfast, where the rest of the men in the mess hall seemed to treat them like lepers, Morgenstern smoked outside the latrines, waiting for Stark. He noticed the other men who were milling about; an Officer here, a Corporal there. Everyone wanted to distance themselves. It was obvious that word had got out. With the Gestapo's involvement, nobody wanted to associate themselves with the three newcomers.

"I'm coming with you," said Stark, reappearing from the latrines and still buttoning his flies.

"It would be better if you waited in the cottage," said Morgenstern, flicking his Juno away.

Stark sauntered off by way of reply. Morgenstern sighed and followed him.

"Let me do the talking then," said Morgenstern, catching up with the other man.

"I'll speak if I fucking feel like it!" said Stark. "But you can start if you have to."

Fair enough, thought Morgenstern. Then they were approaching the guest house. There didn't seem to be anyone around. Stark hammered on the door. A young Grenadier Leutnant eventually appeared.

"What the fuck do you mean by all this noise, eh?"

"So sorry, Herr Leutnant," said Morgenstern, standing to attention. Stark did the same. "We were looking for Hauptmann Eggar, Herr Leutnant."

"Well you won't find him here. Now away with you," said the Leutnant, slamming the door.

Bastard, thought Morgenstern, turning to face the road. Time was, especially in the early days, a young Leutnant like that would be grateful for your help and experience or the mere fact that you acknowledged him at all.

"What about the HQ? That place across from us?" asked Stark.

"Yeah, why not," said Morgenstern. "If they let us in," he added, walking beside him.

When they got there, two different Chain Dogs stood in their way. "Fuck off!" one of them said.

"Hauptmann Eggar told us to report here!" Morgenstern lied.

"News to me," said the other Chain Dog. "Now fuck off!"

"But-."

"Look, you dumb bastards, if Eggar wants to see you, he'll send someone. Now I won't tell you again. Fuck off!"

Morgenstern and Stark walked away. There was nothing to be done. They decided to walk around but after a while and having been met with hostility everywhere they went, they returned to their cottage. Anyway, thought Morgenstern, throwing himself on his bunk and lighting another cigarette, the Chain Dog was right. If Eggar wanted to see them, he'd send someone to collect them. You couldn't just wander about and expect to see an Officer when you wanted to.

"Poor Theo," said Stark, more to himself than out loud.

"There's nothing to be done," said Morgenstern.

"Fuck you Karl! After all we've been through!"

"And fuck you too!" said Morgenstern, shouting now. "Do you think you're the only one who cares, for Christ's sake! What the fuck can we do? Tell me and I'll do it! It's out of our hands! You can't reason with the Gestapo."

"I'm sorry Karl, you're right," said Stark, staring at the ceiling. "Do you think Eggar will help Theo?"

"I like to think he'll try," said Morgenstern. "Anyway, you should worry more about your own hide! Do you want to survive this? I know I do."

"Should we ask if we can see Theo?"

"They'll never allow that." Morgenstern raised himself up on an elbow. "Wilhelm, try and think of something else. Concentrate on Greta, eh? Think about getting home to see her."

"It's not right, Karl," said Stark. "It's not right what they've done to Theo."

"There's nothing right any more," said Morgenstern.

*

Benz awoke to the sound of voices outside in the corridor. He'd been asleep but had had a nightmare about his Battalion of Skeletons. Then Hauptmann Eggar was coming into the room. Benz sat up; back to the wall. Eggar sat opposite him. Lighting a cigarette, he offered one to Benz, who shook his head.

"I'm sorry," said Eggar. "Sorry that this should happen to you. I've spoken to the Colonel, who in turn has spoken to the Gestapo."

"Am I to be shot then?" asked Benz calmly.

"The Colonel demanded that you should be released. Considering the circumstances," said Eggar, flicking some ash away. "But the Gestapo chap, Kruger? He was adamant. You deserted your Field Hospital, he said, in a time of need. Morgenstern and Stark? Well, they had nothing to desert, it has been reasoned."

"But Dieter," said Benz, his situation sinking in, "If I could take you all back to see this Field

Hospital. The Doctor, the Russian prisoners, the sick and wounded. If-."

"I know," said Eggar. "But Kruger has made his decision. He and his sidekick, Lotz? They're due to leave tomorrow."

"I see," said Benz. That meant that they would want their order to execute Benz carried out first. "Can I see Karl and Wilhelm?"

"They won't allow that," said Eggar. "I'm sorry."

"Alright then Dieter," said Benz, accepting his fate. "Do one thing for me?"

"Of course," said Eggar.

"Write to my mother, would you? Tell her I fell in some heroic way."

"Yes, I will," said Eggar, standing up.

Benz stood also. "Thank you Dieter," he said.

Then Eggar left. Benz sat down once more and wept for his lost future.

The Firing Squad

The next morning at dawn came a knock on the door of the cottage. Morgenstern opened it in his bare feet. Stark bolted awake at this new alarm and sat up in his bunk. Jan stood in the doorway, clutching a rifle.

"Look," he said, obviously uncomfortable. "You're lad is to be shot. I just found out about it. You don't have much time. I'm part of the squad. We're on our way to get breakfast. Get yourselves over to the field behind the Farrier's workshop. That's where it'll be."

"Thanks," Morgenstern managed to say. Jan mumbled his apologies. Morgenstern nodded and shut the door. He sat on his bunk, across from Stark, and lit a cigarette. "That's it then," he said.

Stark stared blankly at the door. Then he got up and reached for his boots. Morgenstern did the same. Finishing his cigarette, he said, "I wonder how Theo took it."

"Let's go," said Stark, making for the door.

Morgenstern was smoking again as they trudged through a persistent drizzle towards the Farrier's workshop. As they got nearer, they could hear the Blacksmith's already preparing the place for the day. Someone barked an order for the fire to be stoked as they passed by.

In the field behind, someone had placed a new fencepost on some flat ground. Lengths of rope, perhaps a half metre long, lay on the grass beside it. Buckets of sand were on the other side, waiting to be thrown on the grass around the post. The Chain Dogs had been busy overnight.

There was nowhere to sit and little shelter, so the two men skulked under some guttering at the back of the workshop that leaked like a sieve.

There was little conversation. "Fucking rain!" said Morgenstern.

"It should rain today," said Stark, shivering. "I can't believe this is happening. Theo didn't deserve this."

Morgenstern stayed silent, chain smoking for the duration. Eventually, after about 40 minutes, the same young Leutnant from the guest house the day before, led a firing party through the rain to their positions in front of the post. Next in tow came four Chain Dogs with Benz followed by a Padre, who read aloud with some difficulty from a bible. Benz' hands were tied and he tripped over as he was marched across the field. Two of the Chain Dogs pulled him upright from the wet grass and continued towards the post. They tied him to it around his neck and feet, before scattering the buckets of sand around him. Standing back then and to one side, everyone waited for the Padre to finish. When he closed his bible and nodded to the Leutnant, Benz was offered a blindfold, which he refused. Good for you, thought Morgenstern.

Stark thought he could see Benz breathing hard as he faced the eight man firing squad, who stood at loose attention. The young Leutnant pulled out his pistol, letting his arm hang by his side as the Chain Dogs finally retreated and disappeared without a backward glance. It was hardly the first execution they'd attended after all.

The young Leutnant barked a series of commands and suddenly eight shots rang out. Benz slumped forward, dead immediately, but nonetheless, the Leutnant approached him, shooting him in the back of the head. That's the Wehrmacht for you, thought Morgenstern, following regulations. Make sure the poor bastard is dead. He was proud of Benz though. The young man had died well.

More commands cut through the rain and the firing squad left the field. They would have a free day for their efforts and looked forward to games of cards later and maybe even a beer. Once they left, Stark made to move.

"Where are you going?" Morgenstern asked him.

"I want to pay my respects," said Stark, tears streaming down his face.

Morgenstern didn't notice in the rain. He held Stark back, pointing with his chin. Two Medics had appeared with a hand cart. They untied Benz and placed him face down on the cart. One of them felt his neck for a pulse before they wheeled him away. Stark moved again, but Morgenstern strengthened his grip on his arm.

"Don't," he said.

"But they can tell us where he'll be buried," said Stark, pleading to be let go.

Morgenstern released him, sighing heavily. He stood for a long while where he was in the rain. When he ran out of cigarettes, he pulled his greatcoat collar around him and moved off, back towards the cottage. Then he was back lying on his bunk, reaching for a new tin of Junos. He didn't feel like breakfast today.

*

The Colonel Doesn't Want You

Stark came back to the cottage towards midday, finding Morgenstern asleep. He threw off his wet greatcoat, letting it crumple to the floor, and sat on his bunk looking at his companion who snored gently, his mouth wide open as if stunned by something.

Stark was breathing hard. He raised a hand to his face. His nose was broken, and still bled a little. His upper and lower lips were cut also and he spat a mouthful of blood to the floor. There were cuts above and around his eyes and what looked like the impression of a boot print across one cheek. Even though it was bitterly cold, he took off his tunic jacket, wincing in pain as he felt around his ribcage, where he only had to gently touch those points that were painful to cry out.

"What happened?" asked Morgenstern, looking over at him now. He hadn't moved but he was wide awake. "Where the hell have you been?"

"I was trying to find out where they'd brought Theo," said Stark. "No one would talk to me. First I went across the road. Bastard Chain Dog smacked me in the mouth with the back of his hand! I lost a fucking tooth."

Morgenstern lit a Juno and closed his eyes, rolling onto his back. "What did you expect?" He sighed. "Looks like that's not all you got."

"That was later," said Stark, buttoning his tunic. "I just wandered about. Avoided the mess hall. I went back to the field, Karl. The post is still there."

"Yeah, well maybe they haven't finished with it yet," said Morgenstern, getting up. He reached for Stark's greatcoat. "Here, come on, stand up," he said, helping the man put it on. Then they were sitting on their bunks looking at each other. "Why Wilhelm, in God's name, did you have to run around agitating people and asking stupid fucking questions? Will it have helped us? Helped our situation? It might be you or me tied to that fucking post tomorrow or the next day!"

"I'm sorry Karl, I know."

"Who did this to you?"

"I walked all over. Found an artillery battery down by the river. Told me to fuck off of course, like everyone else. I snapped I suppose. Gave as good as I got, didn't I? Well, it got out of hand. They beat the shit out of me. I hurt a couple of the bastards though," said Stark, chuckling then grimacing. He held his left side and lay down.

Morgenstern stood up and stared out a window. Bastards, he thought. Bastards for doing that to Stark. Still, he'd been more than an idiot to wander around getting under people's noses and asking stupid fucking questions about a deserter who'd been shot while over a million of our lads lie dead out there in the fucking snow. Deserter, that's how they'd see it, without knowing the truth. And the same bastards don't know *yet,* that they've been lied to over and over again already, and that this war is lost! Everything that happens from this day on is just going to be a slow, torturous journey to damnation, humiliation and catastrophe.

"I saw Eggar," said Stark then.

"Oh yeah," said Morgenstern, sighing heavily, lighting another cigarette and turning around, in that order. "He see you? Say anything?"

"Nah. I didn't feel like following him into HQ by that stage. Those bastards! Who in their right minds would join the Chain Dogs, Karl?"

"Well, there, you said it. 'In their right mind'. They're not, are they? Most of the bastards were small town cops who eventually joined the party. Thought it would be a great idea to join the Army where they could really throw their weight around. Probably turned down by the SS and 'Stapo first, and shit scared of being real soldiers. Then you have all the nutters and sadists who ran all the way to the recruiting offices back in the day."

"Well that bastard who belted me in the mouth is a complete swine!"

Morgenstern sat on his bunk with his back to the stone wall. "After we got to Poland in '39, there was one of 'em who kept picking on one of our lads. He was one of life's cheeky sods, you know what I mean?" Stark nodded, a brief smile crossing his face. "Anyway, what was his name? Helmut, I think, yeah. Second name was..", Morgenstern fought to remember, "something funny as I recall. You laughed every time you heard it." But he couldn't for the life of him remember.

"Doesn't matter, go on," said Stark.

"So Helmut was the company clown. Always sticking his neck out and getting into trouble. Eventually he was up on a charge for being AWOL. Stupid bastard was chasing some Polish girl. Left the barracks one night to go and find her. Came back in the morning, mind you, victorious! We heard all about it over breakfast. Next thing, two Chain Dogs came into the mess hall and dragged him away, still clutching his fucking spoon!"

"Shit! What happened?" asked Stark, dabbing at a cut on his face with a rag.

"He showed up the next day much the worse for wear. We had a good Stabsfeldwebel who looked after us in those days. Got Helmut released. Promised he'd be dealt with, etc. etc. The Dogs had really worked him over though. Poor Helmut was never really the same.

"We had a friend or two elsewhere though. Especially some Artillery boys. One of them was a fellow called Ironman. Seriously! At least, that's how he introduced himself. What everyone called him. Wilhelm," said Morgenstern, swinging himself around to sit on the edge of his bunk. It was obvious to Stark that he was recalling a fond memory. "This fellow was the biggest, meanest bastard I have ever seen! Used to box for his regiment! Never beaten!"

"Jesus," said Stark. "What did he do?"

"Ironman could pick up, on his own, 88 shells like they were made of cardboard. Used to toss them around like logs of wood. One time, the Blitz they were riding in, towing their 88, got a puncture. This was early on, when we were marching 30km a day. All about speed in those days."

"Jesus Christ!" said Stark. "30 km? A day?!"

"We often covered more. It was hellish really," said Morgenstern, remembering the blisters and sheer exhaustion. "Anyway, Ironman and his gang pile out of their truck to change the punctured wheel. Some Officer roars past in a Kubelwagen screaming at them to get a fucking move on. Trouble was, they couldn't find the sodding jack! Time was ticking by and their in a panic now, watching all their mates and us disappear from view. They didn't want to be left alone where we were, I can tell you! So what happens? Ironman grabs the wheel arch with his bare hands and lifts the truck up high enough for the rest of them to change the fucking wheel!"

"Ah bullshit!" said Stark. "He'd tear his insides to pieces!"

"It's true, I swear. Heard all about it later."

"It's not fucking true because 'you heard about it later'!" Stark laughed, then winced in pain.

"Well, after the episode with Helmut, Ironman and his lot found the Chain Dogs who'd roughed him up. Don't recall the details, but one of the Dogs died in hospital. Two or three more were sent home to recover. There was a fucking big flap over it of course, but they never found out what really happened. Wall of silence among out lot."

"Jesus Christ!"

"And bear in mind, the Dogs aren't a bunch of pussies. They might be crazy ignorant bastards, but their tough with it. They have to be. Goes with the job. I can't see Ironman's mates making much headway with the Dogs, as I remember both sides. But it was said that he handled them all himself. The Dog who died in hospital didn't make it out of the operating theatre. Ironman only hit him once but drove his lower jaw out the back of his neck. I got that from a Medic who was there."

"Now you are kidding!" said Stark.

Morgenstern shrugged. He could have said how he and a couple of his friends joined Ironman's gang to go looking for the Chain Dogs after a night's boozing during a rare rest day. How he'd seen this giant pick up a 90kg opponent by the scruff of the neck and toss him across the street like a rag doll. But he left it there. Memories. Memories. You had to know when to leave the legends alone. Besides, Ironman and his 88 crew were all killed in a Polish attack three days before the Germans reached Warsaw. A simple one shot stomach wound did for Ironman in the end, though it was said that he lingered for twelve days first…

A harsh knock on the door brought Morgenstern back to today. What now? Stark's face read as he looked at him. Morgenstern held a finger to his mouth before opening the door.

"You're to come with me," said a Corporal, soaking wet and standing back from the doorway.

"What's up?" asked Morgenstern, frowning.

"Hauptmann Eggar wants to see you. Is the other one here?"

"The 'other one'?"

"Gefreiter Stark," said the Corporal.

"It's Obergefreiter," said Stark, joining Morgenstern.

The Corporal grunted loudly in a mocking way. "Follow me," he said, walking away.

They followed him across the road, past two Chain Dogs and into the HQ building. The MP's seemed oblivious to the three men as they went by. The Corporal showed them to a room where Eggar sat on a chair behind a bare table. Morgenstern and Stark were left alone with the Hauptmann by the Corporal who shut the door behind him. The two men stood at ease. There was nothing else in the room to sit on.

"I'm sorry," said Eggar, looking at the closed door. Morgenstern's heart sank. Was this it? Stark went pale.

"Herr Hauptmann?" said Morgenstern, his mouth dry.

"I'm sorry for your friend, Benz. I had no part in it. The Colonel fought hard for him. But Kruger had his orders too. A directive from Berlin, apparently."

"Yes, Herr Hauptmann," said Morgenstern, relief swamping him.

"Then you understand."

"Very well," said Stark bitterly. He didn't add the respectful, 'Herr Hauptmann'.

Eggar let it go. He sighed and looked out the room's only window. "We're leaving," he went on. "Tomorrow or the next day. A new salient has opened up I'm told. North East of here." Morgenstern was curious where, but didn't bother asking. He knew Eggar wouldn't tell him.

"What is-." Stark began.

Eggar held up a hand. "Quiet now," he said. "And listen. Ordinarily, we'd take you in, as per regulations, and you should count yourselves lucky for that alone. Kruger thought the best solution was to have you follow Benz into the ground."

"That was nice of him," said Morgenstern, biting his lip.

"Quiet Sergeant, I said! And listen!"

"Yes, Herr Hauptmann," said Morgenstern, suitably admonished.

"No one even mentioned sending you home on leave. But the Colonel and myself stuck our necks out. The Colonel more than me. He said he didn't want you. Either of you. He told Kruger it wouldn't work, keeping you on here. So, you are to leave in the morning, *early.* You'll be driven to Gobulinskiy; there's a train depot there. You might have to hang around for a bit, but I have papers for you and tickets."

"T..tickets?" said Stark, hardly able to speak.

"Yes, tickets for home lads. You'll have to change two or three times of course, but you'll get there in the end. It'll take you a couple of days I think."

"And when we do?" asked Morgenstern, adding, "Herr Hauptmann?" He couldn't believe it. Was this another fairytale? Where were these tickets and papers?

"You're to report to Army HQ in two weeks. It's all been arranged. Kruger agreed and signed off on it. You'll have all the papers and passes you need, as I said."

"Thank you, Herr Hauptmann," said Morgenstern. Two weeks! That would give them around ten days at home first! "I don't know what else to say. We don't know what else to say," he said, looking at Stark, who was overcome and in tears.

Eggar stood up. He smiled. "There isn't much more to say, is there? Go on now," he said, waving a hand towards the door. "I'll have your papers sent over tonight, or you're driver will have them in the morning."

"Thank you again," said Morgenstern, helping Stark out of the room. He turned to close the door. He and Eggar exchanged a look.

"In memory of my brother," Eggar said quietly.

Morgenstern nodded, and shut the door behind him.

*

<u>Really Going</u>

The two men found themselves back in their cottage. They were dazed and overwhelmed and trying to come to terms with what had just happened. Not only were they to live, instead of being shot as deserters, they had also avoided being absorbed into a new Regiment with new people who were hostile to them. And with that of course, came the bonus of not being sent straight back into inevitable combat. But most of all, they were being given home leave! That rare and precious commodity, so coveted by others that it was responsible for almost 20,000 men in the Wehrmacht, across all fronts, deserting every month.

Morgenstern and Stark soon discovered a new, frightening anxiety. What if something happened to them before they departed for Gobulinskiy and the train that would take them west?

"Relax, Wilhelm!" said Morgenstern, lying on his bunk and smoking. He stared up at the ceiling beams above him as he thought of all the possibilities nine or ten days at home with Elke and little Marta promised. He smiled. He was probably *less* relaxed than Stark. He was just better at hiding it.

"How can I fucking relax?!" said Stark, who was in turmoil. He just wanted to leave, *NOW!* "Don't you realise what this means? Home to Berlin, Karl! Home to Greta! And you? Well, it's home to your wife and daughter!"

"Well I fucking know!" said Morgenstern, chuckling. "Where did you think I was going? Stuttgart? Dresden maybe? Visit my grandmother instead?" He laughed again.

"How did this happen Karl!" said Stark then. "I can't get my head around it!"

"Eggar," said Morgenstern simply. "We were lucky; yes, lucky. I admit it. Nothing like a bit of empathy, or sympathy for that matter."

"What?" asked Stark, confused.

"Look, Eggar mentioned his brother, didn't he? Panzer Leutnant? 24th Panzers?"

"Yeah, what of it? What happened to them anyway?"

"They were holed up in the Industrial District. Down to six tanks I heard, and not one of 'em mobile. Tracks shot to pieces. So the lads fire on the Reds where they stand. Some of the tank's turrets were damaged too; unable to rotate, weren't they? It was said a relief battalion were on their way, but nobody knew when. And really, the lads of the 24th didn't have a ghost's chance in hell, the numbers they were up against. But they still held the Reds off. Rumour has it, the relief column's advance party saw them still firing at the Reds when they first caught sight of them."

"And they were wiped out?"

"Yeah," said Morgenstern, sighing. "By the time the relief column got there, the Reds had fucked off and every single man left of the 24th was dead. But it was a damn close call. Had the relief column turned up a couple of hours earlier? Well, who knows? Anyway, my guess is Eggar here is mourning his brother and since he knows we're good sorts, he's decided to help give us a second chance. It's good of him really. I won't forget it."

"And the Colonel?" said Stark. "We don't even know his name."

"Probably true about him not wanting us," said Morgenstern. "Not surprising when you think of it. And how long would either of us have lasted anyway with these bastards? But all in all, yes, it was good of the Colonel to stand up to Kruger."

"How do you mean?" asked Stark. As a Cook, a lot of this was beyond him.

"Eggar told me that if Kruger had had his way, we'd have been shot like poor Theo; to keep things neat and tidy!"

"Jesus Christ!" said Stark, laying on his bunk. He wanted to forget all the intrigue, the horror, the luck or lack of it. He also wanted to forget what he had been through. What they had all been through. Not just in the last few weeks, but everything since they arrived in this hell hole of a country. He was 24 years old and had lived a lifetime's worth of the worst experiences you could imagine. But he was still young enough to get over it perhaps. Now he thought of the six men who had died since they had walked out of Stalingrad. "Do you think about the others, Karl?" he asked.

"I try not to," said the Veteran. "No more than I try not to think about the million lost souls they're part of."

"But we shared something with them for God's sake! Something unique Karl."

"Unique? Are you serious?" said Morgenstern. "We shared a moment in time with a group of men who didn't make it! Does that sound unique to you?"

"You know damn well what I mean!"

"Yes, Wilhelm, I know what you mean. I'm sorry they're not here. Here with us now, looking forward to seeing their loved ones again. But they're not. That's how it is. What-."

"Alright Karl," said Stark, sounding dismayed.

He closed his eyes. Reuters, the teenager, who died horribly. Wagner, whom he buried himself and none of the others knew. Voss, the broken Panzer Commander. Huber, the Padre and perhaps the most pitiable of them all. How he suffered, tormented by guilt. And old Jürgen. Well, not old really, but worn down by the war. Practical to the end. And Benz, whose fate would haunt him for a long time. He'd come so close.

Eventually, the two men slept. Later, feeling hungry, an experience they were both getting used to again, they chanced a trip to the mess hall. After a difficult series of altercations that mostly involved shouting and threats, they were allowed to help themselves to some bread and sausage. Morgenstern took some cheese and Stark managed to grab a pot of coffee also. "Bastards!" someone in the kitchen shouted after them as they left the kitchen to sit down. Morgenstern thought briefly of bringing everything back to the cottage, but knew the Chain Dogs wouldn't allow it. The last thing they wanted was trouble from them when they were hours away from getting out of here.

So they ate quickly. They were anxious too about the men who would start showing up here soon for their evening meal. Stark wolfed down his food. He didn't like being exposed here, only feeling comfortable in their cottage. Morgenstern broke the silence.

"What'll you do Wilhelm, when you get home?" he asked.

"Dunno really, now that you mention it," said Stark, chomping on some bread. "Haven't really thought about it. Just be glad to get there and see Greta. Take it as it comes I suppose. As long as I'm with her, I don't really care."

"Yeah, absolutely. Me too. Shit we can't tell them we're coming."

"It'll be wonderful, Karl! A great surprise for them."

I hope so, thought Morgenstern. I do hope so. I hope they're well and everything is ok. "I'm sure it will," he said for Stark's sake.

"Should we look Eggar up?" asked Stark, his food nearly finished.

"For what!"

"To check on our papers and tickets. Jesus!" said Stark, draining his coffee mug. "What if he's looking for us right now! While we're in here, feeding our faces!"

"Relax Wilhelm, for Christ's sake," said Morgenstern. "You're enough to give a man indigestion. If that's the case, he'll find us alright. Anyway, he'll send a Clerk. He said so, remember? This evening or in the morning."

"And who's going to drive us? One man do you think, or will we have to share a truck with others?"

"How the fuck should I know? What difference will it make? As long as we go right?"

"I suppose so," said Stark.

They stayed for a few more minutes. Eventually, Morgenstern leant back on his bench and lit a cigarette. It was Stark's cue to stand up.

"Come on Karl. Let's go, eh?"

Morgenstern sighed. He got up, buttoning the top button of his greatcoat and followed Stark back to the cottage. Going inside, they could hear the sounds of trucks, tanks and other assorted transport, moving around the town. Laying on their bunks, they both soon became anxious. Dusk was approaching which meant they probably had another twelve hours or so to wait.

It was a long night. Around 9pm, came a knock at the door. A Chain Dog neither of them recognised shoved a thick brown envelope towards Morgenstern who'd answered it. He turned and left without a word. Slamming the door after him, Morgenstern emptied the contents of the envelope onto Stark's bunk.

"My God!" he exclaimed. There were travel passes for both of them, with their full names and units. These allowed them one month's travel. Train tickets for Gobulinskiy to Kiev. More tickets for Kiev to Warsaw, and finally, tickets for Warsaw to Berlin. Then there were two smaller envelopes with their names on the front, addressed to a 'Desk WH/III/2A' in Army HQ, Berlin. These would verify their current status and allow for them to be transferred to other Regiments or re-absorbed into their original units if they still existed. There were also temporary 'papers' for both of them, which in effect were their all important *Personalausweis* or Identity Document. Without it, they could be arrested, imprisoned or even shot. Finally, there was a small unmarked envelope that contained a generous amount of money for presumably, their expenses and food.

Now Morgenstern *was* stunned. The reality of it all was finally brought home to him. "My God!" he said again, sitting on his bunk and staring at the papers. He fumbled for his cigarettes. Stark was in a semi-stupor. When he gathered himself, he began looking through the assortment of paper.

"We're really going!" he said finally. "We're...really going...home! Everything is signed by the Colonel. Oberst Heinrich Muller. Stamped too!"

"Anything from Eggar?" asked Morgenstern then. "A note? Anything?"

"No," said Stark. "Nothing."

"It's going to be a hell of a trip. A real trek."

"Where did the money come from, Karl?"

"Regiment funds? Who cares?"

"There's forty Reichsmarks; civilian."

Then it's not Regiment money, thought Morgenstern. Someone slipped that in personally. Eggar, he decided. Military banknotes were printed especially for the Army, Navy and Airforce. The notes were marked as such and looked differently from civilian banknotes.

"That's twenty each then," said Morgenstern. "More than enough for food and a few beers."

"Will we get more money at Army HQ?" asked Stark, thinking ahead. "We're going to need more at home."

"Maybe," said Morgenstern. He tried to remember when he'd last been paid properly. "I don't know about you, but I'm owed about eight months back pay!" he said, not expecting to see anything like it. "Perhaps they'll let us have half? Who knows?"

"I haven't been paid since I left Greta back in Berlin. Jesus Christ, that's almost a year ago now! Do you think they're being looked after?"

"I damn well hope so," said Morgenstern, who remembered the street food kitchens back in the early thirties. "Credit notes probably. Like they dished out when we were in France."

"Mmmm," said Stark. He'd know soon enough, he told himself, brightening at the thought. "We should get ready."

"We've got hours yet. It's not like we have any packing to do," said Morgenstern, chuckling. "Besides, nothing will happen till after dark. I'll bet they'll want us to slip away unnoticed. Anyway it'll be up to the driver. My best guess would be after midnight at the earliest. Around 4am at the latest. You should get some sleep."

"How can I fucking sleep!" said Stark, handing Morgenstern his papers, tickets and money. "I can't even sit still! I'll sleep on the road or the train."

"Well," said Morgenstern, "you won't mind if I do." He folded everything neatly and put them in a tunic breast pocket. They were more precious than gold bars. Lying down, he said, "I hope we get going sooner rather than later. Be just our luck for the Reds to attack the town before we leave."

"Goddamn you Karl for even saying that!"

Both men laughed. "Sleep, really," said Morgenstern. "It'll help pass the time."

"Maybe later," said Stark. He was rereading every word on every piece of paper set out in front of him on his bunk like a makeshift game of solitaire. He was still reading when Morgenstern started snoring.

*

Road Trip

Morgenstern woke around 2am to the noise of heavy traffic, and shouts and commands being barked by a variety of voices. "Been at it for a couple of hours," said Stark, looking over at him.

Morgenstern sat up and found himself instinctively searching for cigarettes in his coat pockets. But then he threw off his blanket and sat on the edge of his bunk looking for his boots. He went outside, the sound deafening now from the Regiment moving out of Marinovka. He relieved himself in the same bushes as always and lighting a Juno, he stood and watched the commotion around him. Trucks, some full of men, some full of equipment, roared past him. He could hear but not see, tanks and half-tracks, somewhere not far away, grinding their way through the night. Then there were columns of men marching. Morgenstern recognised the downward look of most of them. It was a look of uncertainty, apprehension and trepidation that every soldier who'd experienced combat knew well.

"Well, they're on their way," he said, coming back inside and closing the door. "Did you sleep?"

"An hour maybe, earlier," said Stark. "Where's our ride?"

"It's early yet; there's time," said Morgenstern. "This won't end today. There'll be people left behind who'll follow on later. Especially the brass."

"I couldn't stand waiting another fucking day!"

"We'll have to if it comes to that. Haven't you had enough of trekking through the woods? Aren't you used to a soldier's lot by now? Spend half our sodding time waiting around!"

"I'm not a soldier, am I? I'm a Cook! When you lot get to where you're going, who's always fucking there with a meal ready for you?"

"That's true," said Morgenstern.

"Anyway, this damn place is driving me mad! I keep expecting something to happen -."

"Look, if they went to the trouble of providing us with papers, which would have been a morning's work by the way, they're not going to forget our ride. Just relax, he'll be here."

Stark stretched out on his bunk and leant on an elbow. "What's the last thing you did with your family Karl, before heading out here?"

"Oh now, let me think," said Morgenstern, lighting a fresh Juno. He too leant on an elbow to face Stark. "I assume you mean before leaving them at the station?"

"Well yeah, of course."

"The day before I left we just stayed at home. An ordinary family day, you know. Marta was what, three years old then, yeah, in '41, three! Wait till you have kids, Wilhelm. Time passes so quickly. Suddenly, they're so big and running around, getting into all sorts of mischief. You have to watch 'em like a hawk!"

Stark smiled, enjoying Morgenstern's obvious delight. "What were her first words?" he asked then, still smiling. Morgenstern lay on his back and drew on his Juno. He suddenly realised he had never told anyone before.

"My daughter's a mute Wilhelm. She will never speak and she will never hear me tell her how much I love her."

"Oh Karl, I'm sorry," said Stark. "I shouldn't-."

"Why is everyone sorry?" said Morgenstern. "Like it's a curse or something?"

Stark nearly said sorry again. "I was just-."

"It's ok, Wilhelm. When she was born, I was sorry too. It's a natural feeling, but do you think I would swap her for another? She is the joy of my life, together with Elke. She is happy and so far unaware that she is different to other kids. Hell, she plays with enough of 'em on our street. They don't treat her any different; least, not yet. You know Wilhelm, if we left things to the kids, this world would be a better place."

"Couldn't be any worse," said Stark, chuckling. "But this will end one day Karl, and we can live our lives in a better world."

"Well, we'll see," said Morgenstern, not believing it. He didn't expect to survive the war anyway.

"So," said Stark, "I took Greta to the zoo!" Morgenstern looked at him and smiled. "What?" asked Stark, smiling also.

"Nothing," said Morgenstern. "I was just thinking about what you could have been doing with a pretty wife, instead of going to the zoo!" He laughed; Stark joining him.

"Well, there was that," he said. "Later. But Greta said let's have a day out. So, the zoo it was. She loved the monkeys! Said they were like little people. She kept saying this one reminded her of a neighbour. That one reminded her of someone else. We laughed so much that day."

"That's good, Wilhelm," said Morgenstern. "That's a nice memory to carry in your heart. There will be others."

Stark suddenly wept. "The others," he said then. "Theo, Huber, poor Hugo. All of them. Do they still have their memories?"

Morgenstern said nothing for a while. He wasn't sentimental, or religious, and thought carefully about what he should say. He wanted to stop Stark thinking this way. So far, there were a million German casualties in this part of the war. All of them had families, parents, loved ones. It wasn't just a tragedy; it was a national catastrophe. And what of the Russians?

"Wilhelm," he said eventually. "All one can do in this life, is concentrate on what we have, what brings us joy. For me, it's my wife and daughter. For you, it's Greta, and the family you *will* have. If we think about things too much, well, where will it end? Think of the future, not the past. You said it yourself, just now. This will end one day."

"Yes, you're right," said Stark, trying hard to take Morgenstern's advice.

There was little else to do but wait. Both men checked and rechecked their tickets and papers. Morgenstern counted his Reichsmarks over and over as if making sure they were real and actually in his hands. He stuffed them in a tunic pocket and lit the last cigarette from his second last tin. He made sure the last tin was in his coat pocket.

Stark got up from his bunk and paced the room. "Come on for fuck sake!" he muttered to himself. Morgenstern ran a hand through his hair. The single candle that lit the room was almost spent so he got up to get another from a box on the windowsill near Stark's bunk. He lit a new one and jammed it down on a table beside the old one, wedged between a gap in the wood.

Not long afterwards, their ordeal ended. A Kubelwagen pulled up outside. They waited. Nothing. No knock at the door. Stark looked at Morgenstern who shrugged, making to get up from his bunk. Stark opened the door slowly. Two Chain Dogs sat in the front of the small car. There was no roof and one of the rear doors facing them was open.

"Come on then for fuck sake! Haven't got all day!" the driver shouted.

They got in the back; Stark first. Morgenstern couldn't get the open door to close, which explained why it was open. Once settled, he looked at Stark, who still wasn't fully convinced they were going anywhere and this was all a great big lie. He tried to block out the thought that they were to be driven into the woods and shot!

The car pulled away abruptly; the open rear door banging against it's frame. They were at least not following the main column of vehicles and men but instead, took a turn that led them away from the town in almost the opposite direction on a narrow road that went into the darkness. The driver flicked a switch somewhere and dim headlights came on to help light their way.

"Where are you taking us?" asked Morgenstern, exchanging an anxious look with Stark.

"Gobulinskiy," said the Chain Dog passenger. "That's where you're headed isn't it?"

"How long will it take?"

The Chain Dog pulled a watch from his pocket. "We'll be there for breakfast." The driver chuckled. Morgenstern leant back in his seat, grabbing the door to stop it banging.

"What time is it now?" asked Stark.

"Questions, questions," said the driver, looking over his shoulder.

"It's just after three," said his companion.

So about two and a half hours, give or take, thought Stark. Could be worse, the look on Morgenstern's face was saying as they exchanged another look.

The freezing onrushing air was quickly becoming unbearable and they sank low in their seats to try and escape the worst of it. But there was no keeping warm and as usual in this winter hell of a country, they resorted to tried and tested methods of not freezing to death. Morgenstern remembered the early days of the first winter he experienced in Russia. Back then, he had been in Rostov, on the Don river. No one was prepared for the sudden brutal temperatures and by November 1941, he and other NCO's had learnt to replace sentries every 10-15 minutes, otherwise they would freeze to death.

The two MP's upfront, with the benefit of the car's windscreen and proper winter clothing, chatted among themselves. It was impossible to hear them through the noise of the crude vehicle.

And you had to shout to make yourself heard. Morgenstern persisted though. Thoughts of Kruger and his 'solution', urged him on.

"Where are you two headed?" he asked.

The driver shook his head as his companion swung around in his seat. "Look, I don't want to talk to you. He doesn't want to talk to you," he said, jabbing a thumb towards the driver. "All you two need to know is we're bringing you where we were told to bring you. It's just an errand for the Colonel. Where we go after that is none of your fucking business! Unless you fancy a detour!" He swung back around. The driver chuckled. That word, 'detour', was a reference to trips made off the beaten track, usually to execute prisoners or deserters. They were almost always inevitably one way.

Morgenstern eyed the man in the dashboard mirror. "Why do you have to be such bastards," he muttered. The Chain Dog heard him though.

"Don't push your fucking late mate," he said, glowering back. The driver looked at him.

"Perhaps he'd like to hear about their chances of getting to Kiev," he said, chuckling again.

"Yeah, fuck it, I forgot to tell you," said the driver's companion. "You've got a slim chance of getting to Kiev, mate, on account of the Reds' fly boys shooting up the train regular like. Even if you get to Kiev, you'll *never* get to Warsaw and you've got fuck all chance of getting home from there anyway! Only trains running back and forth are full of men and cargo coming this way!"

Both of the MP's laughed. Morgenstern hadn't thought about that aspect of their trip. He berated himself for forgetting about that danger. But when he thought about it, would it stop him getting on the train? Would it stop him trying to go home to Elke and Marta? *Tausendmal Nein!* he thought.

Stark looked at him, his face full of dread. "Is that true?" he asked.

"They're just being bastards," said Morgenstern, as low as he could to be heard. "It's bullshit," he added, trying to calm the Cook. "The Reds have hardly anything left that flies. And anyway, our own fliers won't let them get off the sodding ground if they do!"

In fact, after the initial invasion of Russia, which saw most of their air power decimated, the

Russians had amassed a newer, bigger and better airforce. They were still no match for the Luftwaffe, but again, it was all about numbers. No matter how many Russian planes were shot down by increasingly exhausted German pilots, there were twenty more to replace them. And new Russian pilots were taking to the air with perhaps ten hours of flight training. Numbers, numbers. The German state couldn't compete with Russia's industrial production of planes, tanks or anything else for that matter. Least of all men.

Morgenstern bit his lip which bled and froze immediately. He convinced himself that what he'd told Stark was true. No Russian planes would be in the air that far west, would they? Still, it nagged at him. Stark, he knew, wouldn't be convinced, but what could he say to appease him? Fuck these two bastards for bringing it up, he thought. He thought quickly what it took to become a member of the Feldgendarmerie, or Military Field Police. Nicknames among the Wehrmacht rank and file, apart from Chain Dog, or *Kettenhunde,* included *Heldenklauer,* or Hero Snatcher, because they scoured hospital trains looking for malingerers, who they would summarily execute. And for tracking down deserters, some called them *Kopf Jagers,* or Head Hunters.

Morgenstern decided they started out as school bully's, later graduating to prison warders or sanatorium staff, where they could bully the 'lunatics' or 'inmates' to their hearts content. Some of the moderately educated became small town policemen who would later join the Military Police. An ideal job for the average coward who enjoyed bullying others who couldn't defend themselves, while at the same time avoiding the danger of front line action.

The rest of the road trip to Gobulinskiy was uneventful, if not torturous in the freezing air. But eventually, the battered Kubelwagen pulled up outside what looked like a freight train yard. Morgenstern and Stark could see two trains on two tracks, facing in opposite directions and further away, what might have been a small platform.

"Out with you!" said the driver. "Come on!"

They got out and stood at the side of an empty road. Everything looked deserted, not least because there wasn't a light to be seen anywhere.

"What a pair of bastards," said Stark, watching the two Chain Dogs disappear into the night.

"Least we're rid of them," said Morgenstern, lighting a Juno. "Come on, let's hope we're in the right place!"

Stark followed him and they stumbled around in the dark, looking for some kind of entrance. After a couple of wrong turns and dead ends, they managed to find the platform which seemed to be a temporary structure put together in a hurry. There seemed to no one around; no guards, railway staff or anyone. Then Stark noticed a dim light coming from a shed further down the walkway. Inside, they found an *Ostbahn* train guard who seemed startled to see anyone at this hour of the day. A clock on the wall read 05.40. The guard relaxed when he saw the uniforms in the light. Morgenstern and Stark were equally relieved to find someone around.

"Is this Gobulinskiy?" asked the Veteran, sitting on a crate. Stark sat on another.

"Yes, it is," said the guard, his German accent obvious. What was his story? Morgenstern thought absently.

"When is the next train to Kiev?" he asked.

"Around eight o'clock," said the guard, getting up to attend to a pot of boiling water bubbling away on a stove. He noticed the relief on the faces of these two. Where the hell have they come from? he wondered. "Want some coffee?" he asked, satisfied they were no threat.

"Yes please," said Morgenstern and Stark together.

"Okay. Be right with you," said the guard, reaching for several tin mugs. "Where have you two come from then?"

*

Heroes and Thoughts of Home

It was almost 8.30 when the train pulled out, heading for Kiev. There seemed to be a delay in loading some crates into a boxcar at the far end of the train. Morgenstern and Stark watched the process from the platform, standing in front of one of two actual passenger carriages. The rest of the train was made up of boxcars and flat-bed wagons.

When it looked like they were about to get going, the two travellers went back inside their carriage and retook their seats. There were a few military men scattered around who were obviously homeward bound as well. All of them were Officers and Morgenstern and Stark felt a little conspicuous as they faced each on their wooden seats. "Doesn't surprise me," said Morgenstern, once the train was finally leaving. "No leave for the poor bastards doing the real work," he added, winking at Stark, who smiled briefly.

Some Officers had walked past them, to find a seat where they could be alone. There were one or two looks of disapproval, but no one really paid them much attention. While Stark relaxed and looked out the window, Morgenstern made mental notes of their ranks and regiments, trying to place them in the vast theatre of the Wehrmacht's operations with the help of his memory and what he knew.

Then a Luftwaffe Hauptmann entered the carriage. He carried a silver-topped baton that might have been presented to him at some time, but Morgenstern decided he might have bought it as an accessory or even had it made. His stylish and well tailored uniform had the purple and grey flashes of his rank; his tunic covered in badges and ribbons. What really caught Morgenstern's eye however before the Hauptmann buttoned his greatcoat against the cold, was his Iron Cross. It was a Knights Cross, with Oak Leaves and Swords. This meant that he had shot down at least 300 enemy aircraft. Morgenstern guessed correctly that also meant he'd probably flown 800-1000 missions. He wondered for the umpteenth time how a small number of men seemed to be untouchable by danger, fate and death. It was a mystery he would never solve. Still, he acknowledged the real-life walking hero and he was struck by how rare it probably was to see such a man alive.

He joined Stark in looking out the window; wiping a circle of condensation first with his sleeve. Would they ever escape the fucking cold! He stared at dull, grey tree-lined fields that made him think of the Moon and then leant his head back while closing his eyes. Now there was a sudden commotion at the far end of the carriage. The Luftwaffe hero had found a civilian skulking on a seat he had intended to take. "Out with you!" ordered the hero. "Out!" he roared again.

The civilian, perhaps a local of some esteem who had been allowed to board the train, stood up and glared at the Luftwaffe Hauptmann while he adjusted his suit and tie. He tried to leave with the requisite amount of disgust, walking past Morgenstern and Stark with as much dignity as he could muster. But he left all the same and without a word, going into the other passenger carriage. If someone took a dislike to his presence in there, he was in trouble.

"What's up?" asked Stark, coming out of his reverie and looking around.

"A war hero wants to be alone," said Morgenstern, smiling. "He must have an ego the size of a sodding Zeppelin!"

"Look Karl," said Stark, resuming his vigil at the window. "Doesn't it seem normal?"

Morgenstern glanced at the Russian countryside rushing past them. "Yeah, it does," he said. "Strange when you think of the other world only a few miles behind us."

"Wait till we get home," said Stark. "I can't wait to see Berlin!"

"Me neither," said Morgenstern, heartened at the thought. Will we recognise it? he wondered. It's been so long and so much has befallen the city. Even if there had been no bombing raids by the British and Americans, Morgenstern felt sure his experiences would forever distort his view of his home. How do you go from the horrors of Stalingrad to walking down a Berlin street? he asked himself. It won't be easy either trying to carry on at home even with Elke and little Marta, but it's only going to be a week or so and he was determined to try and make sure it went well for everybody. Would Marta even recognise him? Or know who he was? He felt sure she would. He never entertained the thought that he would survive the war and return home for good. That was just reckless fantasy.

Stark thought about Greta. He also knew that life for them both would be forever different and changed, but he convinced himself that things could slowly return to normal. A lot depended on Greta, he also knew, but he trusted her to help them find their way. He sat back and closed his eyes; trying to see her in his mind. Trying to relive his memories of her. But at first, all he could manage was the nightmare of her standing across a vast room weeping as if in mourning; a black veil covering her face.

Morgenstern looked at him and decided to try and sleep. He lay on the bench but it was, of course, not long enough and quickly proved to be uncomfortable. The movement of the train with it's apparent lack of suspension didn't help either, but he nonetheless kept at it, eventually drifting off.

*

Later, a tired and stressed looking Flak NCO entered the carriage abruptly. "Keep your heads down!" he shouted, rushing down the aisle. "Reds in the air!"

Morgenstern bolted awake and sat up. "What's up, mate?" he asked, grabbing the NCO's arm as he went past, and forgetting he wore a Private's uniform.

The NCO quickly pulled his arm free. "What I just fucking said," he shouted, not stopping. "Couple of 'Flying Tanks' coming this way!" he roared over his shoulder, before disappearing into the next carriage. This was not only alarming news, but filled most of those in the carriage with foreboding.

"Shit!" said Morgenstern, looking through the window and up at the sky. "So much for Luftwaffe air superiority around here!"

"Are we in trouble?" asked Stark, gripping his seat with both hands.

"Yeah, you could say that! Red Shturmoviks! Ground attack fighter bombers! Ever seen 'em before?"

"No. I-."

"Lucky you!" said Morgenstern. "Bastards are dangerous! I'm not talking about the old bi-planes they used to have that you could bring down with a slingshot! These are a match for our fly boys and very hard to shoot down! Take a lot of punishment. That's why they're called 'Flying Tanks'!"

"What fucking nonsense!" said the Luftwaffe hero, now pacing up and down the aisle, looking out the windows. "A trench rat's perspective I think," he added, looking down at Morgenstern and Stark with disdain. They exchanged knowing glances but kept quiet.

The train had a flat-bed wagon at either end; one behind the locomotive and it's coal wagon. Each flat-bed had a couple of 20mm Flakvierling 38 light anti-aircraft cannon, surrounded by sandbags. Each cannon required a crew of 6 and there were also four men armed with two MG42 heavy machine guns. Morgenstern didn't envy them.

Sure enough, one then another, lumbering aircraft could be heard getting nearer and nearer to the train. "Get fucking down!" Morgenstern shouted, pulling Stark with him as he ducked under their seats. Now the familiar sound of the machine guns rang out, followed by the repetitive slow dull thud of the Flak cannon.

"Oh Jesus!" Stark cried out, his hands clutching his ears.

The Russian fighter bombers seemed to be directly overhead and then there was an explosion as they seemed to slowly disappear. Next came the noise of Luftwaffe fighters, pursuing the Russians as the train slowly slowed down and came to a halt. The Luftwaffe hero, who hadn't moved a muscle from where he stood in the aisle, now lit a cigarette he took from a solid gold case. He grunted and then sighed heavily, retaking his chosen seat as before.

Apart from him, everyone else piled out of the carriage and stood by the tracks, looking in the direction of smoke that was pouring out of a boxcar at the far end. It had been a close call for the men in the flat-bed wagon beside it, but no one was injured. An Ostbahn guard ran past the group heading for the smoking boxcar. Morgenstern lit a Juno and sat down on a pile of spare sleepers. Stark joined him. "Took seconds," he said, still breathing hard.

"That's all they need," said Morgenstern. He felt the familiar relief of survival. "Maybe they knew our boys were after them. Should have fucked off. Couldn't resist having a go, I suppose."

"Wonder what's in the cars?" said Stark, watching the Ostbahn guard trying to douse the flames with an extinguisher. Other men, from the flat-bed wagon were gathering around him now. Then the train's Engineer walked past; going to see the damage for himself.

"Who knows?" said Morgenstern. "Can't be much of anything important. Going our way? Be a different fucking story when we head back," he added, dreading the thought.

"We should help," said Stark then, standing up and looking anxiously down the track.

"Not now. Please Wilhelm, relax and sit back down. They have it under control. If they want us, they'll shout!"

Now the Ostbahn guard was hacking at the boxcar's door with an axe, and everyone around him jumped out of the way as it collapsed to one side, though still attached to the train. The Engineer was shouting at the guard, who shouted back, throwing the axe on the ground.

"Christ!" said Stark, looking at the boxcar's door, hanging at a hundred degree angle, just off the ground and close to the line's bank. One of the Flak gunners was jumping up and down on it now, in an effort to free it, while the Engineer started screaming at him instead of the guard.

"Come on Karl," said Stark, walking away in that direction. Morgenstern sighed, reluctantly getting up and following him.

"Where's the nearest siding?" the guard was asking the Engineer when they got there.

"Behind us! Next one is about 20 kilometres ahead! We need to uncouple this lot!" the Engineer said, waving a hand at the damaged boxcar and the flat-bed wagon behind it.

"Are you fucking kidding?!" the Flak NCO who'd warned everyone earlier, shouted as he joined the fight. "We can't afford to lose the flat-bed and the fire power! What if the Reds come back?!"

"I'm not fucking backtracking!" the Engineer screamed now, almost hysterical. "And I'm sure as hell not going forward either! See the fucking door?! It'll eventually hit something on the bank and then the whole sodding train will be derailed! And who was the fucking genius who started hacking at the fucking door in the first place?!" the Engineer screamed again, waving his arms around like a windmill. He rounded on the Ostbahn guard.

"Can't we get the door off?" asked a young Infantry Leutnant with one arm in a sling. His other arm was missing. "We could blow it off surely with a couple of grenades."

Everyone looked at him in silence. "Christ Jesus!" said the Engineer. He spat dismissively, grabbed the Flak NCO's arm and dragged him away.

As the gathering slowly broke up amid derisive laughter and quiet mumblings, Morgenstern and Stark peered into the smoky gloom of the boxcar. It was shot to pieces. The fire now out, blackened, scorched straw covered it's floor. Two crates stood at one end. One was untouched and contained a tank engine from a Panzer Mark IV. The other crate, obviously hit by the Russian fighter bombers, had contained a generator, but little of it remained. Huge thick splinters of the crate were scattered around, mixed with parts of the exploded generator; some were even embedded in the boxcar's walls. Both the tank engine and the generator would have gone to Kiev for repair.

"Jesus Christ!" said Stark. "What if the Reds had hit the flat-bed instead?"

"Probably what they aimed for," said Morgenstern. "Lucky bastards really," he added, watching the Flak crews smoking as they relaxed on the bank.

After an hour or so, it had been decided. There was little alternative anyway. The damaged boxcar, with the flat-bed wagon attached, including it's precious cannon, was to be uncoupled from the train and abandoned where they were. Word would be sent back later to have the track cleared.

When everyone had resumed their seats in their carriages, they were completely shocked after finding the Luftwaffe hero had shot himself after drinking a whole bottle of Schnapps. His Luger pistol was in his right hand and he seemed asleep except for the huge hole in the back of his head; while much of his brain, skull and gore still dripped down the window beside the seat that he fought to have to himself earlier.

It took another hour to have him carried out of the carriage while the Ostbahn guard took a bucket of water and cloths to clear up the mess, but eventually the train crawled away, heading to Kiev. Morgenstern watched Stark slowly fall asleep as he pondered the price you must have to pay to receive a Knights Cross with Oak Leaves and Swords. He decided his widow would get little or no comfort from it when it was finally presented to her.

*

So Much For Kiev

"I am so hungry!" said Stark, forgetting already what it was like to be half-starved everyday as they had been for so long. "First thing we do when we pull in is to find some food and a beer!"

"Sounds good, but be careful with your money," said Morgenstern, his mind full of images of litre glasses of lager. He'd forgotten how a good beer tasted. "We've a long way to go and you should keep at least half for when you get home. You're going to need it."

"Yes Grandad," said Stark, smiling.

"Sorry, you're right," said Morgenstern, feeling like an idiot.

Looking out the window, Kiev was a very different place to Gobulinskiy and it's surrounds. It was a bustling city, albeit under German Wehrmacht occupation, not a provincial backwater. Although it was nearly 4pm, it was already dark; dusk had come and gone even at this early hour. The station was a hub of activity and the two men fought their way through the crowd, made up mainly of military personnel. There were civilians but few of these were local Russians.

Morgenstern looked for train times on a board high above the inside of the entrance. It was blank except for some old notices in Cyrillic that he couldn't read. Frowning he glanced around for a Railway Guard. He spotted one beside some gates to their right. "Come on," he said, starting to walk over. Stark followed him. When they got to the guard, Morgenstern asked him for the next train to Warsaw.

"That's it there," said the guard, pointing. "You'd better hurry. Should have left ten minutes ago!"

Morgenstern started to run. "Karl!" Stark shouted. "Fucking wait, can't you!" Morgenstern stopped, but kept looking at the train which was perhaps a hundred metres away on a far platform.

"Wilhelm!" he pleaded.

"When is the next one?" Stark was asking the guard. His first thought was food. He looked at Morgenstern, who was now walking backwards.

"Two trains a week to Warsaw," said the guard tiredly. "Tuesday and Friday."

Today was Tuesday. Stark started to run. "Come on then," he shouted as he tore past the Veteran.

"If we miss it, I'm going to beat you to death, right here, right now!" Morgenstern shouted as he ran, racing after Stark who showed a talent for sprinting.

They came to the gates where a guard checked their tickets. Breathing hard, they began to walk quickly up the platform. The train's air horn blew from the locomotive and then a guard stepped down from the last carriage, ready to blow his whistle. Morgenstern and Stark started to quicken their pace. "Wait!" Stark shouted. The guard seemed ready to do so.

"That was fucking close!" said Morgenstern. "From now fucking on-." His admonition of Stark was interrupted by a high pitched shout from behind them.

"Halt! Zuruck kommt ihr beide. Jetzt!" Back you both come. Now! Morgenstern and Stark froze. They knew immediately who it was from the tone. Morgenstern gestured to the guard, who had his whistle in his mouth now. Please wait! Please! his expression said. Then he and Stark slowly turned around. Two young Gestapo *Kriminalassistents* stood by the gates, looking at them. They weren't going to move. One of them beckoned the two men. They had no choice but to turn back.

"Fucking fucking hell!" said Morgenstern under his breath, as they walked.

"The next fucking train is fucking Friday!" said Stark, almost in tears.

"What?!" said Morgenstern, out loud, aghast.

They reached the two Secret Policemen. "Papers! Passes!" one of them snapped. They handed them over. "Where have you two come from?"

"Gobulinskiy, Herr Kriminalassistent," said Morgenstern, blood pounding in his ears. This kid looked about eighteen!

"I can fucking see that!" said the one on their left. "Before Gobulinskiy! Your point of origin!?"

Morgenstern hesitated. He knew instinctively if he said Stalingrad, they'd be going nowhere today except to the local Gestapo HQ for questioning that could last an hour, or a week. "Marinovka, Herr Kriminalassistent!" he said, remembering the name.

That meant nothing to the young Gestapo man. He in turn not wanting to show his ignorance of Russian geography or where indeed the Wehrmacht were spread across it, remained silent.

The train guard blew his whistle once more. Stark couldn't help looking over his shoulder. He began a silent prayer. The Gestapo men examined their papers as if there was all the time in the world. They seemed oblivious to the train's imminent departure, and couldn't care less if these two common soldiers missed it. What they did care about was the chance to arrest someone for not having the correct papers, passes or anything really. They were golden poster boys for the Hitler Youth Movement.

Seeing however, that Morgenstern and Stark had everything they needed, and that all seemed in order, they reluctantly handed them back their papers and passes without a word.

"Herr Kriminalassistent?" Morgenstern said, as he put his away.

"You can go!" said one of the Policemen. They turned and walked away.

Morgenstern mumbled his thanks after them as was expected and he and Stark turned and ran for the train. The guard, who'd watched it all, climbed up into the carriage and left the door open for them. They thanked him as they boarded the train for Warsaw.

"Should be some seats about half way up," he said, pointing with his chin as he closed the carriage door. Then he leant out, blowing his whistle one last time and waving an olive flag for the locomotive's Engineer to see. The train finally started to move, tortuously slowly, out of Kiev Station.

*

It was very different from the one they had taken from Gobulinskiy. It had many more carriages, with around the same amount of goods boxcars but no wagons or armaments. There was little need because no Russian forces of consequence were this far west; especially their airforce. The train was also near capacity as far as passengers were concerned. Men going west on leave sat with civil servants on official business. Other military personnel were heading west to pick up new equipment destined for the Eastern Front Line. Tanks and trucks could be driven east quicker where they were desperately needed, instead of losing a day or two loading them on and off trains destined for out of the way places. And as far as local civilians were concerned, there were none. To the casual ignorant observer, Kiev might have been any other German city in wartime.

Morgenstern and Stark eventually found a seat after walking through four or five carriages. Sitting opposite them was a Luftwaffe Field Regiment Feldwebel and a portly Panzer Regiment Corporal, who seemed to have lost his left arm. They had been chatting but stopped abruptly when the two newcomers sat down.

"Morgenstern," said the Veteran, by way of an introduction.

"And I'm Stark."

"Berger," said the Staff Sergeant, leaning forward to light Morgenstern's cigarette.

"Ah thanks," he said, leaning back. He glanced at the tank Corporal, whose black uniform seemed to be brand new.

"Er, Scheller," he said. "Gustav."

"You're on leave?" Stark asked, more to break the following silence than anything.

"I am," said Berger.

"And you?" Morgenstern asked, looking at Scheller, who'd remained silent.

"Yes, yes," he said, waving his right arm at his empty left sleeve, which was folded back with a pin. "Permanent leave; at least from the front. I'm to train some new kids apparently."

"What about you two?" asked Berger then. He wasn't sure about Stark, but he knew he wasn't a Front Line soldier. He also knew damned well Morgenstern was. And that he wasn't a Senior Private. This heightened his curiosity as to why they were both wearing the same ill-fitting uniforms.

"Long story," said Morgenstern, tired and trying to think.

"Any food to be had?" Stark asked, trying to change the subject. Berger's eyes narrowed as he looked at Morgenstern.

"We're hungry too," said Scheller, happy to talk about his favourite subject. "Seems we might stop at a place later where we'll be able to get something to eat."

"Long story, you say?" said Berger, not letting up. "Come on then; we've got plenty of time."

Morgenstern looked at him; a thin smile on his lips.

"Very long," said Stark. An uncomfortable silence followed. Berger shrugged, raising an eyebrow. He turned to look out the window, ending the exchange.

"What happened to you?" Stark asked Scheller, looking at his empty sleeve. Morgenstern turned his attention to the Corporal.

"Not what you might think," he said. "Stupid accident really. Slipped climbing into my wagon! Turret hatch slammed down and took my arm off!" He chuckled with embarrassment.

"Well at least you're spared any more of this shit," said Morgenstern. Lucky bastard really, he thought. He wondered briefly if he would willingly lose an arm to escape the madness of going back. He didn't think so.

"It was a close call," said Scheller. "Oh, not my arm," he added. "That healed up well after a spell in hospital. Marvellous surgeon. Highlight of my time out here really," he said, his face betraying a familiar story of horror and personal trauma. "Especially the nurses and the booze ups!"

"How do you mean then?" asked Stark, curious.

"Some bastard Chain Dog officer decided I'd staged it all!" said the Panzer Corporal. "You know, like shooting yourself in the foot. It really was touch and go for a bit. Only for my mates and my C.O., I might have, well, you can guess."

"Plenty of people have done it," said Morgenstern. Berger looked at him again. He bit his lip, wishing he hadn't such a big mouth. "Anyway, you're headed for Berlin?"

"Well, Leipzig eventually," said Scheller then. "Training camp there. But how long will it be before I have to go back? Somewhere."

"By then you won't have to go too far," said Morgenstern.

"That what you think?" asked Berger.

Morgenstern stayed silent. Berger was baiting him he knew. If he wants a fight, he thought, he's picked the wrong man. Instead, Berger looked at Stark.

"Come on Stark," he said. "Where do you two hail from? Kiev? Kharkov maybe? What?"

Stark looked at Morgenstern for help, who sighed.

"We came out of Stalingrad," he said quietly. Berger's expression gave away his surprise.

"Really?" said Scheller. "But how? We've all heard rumours. The Reds can't have taken the place, surely?"

"Probably. By now, yeah," said Morgenstern. "But you won't be reading about it in Der Adler any time soon," he added. This was the Luftwaffe's news magazine. He waited for Berger's response.

"Well you must have quite a story to tell," said the Staff Sergeant, his curiosity satisfied. He held up a hand. "Don't talk about it if you don't want to. I have to say though, from what I've heard, you're damned lucky to be sitting there!"

"You could say that," said Stark, smiling briefly.

"It was another close call," said Morgenstern, looking over at Scheller, who blinked in reply. "We lost some friends along the way."

"Well, now you're going home. At least for a while," said Berger. Mutual respect was thus established.

"Yeah," said Morgenstern. Then he noticed Berger's ribbons and decorations. Among them was an Iron Cross and a Silver Shield on his left upper sleeve. "You were in Cholm?" he said.

"Yes, yes I was," said Berger.

"Then you know about loss," said Morgenstern.

"Loss?" said Berger, frowning. "We held out. We were-."

"I mean loss of those around you."

"Oh yes, pardon me. Of course," said Berger. "It was hellish. But in Stalingrad, how did-."

"Believe me friend," this time from Stark, "everything you've heard is true. If we told you all there is to know, well, you wouldn't believe us."

"I might," said Berger, desperate to hear it. "Try me."

Morgenstern smiled. He is a nosy bastard, he decided. "Tell us about Cholm," he said. "I've heard bits and pieces, but you were there. Quite a time by all accounts."

They all waited. Scheller was eager to hear this new story. He didn't even know where Cholm was. Berger sighed. He was tired of telling the story, at least in length. But in the vain hope that he might hear how these two sitting across from him escaped from Stalingrad, he began.

"We were on our way to Moscow," Berger said, pulling out a pipe that he began to fill from a pouch. "You all know what happened there. We were forced back towards Leningrad. Some others were sent to Cholm. We were supposed to guard and operate the airfield south of Leningrad. Some of our own lads were sent to Cholm too and when the Reds attacked again in January '42, there was the usual confusion and fucking chaos. There had been around 1100 of us. That is, Luftwaffe Regiment men. Then we were divided in half! Half of us stayed in Leningrad; half were rushed to Cholm.

"We thought there'd be enough of us all once we got there, but fuck it, someone must have changed their mind or simply fucked up, because in the end there was barely more than a few thousand and hardly any what you'd call Front Line soldiers! We even had a Battalion of Police Reservists, but where they came from, I never found out."

"How did Scherer expect you to ward off the Reds with a couple of thousand men?" asked Morgenstern in disbelief.

"Oh he knew what he was doing; believe me. Brilliant man really," said Berger, in the way only a survivor could talk of their saviour, General Major Theodor Scherer, who had been in command at Cholm. "There were 6,000 of us to start with, and that figure only went one way. Scherer knew like everyone else that we'd been forsaken. That we were only meant to delay the Reds for a few days." Berger stopped; drawing on his pipe as he stared out the window. Everyone waited in silence for him to continue, if he was up to it.

"It was a fucking nightmare. Words fail me really, or else I'd just end up sounding stupid!"

"I know, we know the feeling," said Morgenstern, leaving Scheller out of that thought. Stark nodded.

"How did it finish up?" he asked.

"We held out and were rescued," said Berger, with little enthusiasm. "There were little more than a thousand of us left when it ended in July '42!"

"My God!" said Stark, looking at Morgenstern.

"We held off over a hundred attacks in those six months!" Berger said casually. "I was at the GPU building with a Captain called Albert Biecker. He got the Knight's Cross for hanging on to the place during March. He was killed four days before we were saved."

"The Shield is something," said Morgenstern then.

"Scherer himself presented them, to us at any rate. I wear it proudly but I would love to forget all about it," said Berger, meaning it.

Stark, who as usual, never said a whole lot, listened intently to Berger's tale while he thought of their old friend, the Padre; Eduard Huber. 'Poor Eduard' as Stark would forever recall him. He often came to mind when Stark heard such tales of heroism or endurance. What would Poor Eduard think about this, or what would Poor Eduard think about that?

Stark would admit to being something of a 'fence-sitter' when it came to God and religion. In the broadest sense, he saw himself as Agnostic, where Morgenstern was a hardened Atheist. He was therefore, happy to be called one of the *'Gottglaubige'* or Believers in God, but not religion. He knew well that this War would vastly increase the numbers of this small minority, and in the Army, and elsewhere, Atheism would become the largest majority. As the silence that followed Berger's short account of Cholm lengthened, he wondered where his beliefs lay.

"What kept you going during those six months?" he asked him.

Berger, who sometimes felt the need to be grandiose, said, "Everyone has their own idea of a God; a crutch if you like. Someone or something that gives them peace; let's them heal. I know, or at least, I knew, men who would read the Bible all day long if you let them. Other men would take to wood carving and one chap I spoke to only yesterday, well, his life is his dogs. He used to breed Shepherds. Some of course would drink anything they could find. Others took to opium, or morphine.

"For me, it was music. Obviously, listening to music in Cholm was….limited. But I learnt to close my eyes and listen to Mozart whenever I liked, from memory. I could hear 'The Marriage of Figaro' in my head as if I was sitting in La Scala, in Milan. I still do.

"What about you?" Berger finished with, looking at Morgenstern.

"What keeps me going? My family; my wife and daughter," he said, without having to think. He felt distanced from this exchange, as he did so often. It meant little to him.

"Yes," said Stark, before he was asked. "My wife..is my life. My dusk and my dawn," he added, with confidence.

Scheller, who had listened, but was naturally reserved, felt Berger looking at him, inviting him to join in and say something. He glanced at Stark. "I'm not religious," he said finally, winking at Morgenstern. That was all he would offer.

The four men stayed silent for another while, pondering no doubt, the madness and horrors that had brought them together. Morgenstern smoked; staring out the window, seeing nothing but the brutal flashes in his head. There'll never be a medal or a fucking shield struck for the poor bastards who passed through Stalingrad. No sir, he decided, you can be sure of that.

*

<u>Dinner at Rovno</u>

The train rolled on. Everyone chatted with each other or with their neighbour. The carriages filled with cigarette smoke quickly. Nobody wanted to open a window because of the cold and anyway, it would have been impossible to do so because the latches were frozen solid. So people played cards, while some others tried to read or even write. Some food was passed around but it was limited to groups of friends. There was the sound of shouts, raucous laughter, anger and even tears. If, however, everyone had stayed silent at the same time for perhaps a minute or so, they would have been able to hear the pitiful wailing and cries coming from the Hospital Wagons at the front of the train.

Originally painted white for winter camouflage, but now a dull grey colour mixed with dirt of all kinds and blackened in places by smoke and coal dust, these boxcars with their red crosses on all sides, were the Devil's own transport. A couple of Doctors would literally spend the whole journey going from one boxcar to the other through connecting doors and walkways. With a Medic to each, these stifling and stench-filled enclosed spaces were testament to the very limits of human endurance. Every conceivable wound serious enough for a poor soul to be allocated a space on the train was here. Each stretcher stacked in rows of bunks on each side, with a narrow aisle in between, represented a personal agony and torment that few people could imagine. It was one reason why Front Veterans wished for a quick and easy death rather than a bad wound. 70% of the men in these wagons would never live to see the train's destination.

But a million miles away in the passenger carriages, men were consumed with their own fears, worries and expectations. Morgenstern shoved Stark off his shoulder again. The Cook had fallen asleep with the motion of the train and not even the frequent jolts and bumps would rouse him now. Morgenstern had stopped smoking. After all, all he had to do was to keep breathing the air around him which resembled a fog wafting through the space. His stomach rumbled and he wondered how much longer it would be before they stopped and had a chance to eat.

Berger and Scheller were now asleep also and he looked around him for someone to ask. Across the aisle, was a young Panzer Engineer Leutnant, who looked up from the thin hardback he was reading to look at Morgenstern, who had caught his eye.

"How much further to Rovno? Do you know?"

The young Leutnant checked his pocket watch. "Not long. An hour maybe? I'm not too sure but I did hear someone speak of it earlier."

"Thanks," said Morgenstern. He closed his eyes which were beginning to sting because of the smoky air. He wanted to sleep to pass the time but couldn't because of his empty stomach and his mind was racing in the background; not allowing him to relax. He thought then of the weeks and months of near starvation he had endured. How also, he had got used to falling asleep, sometimes in mid-sentence with others, as his body decided that it needed rest. How people had really no idea what they were capable of until they were severely tested. This and other thoughts brought him back to thinking how things would be when he got home to Elke and Marta. It was a constant worry that he had pushed to one side since he and Stark had come to terms with the fact that they had been allowed home leave. I won't know till I get there, he said to himself, again.

So he thought of their reunion instead. He imagined seeing the Anhalter Station platform gates as he made his way through the crush of passengers. Little Marta would be five years old now. He would be surprised at how big she'd grown. Then he would spot Elke, who would be waving frantically at him once she'd spotted him in the crowd. As he got nearer to her, would he notice her tears of joy? Eventually he would reach her and dropping whatever he might be carrying, he would embrace and kiss her over and over as she wept with the joy of it. Then he would kneel and embrace his beautiful daughter while Elke knelt beside her and Morgenstern would probably weep then also, as he thanked the Gods and their Angels for this moment.

But it was a cold twist of irony that Elke and Marta would not wait for him at the train station because they were unaware he was coming home. He quickly resolved this in himself by thinking another couple of hours making his way to where they lived made no difference. What mattered was that he was going home at all; alive and relatively well.

A shout from somewhere and he was jolted back to the here and now. "We're here!" There was a slow then sudden commotion as most people stood and made ready to get out and savour the break in the sleepy nowhere that was Rovno. There was nothing to see through the steamed up windows except darkness and while the train took on coal and water, everyone clamoured on the platform while they waited for a seat in the small cafe at it's far end that seemed to be a mile away. Morgenstern had lost Stark in the melee but Berger was with him. Scheller had stayed on the train and he wasn't alone. There were a few men who had probably taken this trip before and were therefore better prepared. "Karl!" came a shout behind him and Morgenstern turned to see Stark fighting his way through the crowd towards him. "Christ Almighty! This is madness!" said Stark as he reached the two men, coughing and wheezing. "The fresh air is a shock!"

"How much time do we have?" Morgenstern asked no one in particular.

"A couple of hours apparently," said someone close by.

"Shit! Won't be enough time!" he said, looking around him.

However, after an hour or so, the crowd thinned out. Patience had run out among most and together with the cold, made most men return to their carriages. Then quickly, Morgenstern, Stark and Berger were inside the cafe. As men left and men arrived, they found themselves being corralled towards a small table near the counter. Four men sat there, but they had finished a meal and empty plates and beer bottles covered the table. When they saw Morgenstern's group approaching, they got up and left after leaving a pile of money behind them.

Sitting down, a small thin man was suddenly in front of them. He dropped a whicker basket on the floor and with one practised movement, cleared the table contents into it. "Three of you?" he shouted over the noise.

"What have you got?" asked Berger, but by then the 'waiter' had disappeared. Morgenstern lit a cigarette while Stark looked around the dingy space, smiling with anticipation. "Looks like goulash?" he said. The waiter reappeared with three bottles of Warsteiner beer which he placed on the table with one hand. Then he was gone again.

"Jesus!" said Morgenstern. "Real bloody beer!"

They drank, smoked and waited. Within ten minutes, three large bowls of goulash were in front of them, with spoons and a small basket of bread. It was a feast. "Two marks, each!" the waiter shouted before disappearing once more.

"My God! It's wonderful!" said Stark, trying a spoon.

Morgenstern thought so too. Berger ate slowly, stopping now and then to take a swig of his beer. Morgenstern finished eating and lit another cigarette, as he savoured his beer, trying to make it last. When everyone had finished, they left their money under a plate and made their way out. Their table was taken before they got back to the platform. Staying where they stood, as there seemed to be nothing happening at the front of the train, which was still taking on coal, they noticed more dead bodies being stretchered off the hospital wagons and piled unceremoniously onto a horse and cart.

"Poor bastards!" said Berger. "I'm heading back in."

"We could be down that end," said Morgenstern.

"Or we could be riding in style on a General's train!" said Stark. "Or better still, flying home! But we're here instead. Come on Karl; I'm freezing!"

Morgenstern followed him back to their carriage. They wouldn't reach Warsaw till the early hours of the following morning and as he retook his seat, he dreaded the thought of several more hours being cooped up in here.

"We've twelve days left of our fortnight," Stark whispered beside him.

"All depends on what they have in store for us at Army HQ," Morgenstern said quietly.

"No need to worry about saving days to come back, is there?"

"Nah, of course not. Long as we show up before our permits run out. They'll give us all the paperwork we need to reach wherever we're going."

Scheller was snoring and Stark glanced at Berger who looked as though he was asleep also. Nevertheless, he kept his voice low. "I can't go back Karl!"

"Why are you suddenly harping on about that again?" the Veteran asked him.

"Dunno really. The food maybe? The beer?"

"Well anyway, you'll fucking have to! You know that deep down! Just enjoy your time with Greta and-."

"I won't be able to, will I? Until I know where I'm going!"

"And you won't fucking know, will you? Till it's over! Jesus, Wilhelm!"

"That's why me and Greta will run! To Sweden!"

Morgenstern turned to face him and gripped his nearest arm. "Don't be a fucking arsehole! You'll never make it! Long before you get to fucking Hamburg! Which by the way, will be crawling with U-Boat men and Chain Dogs to watch 'em! You wouldn't have a chance! Think of Greta man. Do you think they'll give her any leeway? Fuck sake! What do you think will happen to her in Torgau? Or Mauthausen for that matter!" he said, referring to the military and concentration camp brothels.

Stark flinched at the thought. He freed himself from Morgenstern's grip; hating him for what he said. But in his heart, he wept, because he knew with a dreaded certainty that even if he was posted to France or Italy for example, he would not have the strength to carry on and it scared him more than anything else he had seen or done. Closing his eyes then, he tried to imagine running a hand down the small of Greta's back as they lay somewhere. Would she give him the strength he needed in the next few days?

A quiet stillness settled on the carriages. Men used the latrines at either end of them but were mindful not to wake those who slept as they made their way back to their seats. Was anyone aware that they had left Russia and were now heading across Poland towards Warsaw? Did it matter really? Perhaps to some; at least psychologically. But very few on the train that night would be able to shake off the effects Russia had had on them. The best they could do was to forget about it for a while and perhaps pray for a miracle ensuring they would never have to return.

*

Warsaw!

Morgenstern and Stark were walking along the banks of the Vistula river. They had a few hours to kill before their train to Berlin and decided to stroll around Warsaw to pass the time. They had been able to eat a decent breakfast at the station once they had been released by a zealous Gestapo man who had brought them back to the station earlier.

It had taken forever to get off the train from Kiev, and they had spent an hour queuing just to reach the platform gates where their tickets were retrieved by a very tired Ostbahn guard. It was just after 5am. As they got nearer to the gates, it seemed it was a group of Gestapo men who were holding everyone up. The crowd was losing patience and though there were shouts of derision and much complaining, the situation never got close to getting out of control because of a heavily armed unit with the Gestapo that was a mixture of Chain Dogs and SS men.

At the gates, Morgenstern and Stark were told they were to be taken for an 'interview', a Gestapo Inspector not happy with their story of where they had come from. As they were led away, an SS man kept shoving them both in the back with his rifle, hoping to provoke a reaction that would justify his using some form of violence towards them. But they dutifully followed the Gestapo Inspector to an office adjacent to the platform gates. He held the office door open for them to enter and turning then to the SS man, said, "Now you can fuck off!" The Waffen SS Veteran grunted loudly and sneered at everyone before leaving them.

The Inspector gave Morgenstern and Stark mugs of coffee as they sat before a desk. He sat down also behind it and lit a cigarette. "You understand my position?" he asked, leaning back in his chair.

"Yes, Herr Kriminalinspektor," said Morgenstern.

"You are being...evasive, shall we say. Marinovka? And so on and so forth. All well and good. I believe you up to that point. Where you were before Marinovka is my problem. You could have just told me at the gates and now be on your way. What if I let you walk away right now and your names show up on a list of deserters for example? Then it's my neck on the line! You do understand?"

"Yes, Herr Kriminalinspektor," said Morgenstern. "Of course." He hadn't touched his coffee.

In an age where there was nothing as simple as picking up a phone to check something, either in Russia, Poland or Germany, the Inspector had a point. And together with the situation in Warsaw, where German collaborators or rank and file Wehrmacht soldiers were being assassinated regularly by the Polish Resistance or Jewish rebels from the Ghetto, everyone that raised the slightest suspicion was of importance to the German authorities.

"You must be more forthcoming," said the Gestapo man. "Otherwise I cannot help you," he said in that well practised way that he and others like him used so often. A useful ploy indeed, that lulled many a poor soul into a false sense of safety and security in the hope of everything becoming alright because of this offer of apparent 'help'.

Had Morgenstern been on his own, he might have had a better chance of bluffing his way past the platform gates. But Stark's look of dejection and general demeanour gave away the fact that they had something to hide.

"We were cleared and vetted by Oberst Muller himself, Herr Kriminalinspektor. I don't understand-."

"Not good enough! Who is this Oberst Muller? A fucking nobody to me! On whose authority did he send you here? To Berlin? And Kruger? Never heard of him! What will they do with you there, once they have identified you? Hmmm?"

"We had been in a prison camp, Herr Kriminalinspektor," said Stark then. Up to that point, the Gestapo man had ignored him, deciding with one look that he was of little importance and that if these two were bad or wrong, Morgenstern was the one to concentrate on.

"Ours or theirs?!" the Inspector roared across the desk, looking up to the clock on the wall to emphasise the point that his patience was running out. It wasn't lost on Morgenstern.

Morgenstern sighed and lit a cigarette without asking permission. Such was his belief that their luck had run out and that though they were innocent of any real wrongdoing, they would if they were fortunate enough not to be shot as deserters here in Warsaw, be sent to Torgau or some similar place. If they both survived the regime there, and it was doubtful, visions of a very short life in a Penal Battalion somewhere in Russia, flooded his mind as he smoked. Now the Gestapo Inspector was making to stand. Morgenstern looked across the desk at him and then at Stark, who was deathly pale. The Inspector began tapping his lighter on the desk.

"We were in Stalingrad, Herr Kriminalinspektor," said Morgenstern, with an air of resignation. Stark stared at the floor then and closed his eyes. The Inspector pocketed his lighter and finally stood up, going over to the door. Opening it, he shouted for a Guard to come over from the gates. Morgenstern steeled himself but was then surprised.

"Some coffee," said the Inspector to a Chain Dog who had come over. "Something to eat for all of us," he added. They had been in the office for over an hour. He shut the door and sat back down. Lighting a cigarette, he said to Morgenstern, "Please go on."

Morgenstern told him all that he had to. He left out the details of suffering and hardship that would mean little to this bureaucrat, except when it would be wise to by way of an excuse for a course of action or making a decision. When the food arrived, everyone ate and drank their coffee and the Inspector seemed fascinated by their story.

"It was simply a matter of survival, Herr Kriminalinspektor," Morgenstern finished with. "And here we sit, ready to serve the Fatherland once more." He was pleased with himself how that sounded. He sat back in his chair and lit a Juno.

"It's incredible!" said the Inspector. He let that hang in the air as he made up his mind. He believed these two now, but knew questions would be asked at Army HQ in Berlin. They would make enquiries and check every detail of Morgenstern and Stark's trip, including this interview. Without the proper paperwork to cover himself, the Inspector was leaving himself open to some kind of disciplinary action at least.

So in the end, not wanting to sit here for the rest of the day writing this all down, he decided to have these two brought to the Gestapo Warsaw HQ on Aleja Szucha. There, their interview could be transcribed and filed away, ready to be produced for any subsequent enquiry from Berlin or elsewhere.

The Inspector explained this to the two men sitting across from him. "It will delay you for a couple of hours I'm afraid, but it is necessary, you understand."

"Yes, Herr Kriminalinspektor," said Morgenstern for them both. "Thank you for your patience and for your....hospitality." The Gestapo man waved a hand through the air.

Morgenstern and Stark were eventually driven to the Gestapo HQ in a Kubelwagen by a younger Kriminalassistent accompanied by an SS Guard. They spent the rest of the day having to retell their story to yet another Gestapo man, which was written down by a severe looking woman in a small room. When they had finished, they were brought to the HQ's basement, where they spent an uncomfortable night in a prison cell. The Gestapo man had said as they were led away, "A decision will be made soon", despite assurances back at the train station that they would be back there in plenty of time to catch the Berlin train at 9pm.

The following morning, they were woken at dawn by the noise of the basement as it began a new day of terror and intimidation. Soon their cell was unlocked and they were brought back upstairs, after passing men in rolled-up shirtsleeves dragging half-dead civilians in the opposite direction. They were given back their belongings and greatcoats. Morgenstern only started to relax when the same Kriminalassistent drove them back to the train station. He decided stress would one day kill him stone dead, reckoning that he'd used up all his reserves in the last six months. Stark remained silent. It always took him longer to recover than Morgenstern.

Then they were being taken to the ticket hall. The young Gestapo man explained to the ticket clerk they were to be given tickets to Berlin on the next available train and that the tickets were to be stamped '*Geheime Staatspolizei Genehmigung*' or Gestapo Permitted, so as to make things easier for them at the train station in Berlin.

It had been yet another touch and go episode and had it been another Inspector, could have ended in disaster for them both. But now Morgenstern and Stark sat on a bench and watched a barge go by on the river.

"You see why I still think of Sweden, Karl," said Stark, still somewhat traumatised by the recent events.

"I was never blaming you Wilhelm, for that," said Morgenstern, more or less chain-smoking again. He wondered where the barge was headed. "I was simply trying to dissuade you from making a foolhardy decision that would have finished you and Greta both," he went on, referring to Stark's wife. "These are crazy fucking days. We really shouldn't think past the next day or so."

"How many times have I thought it was all over," said Stark later as they walked around Saski Park. "My God, how much can one bear?" he added, sitting on another bench. Morgenstern joined him and soon, they were surrounded by pigeons.

"As much as we can take," said Morgenstern, looking down at the birds. "That's what my mother used to say at least. She was sure we're only burdened with as much as we can carry around with us. Any more and we simply die."

"That makes a lot of sense," said Stark.

"I grew to believe it. Think of those poor bastards in the Ghetto," Morgenstern said, waving a hand towards the Jewish Ghetto almost beside them. "Can you imagine how they suffer? From day to day? The threat of death hanging over them always? The death of their children? Yet, they endure, and somehow survive. I know I couldn't live like that."

"Nor me," said Stark. Never, he thought.

"So I think we all have our place in this mad world. And I believe what my mother said is true."

Towards the evening, they started to make their way back to the train station. They stopped at a bistro for something to eat and maybe a beer. It was still about two hours before their train to Berlin at 9pm. They didn't want to spend that amount of time at the station. They ordered some food and beer but left soon after a group of soldiers entered and destroyed the peaceful silence with their loud voices and laughter.

Then they were finally sitting on the Berlin train, which filled up quickly. They were due to reach Berlin around 6am, after a brief stop at Poznan. Strange we always seem to be on a train at night, thought Morgenstern. Probably just as well, he decided. The less of the world to see, the better.

*

Home at Last

Having slept most of the way, considering their experiences in Warsaw, Morgenstern and Stark missed the chance to disembark at Poznan and get something to eat, or at least some fresh air. Morgenstern woke first; perhaps an hour away from Berlin. After using one of the carriage's latrines, he walked back to his seat and could see German countryside out of the windows, through patches of condensation, for the first time in over a year. He recognised the chemical factory in Rudersdorf then as the train passed close by. He felt a familiar anxiety. We're close to home, he thought. Returning unsteadily to his seat due to the motion of the train, he sat down and lit a Juno. Stark snored loudly beside him and he pondered for the umpteenth time how his home leave would turn out. Just let me heal, he asked no one and nothing in particular. Let me heal enough to have the strength to return to…

Now Stark was awake. He blinked and stretched. "Where are we?" he asked his friend.

"Less than an hour away," said Morgenstern. "Just left Rudersdorf."

"Rudersdorf!" said Stark, surprised. "Jesus," he added, wiping a circle on his window. "We're home, Karl!"

"Yeah," said the Veteran. "I don't know about you, but since I woke, I've felt the tension inside me finally drain away? No real danger now I suppose."

At least for now, Stark thought, but he didn't say it. "Different kind of feeling though, Karl, eh?" he said.

"We'll be fine," said Morgenstern. "You'll be fine, Wilhelm. By the end, you'll feel reborn and everything will work out."

"I do hope so."

"For Christ's sake, stop thinking about next week or next month. Concentrate just on today! When you wake up tomorrow morning, lying beside Greta, concentrate on that day. And so on. Just enjoy the time you have together."

"You're right Karl," said Stark, peering out the window again. "I can't believe it," he added. "We're home! My God!"

Later, they were suddenly minutes away from pulling into Anhalter station, in the centre of Berlin. It was close to 6am on a dreary looking morning that had little effect on most of the men's spirits. And it was cold, but nothing like the cold most could remember on the worst days back in Russia. Few would forget them either.

"What day is it?" someone asked behind them.

"Wednesday, Arnie! Jesus! Are you still drunk?!"

"And the date? February 4 isn't it?!"

"It's the third, you idiot! Don't wish your life away!"

Laughter filled the carriage as men stood up and prepared to leave this train and perhaps for some, take another somewhere, their arduous journey still not over. But for Morgenstern and Stark, they had reached home and they were both beginning to feel a little overwhelmed by it all.

Morgenstern was sure he had become detached from the last few survivors of his Battalion on January 2. He remembered because they had spent New Year's Day in a bunker where he had fallen asleep during the evening, only to wake up later alone in the small hours.

As he stood and stretched again while the train made it's way slowly through Berlin's outskirts, he found himself surprised that so much could have happened in a little over thirty days. Then he was thinking about the next thirty and he quickly dismissed those thoughts from his head. That was far to much ahead in the future to contemplate, he decided.

Stark stood beside him now, staring out the window. "I dreamt of my childhood," he was saying. For some reason it troubled him. It had just been a fleeting memory really of his early years. The scenery didn't help him remember when or where the dream came from. He could see grass; A child's wooden toy, a horse perhaps? That he pulled along on it's wheels and most clearly of all, his mother laughing as she clapped her hands. Sunlight blocked his view of her face, but he knew it was her.

"Home, eh?" Morgenstern said, not hearing Stark. "The times I spent in a foxhole or a bunker thinking I would never see it again," he added, shaking his head at the mysteries of fate.

"Well there it is Karl," said Stark.

Close now to the station, they were suddenly looking at ruined buildings and piles of rubble and debris that were a result of the British and American air raids. "My God!" someone said. Then most of the men were bending down to look out at the shattered landscape. "Was that Wilhelmstrasse?" another asked. "The old tax office is gone!"

Morgenstern and Stark stared out in silence. Everyone knew of and had heard of the air raids, that Goering said would never happen, but to actually see the consequences? Well, that was a different matter.

"Jesus Christ!" said Morgenstern, sitting back down. A knot formed in his stomach. Surely the suburbs were spared from the raids? Surely Wedding, where Elke and Marta lived near his and her greater relatives, was alright?

"I pray God that Heinersdorf is alright," said Stark, as if reading Morgenstern's thoughts. This was where Greta lived near her mother and sister. North East of the city, it was opposite to Wedding in the North West.

Morgenstern stood up again, a new urgency in his voice betraying his building anxiety. "I was just thinking of Wedding," he said.

Others around them were also thinking of their homes. "What about Tegel?" asked one. "Or Spandau?" asked another. But then, the train was crawling into Anhalter Station. Ten minutes later, Morgenstern and Stark were walking slowly up the platform, one of six at the station. The crowds were huge.

"Where is everyone coming from? Or going to for that matter? And at this hour?" said Stark.

"Fuck knows," said Morgenstern. "Wonder is there a quicker way out?"

"No avoiding the 'Stapo at the gates, Karl. You know that."

They were moving a centimetre at a time now, or so it seemed. "Fuck sake!" said Morgenstern. "This is going to take for fucking ever!"

But then they were free of the platform gates and walking towards the station entrance. Free of the requests for permits and papers and the worst of the crush behind them. Morgenstern shoved a Kriegsmarine sailor out of his way who shouted abuse after them. "Relax Karl, we're almost there," said Stark, trying to keep up with him. There were the crowds in the foyer and ticket hall to still get past.

Morgenstern looked beyond the entrance. "Shit!" he said. "See the crowds outside? We'll never get a tram at this rate this side of the sodding weekend!"

"Why don't we eat then?" said Stark. "Another few minutes won't make any difference. Besides, I need time to..." His voice trailed off. Morgenstern took another look outside and sighed in resignation. He followed Stark to a cafe across the hall. As they got nearer, it became clear they wouldn't be sitting down in there either any time soon.

"Christ Almighty!" said Morgenstern, wondering how long it would take him to walk home.

"Come on," said Stark, a food stall catching his eye. "This way."

Then they were standing among a throng of people eating slices of bread centimetres thick and drinking mugs of sweet tea. The stall holder had laughed at Morgenstern when he'd asked for coffee. These days, for the common Berliner, there was none to be had. And good coffee was around the same price as it's weight in gold on the black market.

"It's as if I've never been here before," said Stark, biting off a piece of sausage. "Nothing seems familiar."

"It's different for sure," said Morgenstern. "Notice how the people look?" he asked, looking around him. "Forlorn? Miserable?"

"Already a look of defeat?" said Stark, thinking how hard life must be here; everywhere. That made him think of Greta. "They seem to know what we know."

"It seems," said Morgenstern. "But when you think about it, it's not much of a mystery. First there was the Air War with the British. A matter of time now before our boys in Africa surrender. And Russia? Well, what more do I have to say?"

Stark turned and shouted for more tea. "How did it come to this Karl?" he asked, chewing the last of his bread.

"I'm no General Wilhelm. And I don't understand politics really. All I can guess is that Grofaz bit off more than he could chew and the rest are just making shit of everything." It was indeed so different from the last time he'd been home, but that was a lifetime ago, wasn't it?

Stark shook his head despondently. He began to think of his and Greta's future, if they had one. Then taking Morgenstern's advice, he dismissed these thoughts and concentrated on the now. The two world-weary men finished their simple breakfast. Morgenstern stood where he was and lit a cigarette. He wouldn't be able to walk through the crowd and smoke at the same time.

Stark stood for a while beside him. Like Morgenstern, he decided to walk home. It would give him time to prepare himself. He felt so nervous at the prospect of seeing Greta, it was like going out with her for the first time when he was 17. That was also a lifetime ago.

"Let's part ways," he said suddenly. "I must go Karl."

"Yes, we may as well," said Morgenstern. "You take care, do you here? No crazy trips to Sweden!", he said, forcing a smile. He didn't want Stark to go.

"You take care too," said Stark. "My love to Elke and your little one."

"Marta," said Morgenstern.

"Yes, Marta. You have my address? Good, don't lose it! We must all meet up in the Tiergarten before, well..."

"And you have mine," said Morgenstern. "We will. Count on it."

There were no more words to be found or said and the two men who had been through so much together, embraced as if for the last time. Stark turned and walked away before quickly stopping and turning to look back at his friend.

"I wouldn't have made it without you Karl," he said. "You know that? I won't forget it."

"Go on now Wilhelm," said Morgenstern, their parting wounding him. "Greta waits for you."

Then Stark was gone, disappearing quickly in the crowd. Morgenstern finished smoking and feeling nervous also, took a deep breath and moving slowly, let the crowd around him bring him outside.

*

Salvation

Morgenstern stood outside for a few minutes. He ignored the queues for the trams. Turning right then, he walked up Stresemannstrasse towards Wilhelmstrasse. It was still a dull, grey morning and he wondered how soon it would be before it rained. Then he was walking through Pariser Platz; the Brandenburg Gate an ominous presence nearby. Crossing the Marschall Bridge, he felt more at home now. Everything seemed as it was on the Luisenstrasse, and he stopped for an ersatz coffee in a little place near Karlplatz.

While he smoked again, his anxiety built about seeing his family. Sitting outside on a wooden chair, beside a rickety little table with uneven legs, he watched some traffic pass by. A brewery cart pulled by a huge dray horse, lumbered up the street, weighed down with barrels of beer. There was little other traffic except for an assortment of military vehicles such as empty trucks or Kubelwagens. What caught his eye though was the number of small, black saloons that were seemingly everywhere. They weren't taxis, but government cars. Gestapo bastards, he decided, off to terrorise some poor unfortunate for stepping out of line.

A young woman came out of the cafe and placed his coffee on the table, which nearly leant over, spilling it's vague contents onto a gingham cloth. "Oh I'm sorry," she said. "Let me get you another."

"That's alright," said Morgenstern. "It's less than a mouthful," he said, watching her dab at the spillage with a dishcloth. She was very pretty. 20 maybe? "What's your name?" he asked her, to make conversation.

"Helga," she replied, blushing slightly. "And you?"

"Karl," he said, sipping his drink. It was dreadful. Whatever it was, it wasn't coffee.

"Are you home on leave Karl?" Helga asked.

"Yes, just got back this morning. I'm on my way home now to see my wife," Morgenstern said then.

"Ah," said Helga. "How lovely for you." Her face betrayed her disappointment. Someone shouted for her from inside. "Excuse me please," she said, and then she was gone.

Morgenstern finished his cigarette and took one more sip of his drink before placing a fifty pfennig piece on the saucer. He stood and continued walking up Luisenstrasse, turning right onto Invalidenstrasse. Now the rain started. A light drizzle and he pulled his greatcoat collar around him against the chill.

In no time, he was finally on Mullerstrasse, his home address. Where he lived with Elke and Marta was at the top of the street; just around the corner. All seemed ok here anyway. Normal. No air raids this far north of the city at least. There was a burnt out house though; a fire perhaps? It looked as if only the first floor was damaged, and most of the roof. Then across the street, a group of children stopped playing to watch this stranger pass by. Morgenstern waved, but they didn't wave back. Now a woman passed him, clutching her scarf at her throat. Had she even noticed him? Further on, an old man stood on his doorstep, watching him as he puffed on a pipe, his face expressionless.

There was the corner! Turning it, there was number 27! He stopped and retreated back around the corner, sitting on a low wall as he fumbled for his cigarettes. Lighting one, he tried to gather himself. Okay, he told himself. Now you can go.

He hammered on the door of number 27, it's dull black paint peeling in places. After a few minutes, a man in his fifties opened it and looked up at him. Not recognising the Front Veteran, he left the door open before returning up a bare wooden staircase.

At the same time as Morgenstern stepped inside and shut the door behind him, a door at the end of the hallway opened and there was Elke, wiping her hands on an apron. She looked up the hallway and a hand covered her face as she gasped in a mixture of surprise and shock. Tears welled in her eyes and she put her other arm around her waist and though wanting to rush towards her husband, she couldn't move.

Morgenstern moved for them both. "Elke!" he managed to say. "My love!" He was overcome.

"Karl?!" she said. "I can't believe it!" Elke moved then but her legs gave way and then she was sitting against the wall. Morgenstern was beside her and knelt, holding her in his arms for a long time as she wept. They wept together.

Then a beautiful little girl with black pig-tails came out of the parlour. She stopped when she saw her mother and seemed a little frightened. "Marta!" said Elke, turning towards their daughter.

Morgenstern looked at the child nearby, *his* child. A flower indeed. "Come," said her mother, beckoning her. "It's your father". Marta couldn't hear her mother's words, but she came nonetheless.

"Marta!" said Morgenstern. "Sweetheart!" He tried to lift her chin but she was shy and unsure at first. Then her face brightened and she looked up at him smiling. Did she recognise her father? Morgenstern hugged her gently and felt her hands around his neck.

"Oh my God!" said Elke. "What a surprise! I can't believe it!" she said again.

Morgenstern wiped his eyes. So much emotion had been set free. He was overwhelmed. It was like walking through the doorway of a thousand cathedrals, or the gates of heaven itself. For a while at least, it was salvation and peace.

*

Epilogue

Obergefreiter Wilhelm Franz Stark was reunited with his wife Greta, around the same time as Morgenstern was with his family. That too was a joyous occasion for them both. During his leave, for the love of his wife, he never spoke of deserting and travelling to Sweden. Eventually reporting to Army HQ, within the time of his permit and travel passes, he was granted a further five days leave before being assigned to a new Panzer Grenadier Regiment and posted to...Holland.

Stark survived the war and after a brief spell in a POW camp in Dortmund, returned to Greta and his home in Heinersdorf. They eventually moved to Stuttgart, where Stark found work among the catering staff in a small car factory overseen by the American Occupation Forces. Later, he would form his own catering company and become a successful businessman.

He and Greta raised three children; two boys and a girl. Stark died in Stuttgart, in 1997, at the age of 79, a grandfather many times over. Greta died in 2001, at the age of 80.

*

Promoted to *Oberfeldwebel* in the field, Karl Heinz Morgenstern was reassigned to the 208th Infantry Division, serving under the command of Generalleutnant Rudolf Schmidt and was once more posted to Russia. He was awarded the Iron Cross 1st Class during the Battle of Kursk in August 1943. He fell in action during the battle's closing stages at the age of 32. A friend made sure that Marta's little toy drum was buried with him.

Elke moved to Munich in the summer of 1945 with Marta and Karl, Morgenstern's new son that he never lived to see. Elke died in Munich in 1999 at the age of 84. She never remarried. Marta still lives with her brother Karl and his family, now retired, though previously a prominent lawyer, in Munich.

**

The Battle of Stalingrad is commemorated every year in Russia and will reach it's 80th Anniversary in 2023

*

Printed in Great Britain
by Amazon